GOLDEN RIVER: THE COMPLETE
ADVENTURES OF BEN QUORN, VOLUME 1

BOOKS IN THE ARGOSY LIBRARY:

GOLDEN RIVER
THE COMPLETE ADVENTURES
OF BEN QUORN, VOLUME 1

TALBOT MUNDY

COVER BY
L.J. CRONIN

POPULAR PUBLICATIONS · 2024

TABLE OF CONTENTS

THE WHEEL OF DESTINY

*Talbot Mundy returns to our pages with
a sprightly tale of an American taxi
driver in the sacred precincts of India*

JUSTICE, DESTINY AND love, these three are blind, says one of the lesser known commentators on the Laws of Manu. But he may have written petulantly, like a buzz fly fastened to the Wheel of Things.

At all events, none but a royal rogue and a few hundred thousand simpletons so much as dreamed that destiny had any far seen purpose when it picked up Benjamin Quorn in Philadelphia and plunged him, unprepared, as far as any one could tell, into the polychromatic whirlpool of Narada, thousands of miles away from the United States.

A want ad column in a Sunday paper touched off a spring in Quorn's imagination with a suddenness, and changed his career with a swiftness which might suggest that some unseen mechanism was at work. What more simple and ready tool could there be for destiny than a Sunday want ad column? And there was Quorn's face.

Quorn's face puzzled Quorn himself as much as any one. It was an ordinary sort of face at first glance, but people who looked twice usually looked a third and a fourth time; after that, they usually looked away and utterly forgot him. Some people thought him a crook, so much imponderable purpose peered forth from his eyes; others thought he might be a poet, or a musician, or a satyr, or an anarchist. Whereas Quorn was a man of conservative tendency, who

did not altogether approve of music, and who had not the patience to read poetry.

He led an unsatisfactory, rather sordid life, full of disappointment and hardship, but had managed to retain, if not hope, at least a sort of stubborn optimism, although he knew that his eyes—they had the amber unbelief in ethics of a he-goat's—and something else elusive, vague and undefinable about his not unhandsome face, had kept him from making his way in the world. After trying numbers of sorts of employment he settled down at last to driving a taxicab.

Thus far Quorn is comprehensible. And so is destiny—almost. But why did Quorn like elephants? And *why* did elephants like Quorn? He could not stay away from them when a circus came to town. They fascinated him. It seemed he fascinated them. When questioned about it he would usually scratch his head, just over the pineal gland; which gesture apparently had nothing to do with elephants or destiny, or anything else except thoughtless habit.

Elephants, of course, suggest a link with India, although elephants, so far as any one can prove, had nothing whatever to do with Quorn's decision to go to Narada. There was nothing said about them in the want ad column, and like

most other people, he did not even know where Narada was until he got there. India and mystery to him were synonymous terms, as they are to Indians themselves and to everybody else. Narada is the most mysterious part of India, the very heart of it.

HISTORIANS, PHILOSOPHERS, MYSTICS, missionaries, poets and politicians have invented countless explanations of the heart of India, and the bursting libraries are full of books about it, but they all avoid Narada. It remains unknown. Narada regards India as India regards the rest of us, and as the rest of us regard the Chinese laundryman, concerning whom the more we think we know the less chance we have of understanding.

The tiny state contains one city large enough to amuse a magnificent rajah who rates a salute of one gun and a roll of eighteen drums. Nobody knows why, and nobody cares, but when, once in three years, he pays his official visit to the British viceroy, he rides all the way to Delhi—a journey of three weeks—on the back of an elephant, whose howdah is heavy with gold and silver. He returns to Narada on a different elephant, to be disinfected very expensively by Hindu priests, he being nevertheless not a Hindu by religion but an Animist so far as anybody can discover. But then, what would life be worth without enigmas? The priests can make him do incredibly severe and expensive

penances whenever he breaks a single one of their complicated caste laws—and that is often.

There is an army consisting of a hundred men, most
of whom do sentry duty in the palace precincts, not that
robbers are expected to break in otherwise, but because
there is nothing else for them to do and it keeps the soldiers
out of mischief. They have a colonel and they look fierce,
because they dye their whiskers and they eat rice with
plenty of pepper. They frown savagely at strangers who
come in curiosity to examine the royal treasures, which are
what a guide book would describe as priceless. Mention
of the treasures has, however, been omitted from all guide
books because of an ancient treaty between the government of India and the state of Narada, under the terms
of which no investigation of antiquities and no Christian
missionaries are permitted.

The latter clause of the treaty was long evaded by a
missionary sect whose persuasion is so peaceful that even
Narada's sensitive nerves were hardly conscious of the quiet
intrusion. For more than fifty years a mission flourished,
more or less—or, at all events, there was a mission. The
Reverend John Brown, adopting something of Narada's
method, which included subtlety and breaking laws while
seeming to obey them, bought an ancient palace from a
dissolute heir to the throne who had been banished.

He converted the palace, if nothing else. Behind its
greenish limestone garden walls, he modernized the buildings. He imported plumbing, libraries and school desks.
He established an elementary school of medicine that
would have caused a riot if he had not possessed more than
normal tact. He called it a revival of ancient magic and

offered to supply the Hindu priests with free drugs in any quantity; so that numbers of babies began to be born with unafflicted eyes, and gratitude grew out of that.

A junior priest of an obscure temple, after being suitably protected by incantation, was sent to hang a garland around the Reverend John Brown's neck. It created a scandal, of course, but the Hindu hierarchy lived it down, even though it turned out that the missionary's tenets included such dreadful blasphemy as strong denunciation of the burning of the dead. The Reverend John Brown converted all Narada finally to the use of quinine, and malaria almost vanished. Then he died. He was cremated, Hindu fashion, to lay his ghost before any one could interfere, and his ashes were returned to Philadelphia.

DEATH HAS A way of stopping more than one clock, and of inspiring much diplomacy. In between sighs of relief at having no more missionary in their midst, it occurred to some one that there would be trouble about that cremation, and somebody else thought of the treaty with the Indian government. It was decided to set a backfire, so to speak, and a minister was dispatched by elephant, with sundry secretaries and a band of music, to Delhi to demand that the illegal mission should be withdrawn.

Meanwhile, half of the rajah's army guarded the place, keeping out every one except the birds and bats and sacred monkeys, while the mails went to and fro across several oceans and the international cable carried streams of urgent messages that were taken down by a babu by the name of Bamjee, who knew little and cared less about the mission and the dead John Brown, but who had an eye for opportunity. He mixed up everything, not without some profit to himself, since he bought a Ford car shortly afterward and went into business as purchasing agent for the rajah of Narada. So there was confusion and then compromise.

The mission buildings were allowed to stand as John Brown left them, but there should be no more activity. As a graceful concession on the part of the government of his Highness the Rajah of Narada, the trustees of the mission were allowed to send from the United States and to keep on the spot at their own expense one caretaker, who should have no duty and no privileges other than to see that the mission property was not disturbed; he might remain there until the mission property was sold; and since there was no prospect whatever of a purchaser, it was understood that the caretaker's job might be permanent.

Accordingly a man of parts was selected in Philadelphia by the trustees, by advertisements. Benjamin Quorn was the chosen applicant. He was given a contract, sworn before the vestrymen and a notary public, and dispatched post haste to India, second class.

HE CAME AND lived in the great gate house with a one eyed servant by the name of Moses, an Eurasian, and they two grew gray arguing about Noah's deluge, and the curious statement in the Book of Genesis that light was created before the sun, and what not else. Quorn considered Moses and all his neighbors, from the rajah to the untouchables who swept the street, as heathen; it was the only word he had for them, but it was no worse than the word they had for him, and there was no spite wasted. He became such a well known figure, neatly shaven, rather bent, wandering without much apparent curiosity through sun baked, crowded streets in a ready made Palm Beach suit and a rather soiled white helmet, that soon people took no more notice of him than they did of the sacred *neem* trees lining the streets, or of the sacred monkeys catching fleas off one another, or of the sacred bulls thrusting their way through crowded alleys to better the temple dole by stealing grain from the bags in the grain seller's open fronted shops, or of the sacred peacocks strutting and screaming from walls that guarded sacred mystery.

So many things are sacred in Narada that it is simplest to take the Apostle Paul's advice and hold that there is nothing common or unclean, not even the temple dirt.

And when men had ceased to notice Quorn they grew almost friendly, as men grow friendly with remembered landmarks. They ceased to become darkly silent when he drew near. Moses, having not much else to do, was at great pains to teach him the language, so that after a while he was able to talk with strangers in the street. Then a sort of bewilderment took hold of him, a wordless wonder. It sank into his consciousness that what had hindered him at home was here an asset. It appeared that men understood that strangeness in his eyes, which he himself did not understand.

But the East guards understanding cautiously and hides it with all sorts of subterfuge. When he strolled in the great roofed market place it meant nothing to him that a thousand eyes glanced at the wall at the end. It did not mean much, even, when one day he and Moses had gone marketing together and Moses, half Oriental, half inclined in consequence to keep all secrets hidden, but equally half inclined to lay them bare, led him to that end wall where the sunlight played on broken carving. It was possibly a thousand years old and there was not enough left of it to tell a connected story, even to an antiquarian; but there was an obvious elephant, the lower half of a woman who had jewels on her feet and ankles, and the head and shoulders of a man in a turban.

Farther along the wall appeared the same man riding on the elephant with the lady up behind him in a funny little howdah; but most of the rest of the picture was beyond recognition.

"They say you look like that man," remarked Moses.

Quorn stared, unaware that he was being watched through the corners of hundreds of eyes. The market had almost ceased its chaffering.

"Some heathen god!" he asked at last.

He noticed the resemblance to himself, but it meant nothing to him. It was mere coincidence.

"No, not a god," said Moses. "Some old personage of veree olden time."

Then the Western half of Moses—the half that could not keep secrets—stole a moment's freedom from the other half that could.

"Once," he said, "there was a man named Gunga, whom the gods loved. He was brave and obedient, and yet not absolutelee obedient; and because of his braveree the gods selected him to rescue a princess who was living her life in durance vile. So he came for her on an eleephant, who also was selected by the gods. But because this man Gunga was willing, and yet onlee partlee obedient, he did not finish what he had to do. He got down from the eleephant to see about something or other, so the eleephant supposed he had become faint hearted, and therefore slew him, because an eleephant is not a person of much self-restraint.

"Consequentlee the princess was recaptured by her proud and angree parent and she lived all the rest of her life in the durance vile out of which she had hoped to escape. For all of which the gods were sorree. So the gods said that some day Gunga must reeturn to finish what he had begun, and that carving was made on the wall as a reeminder. That is the legend.

"Now these people say you look like Gunga."

"They're heathen. They're talking bunk," said Quorn, and turned away with his hands in his pockets.

"Oh yes, certainlee," said Moses, and withdrew, tortoise fashion, into the Oriental half of him that was ashamed of the half that tells secrets.

BUT THAT SAME day, as if a trigger had snapped and unseen mechanism moved again, Quorn met the Rajah of Narada and made history—or made it possible for history to happen, which is really as much as Napoleon ever did. Napoleon and Quorn made holes for history to happen through—the difference being that Napoleon knew what he was doing, but that Quorn did not.

It was the rajah's fault. Three of the rajah's wives, accepting astrological advice and knowing that the rajah's moon was in a quarter where it would upset his judgment, had chosen the preceding night to air their views at great length on the subject of a contemplated addition to their number, of whom they had heard rumors. They considered he already had enough wives. And his royal daughter, aged nineteen, with modernist views of her own acquired from reading modern books, who had refused to marry anybody not of her own choosing, and who had not yet chosen because she was always kept behind the *purdah* and not allowed to meet anybody, had added worse than noise—perplexity.

For there were visiting Narada at the moment emissaries from his serene Highness the Maharajah of Jamnuggar—an eighteen gun man of enormous wealth and influence, whose royal ancestral tree was traceable for seven thousand years. He condescended to suggest, through these semi-official intermediaries, that he might be willing to lay his polygamous heart in the dust at the feet of the princess Sankyamuni.

That would manifestly be a fine alliance. The infernal nuisance of it was that these semiofficial representatives were too inquisitive. Like almost all gay gentlemen, the Maharajah of Jamnuggar was a stickler for the very strictest social conventions in so far as they concerned his own womenfolk.

If he should learn that the Princess Sankyamuni held modern views and could only be restrained with difficulty from escaping from the palace precincts and showing her beautiful face to strangers, not only would negotiations be called off but such malicious scandal would be spread by the disappointed and disgusted Jamnuggar as would cause the Rajah of Narada's face to blush the color of his turban. He would almost prefer to have the girl killed, although he was too lazy to wish to murder any one, even his own daughter, except on the deadliest provocation.

It was easy enough to keep Jamnuggar's representatives from speaking with, or even from seeing the princess, since custom provided that royal lovers should not meet each other even by proxy until the wedding day. An expert well instructed as to the type of beauty that the Maharajah of Jamnuggar most admired had been employed to paint the lady's portrait without seeing her. But nobody could keep servants from talking, or the princess either, and she had talked loud enough last night, and long enough to provide every single servant of the scores within the palace with enough gossip to last almost a lifetime. So the rajah rode forth looking for a victim for his royal anger.

He was a rather handsome man, that rajah, and magnificently horsed. He looked rather too lazy to be dangerous, though capable of fighting like a panther if stirred deeply enough or bored beyond the point of patience, and it was noticeable that his mounted attendants kept well out of range of his riding whip. He wore a blood red turban, possibly suggestive of his inner feelings, and it was fastened with a diamond brooch reputed to be worth nearly as much as the Koh-i-noor.

QUORN HAD SENT Moses home to chase pariah dogs and sacred monkeys out of the mission compound. He was still puzzling over the heathenish suggestion that the stone face carved on the wall was like his own, and as usual when puzzled he grew discontented. When discontented he went to see the elephants. There was something about the big brutes that reminded him, nowadays, of foggy mornings in Philadelphia.

They stood picketed at wide intervals beneath enormous *neem* trees in a compound surrounded by a high stone wall, tossing up dust with their trunks in a heat haze like a golden veil and swaying to elephantine music utterly inaudible to man—perhaps the music of the spheres.

He had struck up quite an acquaintance with the biggest one, who was chained by one leg to the picket farthest from the compound gate, a monster named Asoka, a possessor of immeasurable dignity.

The rajah, followed by several attendants, rode into the compound when Quorn had been standing studying Asoka for some ten or fifteen minutes. Brute and man were perfectly contented to look dumbly at each other; neither betrayed a trace of any emotion that he may have felt. Asoka swayed and fidgeted. Quorn stood still. A mahout watched them both from a distance squatting beneath another *neem* tree with his naked brats around him, all dependent for their living on the elephant and all equally ungrateful, but nevertheless aware of obligations.

Quorn's back being toward the compound gate, he did not see the rajah, who occupied himself during the next few minutes with the congenial task of cursing the ancestors, the immediate relatives and the person of the compound foreman, to whom he gave reluctant and ungracious permission to remain living. Meanwhile, something pulled the trigger of the mechanism that propels events.

FOR THE FIRST time in his entire experience of elephants, Quorn had the curiosity to find out whether or not Asoka would obey his orders. He commanded the monster to lie down. To his astonishment, like a big balloon descending with the gas let out, the elephant collapsed and thrust a forefoot out for Quorn to sit on. Quorn did not understand that gesture, but he sensed the invitation and drew nearer. Then, smiling at his own foolishness, wondering what Philadelphia would think of it, he vaulted on to the great brute's neck and thrust his knees under the ears, as he had seen mahouts do. He felt younger and ridiculous, but rather pleased. He thought he could imagine worse things than to have to ride elephants all day long.

It was at that moment, just as Quorn was mounting, that the mahout's brats saw the rajah riding forward down the track between the trees. All five yelled with one shrill voice to Asoka to salute the heaven born. Quorn held on, crying—

"Hold her, now there, steady!"

But Asoka knew no English. Quorn tried to think of ways to get down, but his nerves were suddenly, and utterly for the moment, paralyzed as Asoka raised a forefoot, threw his trunk in air, and screamed the horrible salute that Hannibal, viceroys, kings, some wise men and a host of fools have been accepting as their due since elephants were first made captive. It sounded like paleolithic anguish.

It was a new, young horse that the rajah rode, one not yet broken to the voice of elephants. He reared. The rajah spurred him. Four and thirty elephants at pickets scattered up and down the compound trumpeted a gooseflesh raising chorus; they had been taught to do that when Asoka set example, each of them raising a forefoot and stamping the dusty earth, so that a golden cloud went up through which the sun shone like a great god, angry.

Terror, aggravated by whip and spurs and by the cries of the mahouts, became a thousand devils in the horse's brain. Strength, frenzy, speed and will were given to him to escape from that inferno. He shed the rajah as a cataclysm sheds restraint. He went as life goes fleeing from the fangs of death—a streak of sun lit bay with silver stirrups hammering his flanks, and a broken rein to add, if it were

possible to add to anything so absolute and all inclusive as
that passion to be suddenly somewhere else.

Asoka trumpeted again. The rajah lay sprawling in dirt,
too angry to be stunned, and much too mortified to curse
even his attendants whom panic assured that their master's
royal anger would be vented on themselves. They were too
conscious of far too many undetected crimes against him
to feel able to defy injustice. They must justify themselves.
So some fool struck Asoka as the source of the catastrophe,
struck him across his friendly, sensitive, outreaching trunk
with a stinging whalebone riding whip.

Then genuine disaster broke loose naturally—upward
of five tons of it, with Quorn on top. A green and golden
panorama veiled in smelly haze, with sacred monkeys scampering like bad thoughts back to where the bad thoughts
came from, wherever that is; and a crowd of frantic horses,
shouting mahouts and screaming children darting to and
fro like stokers of inferno, was opened, split asunder and
left gasping at Asoka's great gray rump, that had an absurd
tail like a weary, elongated question mark suggesting that
all speculation was useless as to what would happen next.

The unbelievable had happened anyhow. Never before,
in more than forty years, had Asoka broken faith by snap-
ping that futile ankle ring. He had always played fair. He
had pretended the rusty iron was stronger than the lure of
mischief, thus permitting an ungrateful, dissolute mahout
to spend the price of a new steel ring on arrack, which
is worse than white mule whisky, and more prolific of
misjudgment.

AND NOW QUORN and Asoka were one inseparable entity
as long as Quorn could keep his knees under those upraised

ears. He had never before ridden on an elephant. The only cataclysmic motion he had ever felt was on a steamer on the way to India, and there had been something then to cling to, as well as fellow passengers to lend him confidence. He was alone now—as alone as an unwilling thunderbolt, aware of force that was expelling him from spheres that he vaguely knew into an incomprehensible, unknown but immediate future where explosion lay in wait.

Asoka screamed contempt of consequences, and the dust was vibrant with nerve shattering alarm. Quorn's helmet was down over his eye; he did not dare to lift a hand to push it back in place. He was drenched in sweat. He felt the low branches of trees brush past him and was aware of dim danger colored green that went by far too swiftly to be recognized. The speed was beyond measurement, being relative to Quorn's imagination and to nothing else except Asoka's wrath; they four were one—two organisms and two states of consciousness, with one goal, swiftly to be reached but unpredictable.

They passed through the compound gate like gray disaster being born, with several sarcastic godlets on the gate-posts grinning it good riddance.

And because the road was straight toward the market, headlong forward went Asoka, caring nothing whither, so he got there and then somewhere else. Carts went crashing right and left. A swath of boots and tents were laid low. Fruit stalls, egg stalls, sticky colored drink stalls, booths in which candy was sold and fortune tellers' booths, peep shows, cooked vegetable curry stalls and piles of baskets lined the long street; and because an indignant elephant goes through and not around things, those went down like trash in the wake of a cyclone, each concussion a fresh insult to Asoka, who was red eyed and who undoubtedly loathed himself for having ever obeyed a human being.

Quorn ceased at last to wonder what would happen next, having exhausted all the possibilities and having made exactly one hundred per cent. of wrong guesses. He began, instead, to wonder what to do about it, which is a sign of rebirth of that state of consciousness that makes men superior to elephants. Not that he felt superior—not yet! He felt like nothing on the edge of cosmos.

"What's the big stiff thinking about?" he wondered. "Where does he kid himself he's going? What's he figuring to fix? Who-o-o-a, Irish! Who-o-o-a, Blood! Easy and let me down, you sucker—then get the hell away from here and smash all you want to! Easy, feller, easy!"

MANY CATACLYSMS HAPPENED before Quorn realized that he was speaking the wrong language. By that time there was a black cotton umbrella threaded on Asoka's trunk like a rat preventer on a ship's cable. He was catastrophically anxious to be rid of the incomprehensible thing. So there began to be sporadic variations of the motion and Quorn had to hold on tighter than ever. There began to be concentration now, a deliberate determination to destroy. And they reached the market. Quorn's helmet was struck by a roof beam as they passed in through the cluttered entrance between heaps of baskets; it collapsed around his neck, enabling other people to see him rather better, and disarranging his hair so that he looked even more than usually like the figure on the end wall.

Rumor in the East is borne on bats' wings; but Asoka had arrived more swiftly than the rumor of his coming.

Doubtless he was a monstrous apparition darkening the entrance. There is a pause before a panic, as there is before a typhoon. Even Asoka paused. Men had a moment's opportunity to stare at red eyed anger and the rider who, suddenly self-conscious, dreading to look ridiculous before all that throng, straightened himself and sat majestically, with a sahib's unapproachable aloofness, as if he were there on purpose, obeyed by the monster he rode. Then wrath burst loose again, and Quorn's ears caught no single note in the confusion, his eyes discerned no individual. He heard only the tumult, saw only the kaleidoscopic movement. He was busy holding on.

There is no wrath like an elephant's. It is a prehistoric passion. It is elemental, learned in the dawn of time when Nature was brewing a world in a cauldron of floods and earthquakes, burning trash with white hot lava and obliterating errors with sulphur and boiling deluges. Whatever is made, must be unmade, swiftly, utterly unmade. The taught, trick loaded memory of one short life is in abeyance. Herd memory survives, and with it horror of all things new. There is almost nothing that is not new to such primeval consciousness—new, abominable, loathsome, to be trodden flat.

Down went the market stalls—cloth, eggs, brassware, chickens, crockery, imported clocks, curry and spices, cooked food, benches, baggage, basketry—smashed into a smear of vanity that once was. Humans in white eyed droves flowed this and that way, witless, aimless, shrilling, praying to a thousand gods—as if the gods cared!

There was dreadful din under the roof, like the braying and cracking of battle, until the rajah's soldiers came. They were a gentle soldiery, fierce only of wax and whisker, careful above all things not to harm Asoka, who was expensive, or the crowd that was a lot too cheap, but friendly in its way. They made a vast and most important noise. They brought three bugles into action. They caused the roof, between anvil chorus volleys, to reverberate with hoarse voiced orders. Being well drilled, they avoided danger, setting good example, so that there was plenty of room for Asoka, havoc fully finished, to come avalanching forth and down the steps again into the sunlight, trumpeting for more destruction.

SOME SAID AFTERWARDS that Quorn shouted as he passed outward through the gate, but others doubted that, though all agreed that he moved his right arm, as if his right hand held an *ankus,* and that his gesture, position, attitude were those—exactly—of the figure who rode the elephant amid the broken carving of the old end wall. It was agreed by every one, including numbers who did not see and who therefore knew much more about it, that all he lacked, to make resemblance perfect, was a turban. For his coat was gone; it strangled him; he had thrown it away; he sat in flapping, loose, bazar made shirtsleeves, and his hair, perhaps erect with fright, was not so unlike a turban that men, who believe in such nonsense as destiny, should not glance at the end wall and make suggestions to themselves.

It costs nothing to make suggestions. There is no law against adding two and two together. Men need a modicum of kind, imaginative comfort when they see their stalls and goods and money smashed into a shapeless, many smelling chaos.

And now speed again in straight spurts. Nineteen

dogs, until that moment satisfied to lick sores and scratch verminous pelts, suddenly and simultaneously let themselves be swept into the current of excitement; and having had a nice, long, lazy morning they were as, so to speak, fresh as a pariah dog may be said to be.

They joined in with enthusiasm, an offensive, vulgar, uninvited, unclean pack of yellow curs, each in a little dust cloud of his own, ears up, tail between legs and anatomy tautened in spasmodic curves of speed. Nineteen dogs were enough to make a whole herd of elephants hysterical. Asoka left the city with his trunk outstretched in front of him and his tail outstretched behind—calamity in gray, expelled by Providence, as some folk said, though there were others who do not believe in Providence, unless you spell it with a small "p".

It was the sort of day that would have tamed a locomotive, so hot it was, so merciless the sun. The very palms and mangoes seemed to cast a shriveled shadow. Sound itself fainted with weariness. All masonry became a mirror in which only heat was visible, and when eyes refused to tolerate it, then a mirror from which heat was felt. Sweat dried still born. Oven haze enwrapped all nature and the aching earth smothered even the noise of five ton footsteps, so that Asoka became a great gray ghost bestridden by a wraith, dry throated, talking to himself, with jumbled memories like dreams upshaken into slowly developing consciousness.

"Crashing the gates o' death, I'd call it! He ain't thinking. He ain't looking. He's going, and he don't give a damn where, till he hits what stops him. Gee, there ain't no brakes on this here vehicle! No license plate—no nothing—not even a cop in sight! Who'd ever have thought I'd crave to see a cop! Gee! Guess it was all my doing, climbing on him. Wish I was in Philadelphia!"

But it was no use wishing.

AND NOW BAMJEE—BABU with a keen eye for the main chance, former telegraphist promoted to purchasing agent on commission for his Highness the rajah and, naturally as well as consequently, eager to encourage business… Should an elephant die or grow feeble, Bamjee bought a new one. Did nature forces, behind *purdah* curtains, inspire ladies of high rank to think of jewelry, Bamjee notified the jewelers.

It was even rumored that he split commissions with the court astrologer, who indicated to the ladies which were the proper dates on which to buy such merchandise; but you can trust some people to talk unkindly about everything. Agents for automobiles, gramophones, radio outfits, cameras, clothing, furniture—all had to interview Bamjee. And the rajah paid, when he felt disposed, which was usually after Bamjee had been promised a little extra something for accelerating payment. A very energetic, generous and not intolerent babu, possessed of a college A.B. degree and an enormous fund of cultured incredulity. A little lean man with a big head, gold rimmed spectacles, ingratiating manner and a chocolate and cream hue of skin, accentuated by a rose pink turban.

Bamjee sat in the garden of such a villa as only rajah's dream of, scratching a square inch of the skin behind his ear, a symptom of perplexity. He sat cross legged at the feet of loveliness incarnate in the form of the Princess Sank-yamuni, on whose face there scintillated such emotions as mischief, rebellion, indignation, merriment and daring, all mixed up together—an enticing and exhilarating mixture, likely enough to inspire the heart and bewilder the brain of any one beholding it, as for instance Bamjee did.

It was a lovely garden well supplied by Bamjee with expensive luxuries all purchased on commission. Haroun al Raschid—Shah Jehan—none of the traditional lords of opulence and ease enjoyed such comforts as that villa and its garden held behind the time stained limestone wall.

There were electric fans, unseen, in every hiding place where they could possibly be used to waft cool breezes on reclining lovers. There were fountains, summerhouses, pools in which the lotus bloomed and birds bathed, irrigated trees that shimmered like jade in sunlight, flowers like matched jewels on the breast of mother earth and, in fact, everything that could possibly help to prove how all earth loves a lover, even though the lover love not the proprieties for any one's advice.

One commentator on the laws of Manu makes the possibly irrelevant remark that love is not what lovers sometimes think it is. Perhaps the commentator knew. Bamjee did not; he loved money and intrigue and a certain sort of secret influence that steered adroitly between the reefs of responsibility and the shoals of too much work. A very human person, Bamjee, scratching his head with a perplexed but persistent finger. He was not thinking about elephants.

It might indeed be difficult to think of anything with the Princess Sankyamuni looking at you with eyes such as the East adores with poetry. They were half hidden beneath langorous dark lids that did not even try to conceal excitement. She had pearly skin with just a hint of color, and the great dark pearls that she wore as earrings beneath a turban of cloth of gold were like drops of the juice of royalty exuding from her.

Her dress was the color of dawn on a mountain skyline. She wore her *sari* with the grace engraved by ancient sculptors on the stone of certain temple walls, and there were jewels on her feet and ankles. She was a blossom blooming on the last twig of an ancient royal vine, whose vital force and genius had all flowed into her in one last burst of life before the vine should die, to fertilize a new democracy—perhaps.

"Oh, daughter of the moon," said Bamjee, "this is wonderful, but it is also terrible. Suppose these garden walls had ears!"

"They have," she answered, "but they are dumb to any one except the gods; so talk on, and take care to say only what the gods will enjoy when they ask of the walls what happened."

"Heaven born sahiba, may this babu talk of commonplaces? It is so easy to talk about gods and so difficult to keep the mind on matters of fact in your Highness' royal presence. If the question may be forgiven, does it not occur to your superb imagination that this situation is desperate, that this babu will be accused of aiding and abetting your escape, that I shall not only lose my perquisites and emoluments, but also shall undoubtedly be made to eat slow poison—ground glass, probably."

"Yes, any fool would know that. Use your wits, then, Bamjee."

"BUT I HAVE no wits. Daughter of the dawn star, they are all gone! It is awful! The emissaries of his Highness, the

Maharajah of Jamnuggar—think of it—will learn that she on whom his eighteen-gun-saluted majesty has set his heart has fled from her parental roof. Consider it! They will insult your royal parent. And when Jamnuggar learns of it he also will insult your parent in an expert manner and will tell tales that will make your family name a byword and a laughing stock in every bazar in India! Who could forgive that? Who could possibly forgive it? It is not that your royal parent minds your modern views. I think he secretly enjoys them. But he has to think about the Hindu priests, who have so much influence and who are so conservative, and who object to royal ladies showing their beautiful faces in public.

"He thinks about his own shame, which is to say he thinks about public opinion, about which you do not propose to concern yourself, because you imagine you can run away from it. But how to get away from here? There is no way. To remain here is to be discovered, and discovery means, O Krishna, what does it not mean? Think of the shame of your royal father when the dreadful news is out and all the city talks about it!"

"He is like one of those parents whom one reads about in novels, Bamjee. He has some superficial virtues, but he knows nothing about shame. He can't possibly under-stand, for instance, what my shame would be if I should be married to a man I never saw and whom I would therefore refuse to love, even if he were so lovable that it killed me not to love him."

"O Krishna, in addition they will blame me for buying books for you! What will his Highness, your awful royal father do? What *can* he do, except to incarcerate you? Or possibly he may give you to the priests, to be a temple ministrant."

"Oh no, Bamjee. The priests would refuse to have me. You see, I know too much."

"But, daughter of the moon, we get no comfort out of all this talk! What shall we do? You say you will go to America? Do you know where America is? And do you know about the quota, how they count heads and refuse all immigrants who are not certified as suitable? And are you suitable? And who shall certify you? And how shall you get to Bombay, which is the port from which steamers start? You have neither clothes nor money for such a journey."

"That is for you to attend to, Bamjee. I have made up my mind to be independent and I have run away. I have done my part."

"Krishna! Who shall explain things to a woman?"

"There is no need for explanations. Unless some way is found out of this difficulty, you will be ruined, Bamjee, and that is all about it."

"Daughter of the dawn, if they should find us here—O Krishna! Yet if I should take you to some other place, if we should pass out through the gate, the servants—daughter of mystery, how did you get here?"

"There, over the wall where it is broken. See where I tore my dress? I came while it was yet dark. You kept me waiting an unconscionable time, for which you should be ashamed instead of daring to suggest I did wrong. I did right, Bamjee. I believe in destiny. The astrologer said that I shall marry whom I will, because undoubtedly there is independence in my destiny."

The babu burst into English, by way of mannerly concession to the sex of his tormentor. Swear he must, but not in her language, in her presence, even in that crisis.

"Oh, damn destiny! If there is any such thing as destiny—"

HE WAS INTERRUPTED by the sound of enormous breathing, like a giant's, and titanic footsteps, muffled, as if gods were coming. Bamjee, the cultured unbeliever, sank his neck into his shoulders and turned up his toes, every nerve alert, anticipating evil. But the princess, primed with modern novels and absurd ideas of freedom, could hardly be expected to be wise or properly religious. She was an optimist.

"Something wonderful is going to happen!" she exclaimed, and clapped her hands.

"Yes, any fool could guess that," remarked Bamjee. "My flesh creeps. Robbers undoubtedly are coming to murder me and carry you away. There is nowhere to escape to. Destiny, thou art a devil!"

He was acting bravely for the honor of his sex. There was a moment of ghastly silence, timed into pulse beats by swift, oncoming, muffled footfalls to which the babu's heart beat *obligato,* and by a breathing that suggested horrors reaching forth for some one weak and innocent to horrify. Then suddenly the babu screamed. The horror happened.

There was a shock like an earthquake. The old rotten limestone wall, already broken, shook, lurched, tottered, and fell inward, battered headlong by an elephant blind with exhaustion. Then more of the wall went down, like a dam destroyed by spring floods, opening to left and right and tumbling into dusty heaps. For a second in the gap, enormous and partly stunned, Asoka loomed, an apparition ridden by a phantom. Then the great brute staggered forward, stumbled on the masonry and fell. He lay heaving, sobbing, groaning near enough to the fishpond to smell water and too spent to reach it, an enormous lump of abject misery. Quorn was pitched in an equally woeful heap at the feet of Bamjee, whose turban fell off as he backed away and fell into the pond among the frightened frogs.

The princess was the only one unterrified. She kept her head and lost, in fact, nothing except her imported lipstick, which she was just about to use because she wanted to look lovely in the presence of destiny's messenger; a sudden nervous gesture sent it spinning close to Quorn's hand, and Quorn, not knowing what he did, clutched it, so that three of his fingers became smeared with carmine.

Destiny, though wearing no top hat, as specialists ought, had done to Quorn what specialists do to nitwits in the bughouse. It had jarred loose something that he had not known was there and he was, consequently, coldly sane in some respects. He staggered to his feet and, with his left hand, tore away the remains of his helmet that was crushed around his neck. He refused to believe his eyes yet. There was too much loveliness to look at. He had read of such damsels in story books, but he had never believed they existed.

What with the emotions he had come through, and the shock of falling, he was almost ready to believe himself dead and in another world. This exquisite creature before him, whose eyes were dewey jewels, might almost be an angel, such as his mother had described when he was head high to her apronstring.

Nevertheless, he was sane enough to notice that her

dress was torn and that she looked excited, which no angel
should be. Also he noticed that he did not feel afraid of her,
and he had always entertained a dread of meeting angels.
So there was something wrong about that somewhere.

QUORN FELL BACK on habit. With his right hand, that
had crushed the carmine lipstick, he began scratching his
head, just over the pineal gland that is such a problem to
the scientists, and three red marks appeared, exactly like a
caste mark, in exactly the place where a caste mark ought
to be.

With the same hand he felt for the top of his head, half
hiding his face from the princess. He discovered, as he
suspected, that his skull was almost baked through by the
sun. Then his roving goat's eye saw the babu's turban. He
picked it up, put it on and turned again toward the princess, who saw for the first time turban, yellow eyes and
caste mark.

She screamed, whereat old habit and familiar memories mingled in Quorn's half stunned brain. He began to
think instinctively in terms of Philadelphia, but he spoke
intuitively in the language of Narada, taking great pains
with his grammar and pronounciation. So the speech was
polished, but the thought was this wise:

"You've no call to fear me, missy. Me and him are
committing trespass, but we didn't mean no harm by it."

He turned from her to look at "him"—Asoka, sobbing
and tossing his trunk in futile efforts to reach water, which
was several feet too far away. Quorn suddenly became
aware of Bamjee crawling out of the fishpond, with his
mouth half full of lotus stalks.

"Hey, you!" he ordered. *"Panee lao!* Fetch a bucket quick to give this poor sucker a drink. He's famished."

Bamjee ignored the order; he was too indignant. But Quorn spied a gardener's watering can, imported and expensive, left among the flowers by a home grown gardener who preferred the old fashioned goatskin water bag. He seized the can, filled it, grabbed Asoka's trunk and thrust it into the receptacle.

"There, ye darned old idjit, help yourself."

The water vanished, to be squirted down the great brute's dusty throat, while Quorn refilled the can. A second and a third two gallon dose went sluicing down the gurgling throat. Then Quorn took a drink himself and perhaps the relief it gave him stirred imagination. He sat down on Asoka's forefoot and began to comfort the great brute.

"There, don't you carry on. 'Tweren't your fault. It was all my doing, climbing on your neck, and you not used to a guy like me. There, there, quit grieving. There ain't no special harm been done, nothing but what money'll set right, and there's always somebody got money, even if it ain't you and me. You're bruised a bit, but all of us gets bruises now and then. You've earned yours. You've had your fun, so cheer up. You sure did play the typhoon in that marketplace!"

Asoka seemed aware that comfort was intended, for he left off moaning. He even touched Quorn's shoulder with his trunk. But his eyes did not lose their madness until Quorn began talking in the native tongue, the way mahouts do when their charges are in trouble.

"A prince, a rajah of the hills, a bull of bulls, a royal bull! Did they offend him? Did they offend my pearl of elephants? He shall have great honor paid him. He shall have a howdah of gold and emeralds. They shall paint him blue and scarlet. He shall lead the line of elephants and he shall carry none but kings!"

The poor bewildered brute responded, swaying his head to and fro and permitting Quorn to rub the edges of his ears. Whatever reasoning went on within Asoka's brain, he evidently did not connect Quorn with the cause of his anguish, but rather with relief from it. Quorn was his friend in need, who had dropped, as it were, from the sky to bring him water in extremity. He gurgled for more water. Quorn persuaded him to rise and led him to the fishpond.

BAMJEE MADE THE next remark, quite suddenly. His modern views were weakening. He needed moral and material support.

"Destiny be damned!" he exclaimed in downright English. "That man is a cabdriver from the United States," he added.

His modern views were weakening; he needed moral and material support.

"You lie," said the princess calmly. "He is Gunga. He is sent by destiny to make me free!" Her eyes were glowing orbs of triumph.

Quorn, busy with the elephant, knew nothing, and cared less concerning ancient legends. He was standing in front of Asoka, beneath the upraised trunk, coaxing with whatever argument occurred to him:

"Now don't you act crazy again, you big boob. You've only got one friend on earth this minute, and that's me, you sucker. Lose me and you lose your last chance. They'll shoot you sure, unless I take the blame for all the damage you've done. Don't kid yourself. Many a time I've known what it is not to have a friend in the world; I tell you it's no cinch. You big stiff, thank your lucky stars, instead of looking at me red eyed like a doggone nightmare."

"Bamjee!" exclaimed the Princess. "Do I, or do I not, look like 'her'? Does he, or does he not, resemble 'him'?"

"You do. He does," Bamjee admitted ruefully, as one who hated to concede to himself that he was secretly glad of the incredible, plain fact.

Suddenly the princess seized entire command of Bamjee and the situation.

"Come!" she commanded. "I don't care now who sees us. The more the better. Help me to find some sort of saddle for the elephant. Help me to find servants."

"But this man and his elephant may go away," Bamjee objected.

"No, they will not," she retorted. "This is destiny. There is nothing for us to do but bring a saddle and some servants."

"That is most unmitigated nonsense," remarked Bamjee under his breath. "This is lunacy, but why not be a lunatic if lunatics are happy? To put a saddle on destiny is something altogether new, I think."

Quorn was devoting his entire attention to the elephant. That shock of crashing through the wall had had a strange effect on both of them. It had made Asoka crazy. It had made Quorn sane. It had shaken loose Asoka's memories of tricks learned in his youth a half century before; memory had become mixed up with desire to please his only friend, so he began to dance a sort of double shuffle, bobbing his aching head in time to unheard drum beats and shaking his feet as if bells were fastened to them.

Quorn, with his new found sanity, perceived that if he

would control the elephant he must encourage him to do the things he wanted to. So he encouraged him to dance.

"That's the way to shake 'em. So's the boy! Step lively, you old sucker."

He began to whistle, and the whistling suggested something else to Asoka, who stopped dancing and raised himself on his hind legs. Quorn encouraged that too.

"Now try the other end, old-timer."

Not knowing the proper word of command, he made signals, which Asoka evidently understood, for he came to the ground and then stood on both forefeet with his hind legs in the air.

Presently Quorn had him waltzing around the fishpond, causing devastation of the garden but establishing a cordial understanding, which was increased when Quorn espied a long handled scrubbing broom that some gardener had left amid the shrubbery. He ordered the elephant into the pond and was obeyed so swiftly that more than a dozen fish were splashed out on the wave displaced by five descending tons. Quorn picked up the struggling fish by the tails and threw them in again. The elephant lay on the muddy bottom, reveling amid the ruin of lotus plants. Quorn seized the broom, and, stepping on him, scrubbed him thoroughly, as he had seen mahouts do. When one side was finished, Asoka rolled over and Quorn scrubbed the other side.

A BATH AND scrubdown to a weary elephant are as toast to a poached egg; they belong together, and it is the fitness of things that creates harmonious conditions, out of which events are born. Forth from the pond came a new Asoka, contrite and amendable, who needed only a little something more to make him feel that the world was, after all, the best place ever invented.

Quorn went off in search of sugar cane, because his intuition was now working full blast. Asoka followed him, determined not to lose so soon this prodigy of friendship, so Quorn held him by the trunk and they explored together, neither of them meaning to do damage and yet not estimating heights and widths with accuracy that was any credit to them. They passed under an ornamental wooden archway, six inches too small in each direction for Asoka's bulk. It naturally came adrift and would have started another reign of terror, but for Quorn's presence of mind; he contrived to pretend that the destruction of that arch was exactly what he wanted, and that utmost speed away from there was the next event in order.

They arrived in haste, but not in panic, around the corner of a building, into a stable yard where ancient vehicles and rotting lumber were crowded in confusion against the far wall. Along one side there was a shed, in which Quorn spied sugar cane. He made the elephant lie down in mid-yard, appropriated half a dozen stalks of the tempting stuff and proceeded to baby his charge.

"There now. That's for being daddy's good boy, daddy's pearl. That's what good boys get for doing what daddy tells them." Never having been a daddy, never having even felt like one before, he let the new emotion have its head. "You damned old duffer, you and me's friends, d'you get me? I never knew how bad I needed a friend."

Then more astonishment. Quorn found himself surrounded by the princess, Bamjee and a score of native servants who had dragged forth from a shed an ancient elephant saddle with its small crimson canopy still intact. They proceeded to try to put the saddle on Asoka, who objected. Quorn tried to prevent them, but the princess became furious and he could not manage both her and Asoka, so he chose the simpler task and controlled the elephant, who jumped to the conclusion that Quorn wished him to be saddled.

Anything that Quorn wished was Asoka's pleasure, so presently, after much sweating and shouting the saddle was in position. The princess climbed in. She commanded Quorn to take his place as mahout in front of her. Bamjee, bringing an ancient *ankus* from a shed, placed it in Quorn's hand and Quorn climbed on to Asoka's neck in a sort of daydream. He did not know where to go or what next was expected of him, but Bamjee gave the necessary order and the elephant rose, immediately turning homeward.

Home was what Asoka craved now. That futile picket under the outspreading *neem* tree was as necessary to him as a warm bed and a good book and a towel are to us prodigal sons. He must reestablish his existence on a normal basis. Most of us crave normalcy, and elephants are just like anybody else. So it was best foot foremost, with Bamjee riding ahead on a moth eaten, melancholy looking pony; because Bamjee was a babu with an eye to opportunity, who thought of destiny as the product of keen men's scheming. Bamjee had it all by heart now. He could see the outcome.

And it was even better than Bamjee hoped for. All the inhabitants of Narada City who had nothing else to do at the moment—that is to say almost all of them—had turned out and were pouring along the highway to discover what had happened to the elephant and Quorn. They were excited, hot, breathless, expecting something terrible, and in a mood to be thoroughly entertained by anything, so be it staggered imagination. The sun shone through the cloud of dust they raised, on to a drunken splurge of color all in motion. And they beheld a miracle; no doubt about that whatever.

THEY BEHELD AN elephant that moved as if impelled by an obsessing purpose, holding his trunk rigid as he swiftly shuffled through the dust. They beheld an ancient scarlet howdah on his back, a howdah such as nobody had seen for generations. Riding in the howdah was a gloriously dressed and radiantly beautiful young woman, whom not one of them had ever seen before, because the law of *purdah* had always kept her in strict seclusion.

When Asoka had burst forth in his fury from the city, he had had no howdah on his back. When Quorn had ridden forth, he had had no turban on his head. There had been no princess connected in any way whatever with the incident. So what should anybody think? Quorn sat bolt upright, so exactly like the image on the wall that nobody with any sense at all could doubt him. There was a carmine caste mark on his forehead. And the princess, radiantly lovely, unveiled, looking straight before her, was so thrilling that anybody who had imagination—and who has not?—would be eager to believe the utterly incredible about her, and the more incredible, the better.

Furthermore, they heard the voice of Bamjee crying:

"Way there! Way for the Wheel of Destiny! Behold! The gods now finish what the gods began!"

Could anything be simpler? Could anything be more authentic? Why should anybody not believe it? A roar went up, such a roar as Alexander heard, or Darius, when a multitude acclaimed him king of kings. The crowd began to dance with enthusiasm. They began to shout time honored phrases of mystical meaning. Messengers were sent on borrowed ponies to inform the priests of thirty temples that an ancient prophesy was coming true.

And because there is competition among temples, as in any other walk of life, and no set of priests was willing to let any other set have all the credit—rightly, too, since none of them had earned it—all the priests turned out in full array with drums and bands of sacred music, leading the procession; so that Asoka had to slow down lest he tread on priestly heels. And that provided time for garlands to be woven, garlands that were tossed to Quorn and that fell and draped Asoka's shoulders and the scarlet howdah, until Asoka and his burden were a mass of flowers and the street was strewn with trodden blossoms.

Through Narada's quiet streets there surged such a throng as those ancient buildings had not seen for centuries. The sacred peacocks screamed from garden walls. The sacred monkeys jabbered and grimaced from jade green trees. The parakeets wove bright green patterns in the sunlight. And the sun, in his place, as usual, but having no concern at all with destiny, beamed down his benison on all concerned.

PRESENTLY THEY REACHED the palace gate, because the princess so commanded, and Asoka willingly obeyed the pressure of Quorn's knee. Bamjee had ridden ahead for private conversation with the rajah, Bamjee being a man who had an eye for opportunity as well as a lucrative job to lose. So the rajah, who had had several whiskies to console him for the morning's accident, had time to get into his royal robes and a strategic state of mind.

He realized he had an opportunity to snub the eighteen gun Jamnuggar, which was better fun than being allied to him, and that he could bully the priests, which was better fun than being patronized. Bejewelled then, and pleasantly inspired by potent spirit, he received the thunderous procession at the splendid entrance gate, surrounded by scores of attendants in their best court suits.

The crowd heard nothing, because the crowd itself was making too much noise. But the crowd saw, which was all important, because liberty—whatever the philosophers may have to say of it—is something that the crowd gives or the crowd withholds. Priests, acolytes and temple ministrants were forced to make way, striving to preserve their dignity; Asoka had a one track mind.

Home was what Asoka wanted, but he was aware that Quorn wished him to deliver his burden first, so he hurried to get that over with and made for the gateway through the swarm of priests, as an alibi goes through circumstantial evidence, brushing it all aside, a five-ton alibi, as welcome to the rajah as a catchword to a politician. And Bamjee managed to get the gates shut just behind him, while the crowd yelled itself hoarse.

"She is free! She is free! She has her liberty! The gods sent Gunga back to finish his task! *Bande Sankyamuni!*"

Only a dozen priests had entered behind Asoka before the gates were closed. They grouped themselves around the rajah to prevent him from appearing too important, and Quorn made Asoka kneel before them all. They happened to be priests from different temples, so that they were not unanimous except in determination to snatch all the credit possible; and the rajah was quite a statesman when he had such a man as Bamjee to make suggestions in a whisper from behind.

"You, who are custodians of truth and the interpreters of events," he said, "is this or is it not fulfilment of an ancient prophecy?"

They said undoubtedly it was fulfilment. There was nothing else they could say with the crowd outside the gate all yelling the correct interpretation in their ears. They could hardly deny the full significance of what had happened after permitting themselves to lend their dignity to the procession.

"Then you will inform the Maharajah of Jamnuggar's ministers that destiny has raised my daughter higher than even he may reach?"

They liked that. They agreed at once. It would raise Narada to a hitherto unhoped for eminence, and themselves to the position of censors of royal marriages. It gave them the chance to seize importance for themselves. They said no other course was possible.

"Then you will tell the people," said the rajah, "that my daughter has been set free from the laws of *purdah*, but without loss of caste or priestly recognition."

That was a challenge, which they had to answer on the spot, and they could only answer one way, being jealous of one another and afraid that if one said no, another might say yes. So they agreed.

"Then let there be a celebration," said the rajah, Bamjee prompting him. "Let all the city celebrate with fireworks and colored lanterns. There shall be a banquet in the streets tonight at my cost. And my daughter shall ride through the streets by torchlight, with twenty elephants and all my army, to celebrate her emancipation."

THERE WAS NOTHING for those priests to do but to accept the situation and to study how to swim with the new tide, not against it. They departed solemnly, with dignity, to order garlands hung upon the carving on the end wall of the market place, while Bamjee slipped away to purchase fireworks on commission. Bamjee was happy. But some people are never satisfied; the rajah, being royal, craved the rind as well as the fruit, so to his daughter he was royally surly when the priests were out of earshot and they stood like actors in the wings, without an audience.

"Do you see what you have done?" he snorted. "You have made it utterly impossible for me to govern! You have used one silly story to upset a thousand customs. You will upset me next. Then what?"

"Ask the astrologer!" she answered laughing. "Destiny does strange things! May it make you generous to Gunga!"

And, since her giggling maids had come, she let herself be shrouded in a silken shawl and borne away into the palace to have supper and be bathed and arrayed and hung with jewels to make ready for the evening celebration.

"This rising generation," the rajah remarked savagely, "has neither grace nor gratitude."

But having said that, he began to feel better, so he lighted a large cigar and came quite close to Quorn, who was sitting silent on Asoka's neck. He narrowly examined Quorn's eyes, nodding.

"You're a strange coincidence," he commented. "Do you believe in destiny?"

Quorn sniffed at the good cigar smoke as he met the rajah's royal gaze. There was something, somewhere that they held in common, although he could not guess what at the moment.

"Destiny be sugared," he answered. "I must take this critter home and go and mind the mission."

"Destiny is sugared sometimes," said the rajah. "I suspect this whole thing was arranged by Bamjee for the sake of business, which will make it sweet for him. Would you like a cigar?"

QUORN SMOKED AND they observed each other, until the rajah spoke again.

"I suppose you realize that I must send you back to Philadelphia? You'll be a nuisance in Narada. They say I'm generous. You'll go, of course?"

"Me?" Quorn stared at him rebelliously. "Hell, no!"

"How much?" asked the rajah.

But nobody could buy Quorn now. He had a friend, a new experience. He had to cultivate Asoka. Nothing else could interest him.

"Hell, no!" he repeated.

"Some men don't know enough to take advantage of destiny," said the rajah.

"Maybe. Some men don't believe a lot of nonsense," Quorn retorted.

"Yes, but some men live by nonsense," said the rajah. "People like me, for instance. I enjoy nonsense.

"I enjoy you. But nonsense makes powerful enemies at times. Somebody may poison you, and we'll have to bury you unless I can find some way out of the difficulty. There's a bad lazy devil in charge of my elephants. I could protect

you if you took his place, or you might like to be superintendent and keep an eye on him and all the others."

"Suits me," Quorn said simply. "Do I rate enough to live
on? Very well, sir, if you'll tell 'em to open the gate I'll—
Come on Two-Tails, you old sucker, play up the luck before
it changes on us. Up you get and hit the pike for home.
We're buddies, me and you! We'll go to by-by like a pair
of good boys."

THE BIG LEAGUE MIRACLE

Another graphic tale of Ben Quorn

ONE COMMENTATOR ON the Laws of Manu advises: "If you desire peace, make no miracles."

Those of us who do not know how to make them will be willing to concede the point without getting angry about it. Ben Quorn, on the other hand, grew irritated because all the inhabitants of the Indian city of Narada thought of him not only as the maker of a miracle but as the miracle itself.

"I'm an ex-taxicab driver with a clean record," he insisted.

But if you have eyes like a he-goat, and have tamed an angry elephant, and have had your portrait carved in stone on a wall in the public market place a thousand years before you were bom; and if, because a princess rode the elephant behind you after you had tamed him, and in consequence was released from the law that keeps royal Indian ladies behind curtains; and if, in consequence of that, you are held to have fulfilled an ancient prophecy and have been appointed superintendent of the rajah's elephants, there is no peace for you—none whatever, as Quorn discovered.

It was wonderful at first, with thirty-four great elephants and thirty-four mahouts to do his bidding. Quorn took enormous pride in the elephants because, for some strange reason, they appeared to love him. When he entered the great compound under the *neem* trees within the ancient limestone wall, and the rising sun was gilding everything

with pale gold through which crowds of bright green parakeets wove sudden patterns, then Quorn enjoyed even
the sacred monkeys that were blamed for stealing the
elephants' grain, which of course the mahouts had really
sold, or swapped for strong drink.

The monkeys would scamper away, being reputed sacred,
whereas they knew, of course, that they were nothing of the
kind, so they had guilty consciences and preferred not to
be noticed. But four and thirty enormous elephants would
salute Quorn, raising their trunks in air; and there would
be tantrums and sulking all day long if he passed by one of
them without some sort of recognition. Wordless it might
be, and even motionless; but Quorn had discovered that
there is a bond of sympathy between beast and man, along
which flows mutual understanding if you have the trick.

"You stand still, and you like 'em, and they get you—
same as a girl gets the smell o' roses," was Quorn's way of
explaining it.

"YOU ASTONISH ME with they way you manage
elephants," the rajah said one morning. "Some men born
to the business don't do as well as you. How is it that you
know how?"

"Don't need to know how, sir," Quorn retorted. "It's like
the rajah business. Your ministers know all the rigmarole.
If things ain't working right, I guess you get yourself a new
crew. Same here. These heathen mahouts they all know
elephant; I make 'em do their stuff. That's all there is to it."

The rajah endured that comment on his statesmanship
with royal patience. But whenever he was patient he had
deep motives. Quorn who had learned a lot since he came
to Narada had not discovered that yet.

"Are you good with other animals?" the rajah asked him.

"Had a dog once. Got run over by a truck."

"Did you ever see a tiger?"

"Plenty—at the circus. I've sometimes wondered, sir, whether them brutes aren't overrated. Such as I've seen was lazy. Folks'd think 'em terrible ferocious when they'd yawn and stretch 'emselves, but they look to me like out size pussy cats—good lookers, but not much to be skeered of. Maybe I'm ignorant."

The rajah smiled. He watched Quorn count out stalks of sugar cane to make sure that the mahouts had stolen none of it; he watched him dose a two ton stomach ache with laudanum and then put fly bane on the edge of a ragged ear.

"Tigers," he said presently, "are not half as dangerous as elephants. A tiger can only bite and claw. An elephant can crush. I have seen many a tiger and many a man crushed flat under an elephant's paw. There are three elephants in this compound that have killed both men and tigers!"

After which the rajah rode away. And presently came Moses, who had been watching both of them, but especially watching the rajah's tell tale eyes. Moses was Quorn's Eurasian servant, who, being one eyed, sometimes saw only half of anything; and being half white he only told half secrets; but the other half of him being Oriental, the important part of every secret remained hidden in the dim recesses of his mind.

"If I were you, Mr. Quorn, I think I would return to the United States," he suggested.

"You ain't me," Quorn retorted, "and you haven't ever hunted a job back where I come from."

"Are there temple priests there, Mr. Quorn?"

"Maybe. I've driven most sorts of folks. I reckon priests ain't worse than politicians."

Moses changed the subject:

"Aren't you coming home to tiffin, Mr. Quorn? I've brought your sun spectacles."

Quorn had taken to wearing goggles in the streets because they reduced his strange resemblance to the Gunga Sahib, whose portrait, riding on an elephant, had been carved a thousand years ago on the limestone market wall. He hated to be stared at, and he did not enjoy the thought of looking like a heathen Hindu who had been dead for centuries.

He was usually in a hurry to get home to the midday meal, because the sight of an elephant eating a hundred pounds of hay aroused his appetite. But this time Moses led him down the long street called Pul-ke-nichi, meaning "underneath the bridge", the street where the fortune tellers and the nostrum sellers do a roaring business in between the offices of money lenders and the booths of cheap jack merchants. It is a smelly street, but interesting. Quorn protested, but Moses pleaded—

"It is necessaree that I show you something, Mr. Quorn."

SO PRESENTLY THEY stood beneath the bridge, where Moses shyly indicated the cause of their walking out of their way in the heat of an Indian noon. It is a very ancient bridge, and beautiful because time has smoothed it and obliterated all its builder's sins. It connects two ancient temples built on low hills known as Kali's Bosom. But nowadays the priests of those two temples are not on speaking terms except when they meet to agree on fines and penances to be imposed on other people, so there are no longer glorious processions from one temple to the other, and men have grown so superstitious about crossing the bridge that the grass grows in the cracks of the limestone pavement and the doves build nests on the shoulders of gods and goddesses that face inward from the parapet on either side, cooing there all day long as if there were no such thing as hawks in the azure heaven.

"Will you kindlee look at that," said Moses.

Carved on the wall of the limestone arch beneath the bridge there was a tiger being led into what appeared to be a temple door, by a lady who wore jeweled anklets. The tiger had some sort of collar and she led him with her left hand. In her right hand there were flowers.

"For her funeral, after the tiger eats her," Quorn suggested, but driving cabs in Philadelphia had not made him an authority on mystic symbolism.

"No, that is an ancient prophetic utterance," said Moses. "That is said to be the same princess whom the man named Gunga Sahib rescued on an elephant from durance vile, only he did not finish doing so because the elephant killed him. And it is part of the legend that after the elephant slew the Gunga Sahib, her angree royal parent put her into a tiger's cage in a courtyard of this temple. Nevertheless she tamed the tiger and led him forth across the bridge into that other temple. And people say—"

"Shucks!" remarked Quorn. "People are always talking bunk."

"And people say," said Moses, "that you are Gunga Sahib come to life again, because you look like Gunga Sahib and because you tamed the big elephant and brought the Princess Sankyamuni into the city on his back."

"They're looney."

"And they say that consequentlee the Princess Sankyamuni must be that princess of the legend, also returned into the world to finish that which was begun by Gunga Sahib but not finished, many centuries ago."

"Meaning she's got to be et by the tiger?" Quorn suggested.

Moses preferred to offer no opinion as to that, and Quorn was hungry, so they made haste to the gate house of the abandoned mission where Quorn lived nominally as caretaker, although Moses did the actual loafing around the place, which was all that the task amounted to.

And while Quorn sat eating curry and rice, came Bamjee, the rajah's business agent—Bamjee the ex-telegrapher, with his big head blazing in a flame colored turban, his big eyes observing everything through gold rimmed spectacles, his big mouth showing white teeth in a smile that would have thawed a money lender, and his undersized body resplendent in a gray silk suit. A very prosperous and distinguished *babu,* with a B.A. degree, a platinum watch chain and no advertised prejudices. Being also a person of tact, he took one of the chairs in the shade of the porch until Quorn had finished eating, which gave him plenty of time to consider how to break his rather awkward news; so he was ready by the time Quorn filled his pipe and came and sat beside him. When Bamjee was ready, very often all the unseen wheels beneath the surface of Narada began moving.

"MR. QUORN, THE priests are very much offended with you."

"Me?"

"Because you brought the Princess Sankyamuni through the city on the back of that great elephant Asoka and all the people said you are the Gunga Sahib come to life again. They said also that an ancient prophecy has been fulfilled. Therefore, as you know, the priests were obliged to agree that the Princess Sankyamuni shall be released from *purdah* and may go where she pleases in public without losing caste. The priests could not help it. But they consider it a very bad example to the other Indian ladies, and they are also angry because their hand was forced. So they have revived another ancient legend, according to which the princess whom Gunga rescued was afterwards thrown into a tiger's den. She contrived to tame the tiger and she led him from one temple into another one, across the bridge connecting them.

"Nevertheless, her angry royal parent made her spend all

the rest of her days in lonely seclusion because she wished to go about in public and to do good. But it was prophesied that she should be reborn some day, and that people should know her because she would repeat the taming of the tiger. The priests make the logical assertion, Mr. Quorn, that if one prophecy has been fulfilled, then so must that other one be also. Therefore, if the Princess Sankyamuni wishes to be a modern woman and to enjoy her liberty, she must be put into a tiger's den and she must tame him. They have a very ferocious tiger ready for her."

Quorn's pipe went out.

"I ain't no princess. What has the tiger to do with me?" he demanded.

"You are in a predicament, Mr. Quorn. His Highness, the Rajah of Narada, made you superintendent of his elephants in order to be able to protect you from the priests. The crowd has called you Gunga Sahib, and his Highness foresaw how annoyed the priests would be. He was happy to score off the priests. But his Highness is a potentate of sudden gratitudes and generosities, who very quickly wearies of being merely philanthropic."

"Cheese it!" Quorn retorted. "I've already saved him nearly half his bill for elephant feed."

Bamjee blinked. As purchasing agent on commission, he was aware that purchases had fallen off since Quorn became superintendent. Quorn could quickly see through the mahouts' little tricks, but he needed time to plumb the depths of Bamjee's mind.

"The Princess Sankyamuni," Bamjee went on, "asked her royal parent for advice concerning this new development. His Highness consulted me. I said that possibly

Mr. Quorn, who is so successful with the elephants, can tame a tiger also, and in that case everything might turn out fortunately."

"Trust you not to mind your own business!" remarked Quorn. "So *that's* what he meant this morning when he asked me whether I know tigers."

"Yes, and he wishes you to tame that tiger. Also, the Princess Sankyamuni wants to talk with you," said Bamjee.

"Nix! Nothing doing! I ain't hired to tame tigers! Me, a woman, and a tiger don't mix! Ask the court astrologer; he'll tell you it's in my horoscope."

BUT QUORN WAS playing against destiny and the cards were stacked.

"She did ask the astrologer," said Bamjee. "The astrologer said that, because of the position of the Sun and Saturn in her Tenth House, if she should tame the tiger she will very soon inherit all her royal parent's dominion and you will become her principal adviser."

"Me?"

"And the worst of it is, Mr. Quorn, that being a woman, and therefore talkative, she told one of her attendants, who told her royal parent what the astrologer said. And consequently, he is naturally not altogether anxious that the tiger should be too tame."

"Jee-rusalem! Moses was right. I'm going home to Philadelphia!"

"Unfortunately, Mr. Quorn, if you should try to go away just now the people would say that because you are undoubtedly a reincarnation of that personage named Gunga, therefore you belong, as it were, to them, and they derive great comfort from having you here in their midst.

And of course, there is no railway in Narada, so you would have to go by carriage, which they could very easily prevent. I think they would be so indignant if you should try to go that they might kill you. The priests are most strategic and crowds, being mercurial, are easily influenced, Mr. Quorn. And they are so looking forward to this ceremony with the princess and the tiger that if they were to be deprived of it, there might be riots. And since she can not go through with the ceremony unless you will help her, you would be responsible for the rioting if you should refuse. And if she does not go through with it she will be forced again into seclusion."

"You mean they'd take away her liberty? They'd make her hide behind a curtain all her life?"

"Yes," said Bamjee. "And the princess wishes to talk with you this afternoon at four o'clock."

Quorn could not even light his pipe, he was so upset. Instinct urged him to throw up his job and go home to Philadelphia, disguised if necessary. But he remembered how seasick he had been on the voyage to India. And then, again, there are not many ex-taxi drivers who have an opportunity to talk about a tiger with a princess in her palace while a hundred thousand people almost breathlessly await the outcome.

Pride is subtle stuff, and so is curiosity. He decided he would give his answer when Bamjee should return for him in a royal carriage with two horses that afternoon at half past three. Meanwhile, he would think it over.

But the thinkers are not many. As a commentator on the Laws of Manu says, "They who believe they think are oftener than not like harlots waiting for a lover, knowing neither whence he shall come nor who he may be."

When Bamjee had gone Moses came out from behind the reed blind that hung in the open doorway to keep out heat and dust. He had obviously been listening, which made Quorn unreasonably irritable. And if we won't be reasonable, destiny makes use of our unreasonableness, so says the selfsame commentator, which almost makes it look as if destiny holds the long end of the lever.

"Mr. Quorn, I think that Bamjee wishes to be rid of you because the corn for the elephants no longer is stolen and therefore Bamjee receives less commission. He thinks if you should try to tame the tiger you might be eliminated."

"And you don't want that for fear you might lose your own job cooking for me. Gurr-rrgh! I know you!"

That settled it. Quorn's unreasonable irritation tipped the scale. It caused him to decide to talk things over with the Princess Sankyamuni. He assured himself that a mere discussion commits nobody. But if destiny and a lovely woman are on the same side of the balance, there is not much chance for a man from Philadelphia, or from any other place, to escape without gaining at least experience. Quorn might have thought of that too, but he was angry. Angry men don't think much.

Bamjee arrived silk suited, in a two horsed carriage with a turbaned footman up behind, and Quorn, in his ready made Sunday hand-me-downs and a new white helmet, drove with him to the part of the rajah's palace where the Princess Sankyamuni had already begun to taste the deadly democratic vices. And when the princess came into the great, cool, darkened drawing room, which was furnished in the jazz band Louis Quinze style but looked out on a quiet garden where a fountain played to some thousand year old statues of a dozen or so contemplative gods, there were only nine veiled maidens to protect her from the tongue of scandal; whereas, nineteen surely never would have been enough, when it is remembered that Quorn was the first non-Hindu masculine adventurer to set foot in the palace or to see her face unveiled.

PERHAPS IT IS not quite accurate to say he saw it, because it dazzled him. To Quorn it seemed that she was even lovelier than on the day of her famous ride behind him on the elephant. She paid the subtle compliment to liberty of wearing only half her jewels, so that there was less to distract attention from her eyes, which, according to Quorn, would have melted cast iron if she had looked at it long enough.

They melted Quorn's heart, timed by his heart beats, in eleven seconds. Trying to describe her afterward to Moses, and remembering the color of her *sari* and the turquoise bracelets on her beautifully modeled feet, he likened her to a nosegay wrapped in tissue paper. But Quorn never had the patience to read poetry, which he regarded as sinful waste of time. His metaphors were like a one horse hearse, suggesting the simplicity imposed by limitations.

The princess sat on an armchair, quite uncomfortable because she was used to lolling on sandal scented swansdown cushions; and her maidens sat around her in a semicircle, blushing behind their veils because they could not hide their pretty feet unless they sat upon them, and there was not room to sit upon them on those French plush covered chairs. Quorn stood, hiding his hands inside his helmet.

Bamjee spoke first, although that was against the court rules as laid down by all palace chamberlains since royalty was first invented; but the silence was becoming awkward.

"Daughter of the Dawn, this *babu* begs you to remember—"

"You may leave us, Bamjee."

He went out bowing, backward, utterly disgusted to discover that a wad of paper had been firmly wedged into the key hole and that the door made too much noise when he tried to clear the keyhole with his fountain pen.

"Shall I call you Gunga Sahib, or do you like your funny foreign name?" the princess asked.

She had a voice like honey oozing from the tips of rose buds. It suggested a virgin's dreams of paradise. It hinted at passion, ripening but not yet ready to be revealed.

"My name's Quorn, miss—beg pardon, miss, I mean, your Highness."

"No, I like miss better. It sounds modern. Won't you sit down?"

Gingerly Quorn arranged himself on a row of brass headed studs at the edge of an imported plush and gilt chair. He hesitated, but decided not to lay his helmet on the floor because, for the first time in his life, he felt ashamed of his horny hands and preferred to hide them. He kept twisting the helmet by the sweat band, as if it were a receptacle in which he hoped to catch some sort of comfort.

"Can you tame a tiger, Mr. Quorn?"

"Me, miss?"

"You did so wonderfully with Asoka, and an elephant

is so much bigger than a tiger. Besides, everybody knows that elephants can kill tigers if they can only catch them in a corner. So it stands to reason that whoever can tame the greater can tame the lesser. You have to admit that, Mr. Quorn. You must be logical, now mustn't you? I must have a very savage tiger tamed almost instantly. He has been purposely taught that all men are his enemies, and he is probably rather hungry."

"Gosh, miss, why not feed him?" It was cooler in that room than outside, but Quorn wiped the perspiration from his face.

"That might help, but the priests won't allow it. You see, they suspect I will ask you to help me, and they know you have lots of laudanum for the elephants when they have stomach ache, so they are afraid you might put laudanum in the tiger's meat. I have to lead that tiger out of his den, across the bridge, and into a cage in another temple."

"Asking your pardon for the question, miss, but isn't this proposition kinder crazy?"

"Oh, no. It is just symbolical. I lead hate out of Kali's temple into Siva's, where it is transmuted into love. I have consulted the astrologer. Isn't that what your Christian Daniel did before they threw him into the lion's den?"

"Tigers is different," Quorn objected, groping blindly for an argument. "Miss, isn't there a British political resident in Narada? Do you suppose the British Government 'ud allow a beautiful young lady to be pitched into a den o' tigers? I've heard a lot of criticism of the British, but nothing that bad."

"I believe there is such a person as a resident," said the princess, "but he is absent, fortunately. It would be unendurable, if he should interfere. I am quite sure I am a reincarnation of Sankyamuni; you see, I even have the same name. I am equally sure you are a reincarnation of Gunga Sahib, though you probably did some bad deeds in former lives that merited the *karma* of forgetfulness. I don't remember very clearly either. But I know the legends and the prophecies. You and I have seen one come true, so now let us tackle this one boldly."

QUORN DID NOT feel even slightly bold, but he hated to admit it.

"Tell me about it, miss."

"Didn't Bamjee tell you? The priests say I must lead their tiger over the bridge from Kali's temple into Siva's, symbolizing the transmutation of death into life—of evil into good—of passion into ecstasy?"

"Why not let them priests do that transmuting, miss?"

"Oh, no. They couldn't possibly. They are only poor priests. You and I are blossoms on a branch of destiny."

"Miss, I haven't done no blossoming since mother used to scrub my ears and pack me off to Sunday school with ten cents for the missionary box."

"If you don't believe in your destiny, then destiny will force you to believe," the princess answered. "For instance, the rajah, my father, insists somebody told him what the astrologer said about my becoming Ranee very soon, and your becoming my confidential adviser, if we face this ordeal bravely. My father hopes, of course, that you will be killed trying to tame the tiger, and that I will be afraid at the last minute. Then he could simply force me back into seclusion, and that would be the end of me. He would marry me to some one I have never seen. But I would rather die than that. I don't intend to be afraid. I am going through with this—with you or without you, Mr. Quorn."

Admiration took Quorn by the reins with which a man may govern judgment when he is not in the presence of incarnate youth and loveliness—and not for the first time in his life within a palace—and not indignant that a parent should be willing to toss that marvelous young woman to a tiger—and not almost equally indignant because he himself is to be included in the tiger's meal.

"Gosh!" he exclaimed, "I'd like to put one over on 'em!"

And the princess seized that opportunity as naïvely as she proposed to accept the other one. She sketched the situation swiftly for Quorn's benefit.

"You see, Gunga Sahib—I mean Mr. Quorn, if we succeed in this, we shall have defeated the priests forever. They will never again be able to challenge either of us, because they will have used up all the legends. The priests hate you as much as me. They can't endure to have the crowd regard you as the reincarnation of Gunga Sahib. And yet they themselves have said you are that, because the crowd insisted on it when they saw you ride Asoka. Sooner or later the priests would find some way of killing you, unless we put this over on them as you say. Afterward, when I am ranee, I will be able to protect you and we will do wonderful things."

"And when is all this supposed to happen, miss?"

"Oh, any time. Tomorrow would do nicely."

Quorn scratched his head. He felt like a man in a dream. His reeling brain could suggest no way out of the dilemma. But he was partly Scotch and had to bargain, as he would bargain at the trumpet of Judgment Day.

"Time costs nothing, miss—leastways, not here in Narada. Supposing you was to name a date a little later on. That special bad tiger might up and die on 'em. He might bite a priest and get ptomaine. That'd give us a bit better break. We might ring in a circus tiger, if we had time to shop around a bit, and maybe some o' them half fed subordinate priests might listen to the chink of money."

"The astrologer says we have until the next new moon," the princess answered. "We can't fail if we act before then. But if we wait until after the next new moon we can't succeed."

"Let's see—that's eleven, twelve, thirteen days."

Quorn hated the number thirteen. It invariably made him nervous. It made him so nervous now that he could think of nothing except that glorious pair of eyes that did not know what fear was. He was glad his insurance was paid up.

"Miss," he said, "this proposition is the darn' craziest I ever heard of. But I kinder like you, miss, if you'll excuse my saying so, and if you're all that set on taking such a crazy chance, I'll go you, provided you claim every one o' them thirteen days to give me half a chance to think in, and provided you act the way I warn you when the time comes."

HE KNEW HE was behaving like a lunatic, but almost before he had finished speaking he was actually proud of it. The princess gurgled with delight. She rose, and he rose, and he dropped his helmet. Before he could prevent her she had seized his right, rough, horny hand in hers and was kissing it.

"There, there, now, missy, don't you carry on. We'll manage somehow."

She was crying, she was so delighted, and Quorn felt like a man who has been knighted on the field of battle. He trod on his helmet but contrived to pick it up and then backed away toward the door, where he stood holding the crushed helmet in both hands until the princess and her ladies had gone out past the gilt and enamel screen at the opposite side of the room. Then he opened the door and almost stumbled over Bamjee. The relief was instant. Swift reaction followed upon its heels. Thought flowed in as water flows into a dry sponge. An idea came to him. It was no more crazy than all the rest of it. He seized Bamjee by the throat and shook him, to the exquisite but suppressed delight of several palace servants, bitterly jealous of the business agent.

"You scheming rogue! This is your doing! You've got me into this mess. Now help me out of it! Listen, unless you want to be a legend and a prophecy and walk into that tiger's den ahead o' me, you do exactly what I say and hold your tongue about it. Get me a good tame circus tiger. Get him quick. I'll give you two days. I want him dumped there back of the elephant lines, in the cage in the old shed back of where Asoka's picket is. If he ain't tame, you'll be the first meal he tastes after I take one look at him. Do you get me? One tame tiger, paid for by you and delivered to me in the old shed back of the elephant lines, and not a word said."

Bamjee wished for the use of his windpipe. And, being a person without prejudices, he was quite willing to play anybody's game and sit on either side of anybody's fence. Also he had imagination. There would be a nice, inaudit- able profit on the tiger; he felt quite sure the princess would pay the bill, even though Quorn should advise her not to. And, being a rajah's purchasing agent, he knew where to shop for every kind of unconventional extravagance, from zoos to Parisian underwear. Bamjee agreed instantly, nodding as well as he could until Quorn let go of his throat.

As they drove away in the two horsed carriage it occurred to Bamjee that Quorn might prove to be the joker in destiny's pack of cards. He had played poker at Calcutta University, where Hindus like to be as debonair and devilish as anybody else. He knew how a joker upsets all calculations. He had once filled a flush with the aid of the joker and won all the other students' money.

"Mr. Quorn, I think you might be wise to trust me," he suggested.

"I'd as soon trust a snake," Quorn assured him.

"But a snake who bites one's enemies is a trustworthy accomplice," Bamjee answered. "Like you, I admire the Princess Sankyamuni, Mr. Quorn. Also, you may remember when you rode on the great elephant Asoka through the city with the princess up behind you, it was I who caused the crowd to recognize you as the Gunga Sahib."

"Yes, you've caused me a heap of trouble," Quorn retorted. "However, let's look at it this way: if you help me and hold your tongue and if we fail, nobody will know you had a hand in it, so you'll make no more enemies than you have already. If you don't help, and if we win, then your job's gone, for I'll guarantee that. But if you do help, and we win, then you can look to the princess for all the patronage you can wallow in, you durned percentage grafter."

"I wish my education had included the art of graceful speech," said Bamjee. "I have only an unpolished smatter-

ing of English. Suppose I put it this way: I will scratch your
back if you will scratch mine."

"Very well," said Quorn. "I'll go you. But mark my words,
I'll have the tiger scratch you good and plenty if you fail
me in one particular."

BAMJEE DID NOT mention that he, too, was a target of
priestly indignation. Quorn had only perpetrated and
unwittingly become a miracle. Bamjee was the man who
had proclaimed him, which was worse, and the priests
were sure to get him for it some day unless he looked out
for himself.

So Bamjee, after depositing Quorn at the elephant lines,
drove off with all his ingenuity concentrated on getting the
nice tame tiger that Quorn had set his heart on. He knew
of a Jain temple where they had a hospital for animals,
and where there was a convalescent tiger that caused the
benevolent Jains anxiety because he disliked vegetables.

The Jains refuse to kill for food or for any other reason.
He could get that tiger, it occurred to him, for nothing
more expensive than a promise to treat the dumb brute
kindly. And he could charge for it at market price, which in
the case of tigers is elastic and depends on what you want
the tiger for, and how badly you want him, and how soon.
Bamjee was an excellent man of business, which the Jains
reputedly are not, though they can win the heart of any
injured animal that is brought into their temple compound.
A beautiful, milk fed tiger, reared from a cub in captivity,
changed guardians that very evening, and without too
much mendacity. Bamjee simply told the venerable Jains
that a rajah's daughter desired the lovely creature for a pet.

And so it came to pass that Asoka, the biggest of all the

elephants, fidgeted and trumpeted because he could smell tiger somewhere near him. There was a wall between them, and the tiger was locked in a cage in a shed, but the new surroundings had made the tiger restless, so he was vibrant as well as smelly, with the result that the great elephant plucked nervously at his new steel picket ring. Moreover, Quorn neglected him, and an elephant is jealous as well as nervous. Restlessness and a sense of impending trouble spread all through the elephant compound, so that the mahouts were kept busy cajoling and commanding.

Quorn, with only twelve days left in which to make a plan to outwit priests who think in terms of centuries, had a chair in front of the tiger's cage in the shed, and was trying to think.

"Dammit, a man can't dig without trying," he reflected, "but thought seems different. The more I try to think, the less thought comes!"

The tiger paced up and down behind the bars, rising on his hind legs as high as he could reach at each end before he turned. Quorn had watered him and fed him good fresh meat, but when he had gone up close to the bars afterward he had had to jump back to avoid the swift, out reaching claws. The sight of the snarling fangs had nearly paralyzed him.

"Tame!" he muttered.

According to Quorn's idea the tiger should be sleepy and contented after that good meal, but there seemed to be something wrong with the calculation. He pushed the chair away and began to pace up and down with his hands behind him; and because he was trying to think of one thing, and one thing only, every conceivable thought occurred to him except the one he wanted. He was like a drowning man, reviewing all his past life, only that it took much longer.

It was possibly an hour before he realized that he was pacing one way and the tiger the other, each turning when the other turned and each making exactly the same pause before resuming the patrol. But when he had become conscious of what was happening he kept it up, until it dawned on him that the tiger seemed to like it.

He ventured slightly closer to the cage. The tiger took no notice, so presently Quorn walked up and down so close to the bars that the great claws could have reached him through them easily. But the tiger kept on pacing up and down until Quorn grew weary of it and turned away at last. Then the tiger ceased and lay down, watching him.

"Seems what you want, you sucker, is entertainment," said Quorn, and scratched his forehead.

He went out to see how Asoka was behaving and spent a long time soothing and calming the enormous beast. The sound and smell of tiger stirred and alarmed every nerve in Asoka's being, so after a while Quorn moved him to another picket beneath a *neem* tree more than a hundred yards away on the far side of the compound, where he soon settled down to dusting himself and behaving reasonably.

"I think you've given me a thought," said Quorn, "you big old bag of notions. Me, I ain't no ornithologist. I don't know a tiger from dynamite, but—"

He did not dare to try to hook that thought yet. It was, so to speak, nibbling. He studied Asoka's forefeet for a while.

"They could crush a few eggs. They sure would make

some omelette," he muttered. "Mebbe you could kill a tiger if he'd stand still. Mebbe."

Then he went back to the tiger, which appeared to have been sleeping. But the moment he entered the shed the tiger got to its feet and, appearing to recognize him, resumed its pacing up and down. It stopped at the end of half a dozen turns.

"WHAT'S WORRYING YOU now?" Quorn wondered. "If you'd only eat sugar, same as elephants, I'd be on the soft side of you in no time."

Hands behind him, in a brown study, he began to pace the floor. Before he had made one turn up and down the tiger was doing the same thing. He stopped when Quorn stopped. He resumed when Quorn resumed.

"Seems you're teaching me—not me you."

He decided he could learn, perhaps, and tried a few experiments. He found that when he rubbed against the bars the tiger did the same thing, like a great well fed cat who wanted stroking. But he did not dare yet to put his hand inside the cage. Instead, he set the chair close to the bars and sat down where the tiger could not quite reach him with its claws but could smell him and grow used to him. After a while the tiger lay down in a corner and went to sleep. Quorn took advantage of that to put the chair inside the cage. The tiger awoke, examined the chair suspiciously, decided that it smelt like Quorn, and went to sleep again.

So Quorn left the chair inside the cage and went out into the sunlight to consider. Did he dare? Had the tiger already decided to be friendly? It was evidently a tame tiger, who was used to being handled, and there was a mark on the hair of his neck, which suggested he might have worn a collar not so long ago.

One thought led to another. Quorn remembered having seen, at the back of the shed where they kept all the elephant harness, a collar that was much too big for any sort of dog he had ever heard of. He went and fetched it. It was a splendid collar with a strong brass buckle and an equally strong ring to which a chain or a lead could be fastened.

"Things are working out too slick, like 'rithmetic, for me to quarrel with 'em yet," he said to himself.

He recalled then that he had bought a second hand revolver in a pawnshop on the eve of venturing to foreign parts. He walked all the way home and fetched the thing. It was loaded and he hoped it would go off at the proper moment if required, although he doubted being able to get it out of his hip pocket very quickly.

"Nothing venture, nothing win," he told himself. "And what do you stand to lose, Ben Quorn? Only your life, and you're bound to lose that sometime. Getting chewed by a tiger won't hurt worse than being seasick."

He returned to the shed and, summoning every last ounce of courage, slipped quietly into the cage while the tiger was lying in a corner, not asleep but licking himself lazily. Quorn sat on the chair, listening to his own heart beats.

It was several minutes before the tiger strolled over to investigate. He sniffed, assured himself that the smell of the man on the chair was the smell that he knew, and began to pace up and down before the bars. Quorn sat still, simply paralyzed with fear. Two or three times the tiger came quite close to him—once actually brushing against his legs in passing. Two or three more turns up and down the cage, and then the incredible happened. The tiger came and lay at Quorn's feet, sprawling with his legs in the air, as if inviting Quorn to scratch his stomach. The tiger lay head toward him, tail toward the bars.

Courage is relative. Quorn was a man to whom an altercation with a traffic cop had been a desperate adventure until he left the United States. If he had really known how dangerous a tiger is he might have leaped out of the cage that minute, while he had the chance. It was surely something more than courage—perhaps sheer luck and ignorance that made him rub the tiger's ears. But it was courage and nerve and almost nothing else that enabled him to slip that heavy collar around the tiger's neck and buckle it. Then fear took hold of him again. He had not the remotest notion what to do next, so he sat still. And the tiger lay still, with his great gleaming fangs within six inches of Quorn's legs, and every inch of Quorn's skin tingling every time the tiger breathed.

That strain was too great. Quorn pulled out the revolver, intending to make his escape and to shoot if he had to. The tiger rolled over and raised himself, staring at Quorn's face as if wondering whether or not to kill and eat him. And then, unable to endure fear any longer, Quorn did the craziest thing he had ever done in all his life—even crazier than throwing up a good job taxi driving in Philadelphia.

"Here, pussy!" he said, "pretty pussy! Nice puss!" And he tossed the revolver into the farther corner of the cage. THE TIGER LEAPED after it. Quorn leaped for the door and slipped out, bathed in sweat. The tiger played all over the cage with the revolver, as a cat plays with a mouse, until the weapon slipped out under the horizontal bottom bar and Quorn picked it up.

"Why, durn it," he muttered. "I may be born with a gift o' training tigers." That thought brought awakening self esteem. It stirred the imagination.

Presently came Bamjee to inquire whether or not the tiger was up to specifications. By that time something new, strategic and dynamic was aroused in Quorn. He was no longer the bewildered taxi driver. He had emerged into Machiavelli's class, alert and bending every intellectual resource toward an end in view.

"He already eats out o' my hand," he answered. "And so do you unless you want your head broke. Go you to the palace and get some clothes belonging to the princess. Bring 'em here. Act secret. And remember to lie like hell to any one who asks questions. Make it snappy now."

That evening Quorn draped the chair inside the cage with dawn hued clothing that was perfumed with scent so subtle that it suggested a palace roof, a muted instrument beneath the stars, and a song sung to a sweetheart. It was strange bait for a tiger, but the tiger soon grew used to it and after a while seemed even to like it. And the following afternoon Quorn had the princess herself in the cage. The tiger recognized the scent and behaved admirably. The only difficulty was that the princess was utterly fearless and wanted to take too many chances.

"Why, look!" she exclaimed suddenly. "This is the tiger who used to pull the two wheeled cart in the durbar processions. He was so tame that he let a frightened horse kick him. And he was hurt so badly that they gave him to the

Jains. Quick, give me a whip! I'll show you how he jumps over a person's head."

Quorn almost sulked. Gone was the glory of having tamed a ferocious monster! But the sight of the princess holding the brute by the collar excited his admiration for her at any rate and again set imagination working. So far he had only the ingredients for a miracle. Next he had to set the stage, and then to turn the trick. When he had persuaded her at last to come out of the cage he suggested a plan to the princess; and she was so delighted with it that her eyes became azure pools of laughter and she said that if Quorn were not verily Gunga Sahib, then the gods must have made two of them and lost the other one.

"I am only sorry I agreed to wait thirteen days," she objected.

But Quorn needed every hour of all those days to make his preparations. The princess was brave and impatient and merry, but no good whatever at details, so Quorn had to think of everything—with the aid of Bamjee, who undertook to do the necessary propaganda. Quorn's blood was up. He was not only eager to risk everything for the Princess Sankyamuni's sake, he was blazing mad, indignant with the priests, with the rajah, and with the entire population of Narada because it was willing to let the princess run that awful risk.

"Don't you give those priests a chance to back down!" he instructed Bamjee. "They've got to take a licking, or we're out—one way or the other, and no alibi! You keep the crowd so pepped up that the priests won't dare to call it off!"

IT WAS THE rajah who grew frightened as the day drew

near. It occurred to him that he stood to lose whichever way the tiger jumped. Public opinion, that was now excitedly in favor of the ceremony, would undoubtedly condemn him afterward, even though the incredible should happen and the princess should come through the ordeal successfully. He would be regarded as a heartless parent; and because he was exactly that, it was the one thing that he wished not to be called. He tried to bargain with the priests, offering them all sorts of concessions if they would dig up another legend, or come out into the open with another contradictory prophecy that would serve as an excuse to cancel the proceedings.

But the priests were in no position to oblige him. What they hoped was, that the rajah would forbid the ordeal, thus forcing the princess back into seclusion and leaving the priests more influential than ever. But the rajah knew that if he should do that, not only would the priests have triumphed, which would be galling, but the crowd would blame him for the disappointment.

He consulted Quorn, while Quorn was sitting on Asoka's forefoot with mallet and chisel, trimming Asoka's toe nails.

"Can you tame that tiger, Mr. Quorn?"

"Haven't seen the crittur yet, your Highness."

"It's an enormous one and venomously savage."

"Priests won't let me see him, sir. I'd like some sort of pass that 'ud take me into the courtyard where they've got him caged."

"Do you propose to—er—er, dope him?"

"No, sir." Shade of Machiavelli! Quorn saw suddenly

how to fit the last piece into the puzzle. He went on chiseling Asoka's forefoot.

"I'm afraid the priests might dope him, sir. Can't do nothing with a tiger that's been doped. He's undependable."

"You mean, then, you can manage the brute?"

"If I'm let. But I don't trust them priests. I'd like that tiger watched. I'd like leave for Bamjee and my man Moses to spell each other keeping tabs on him from outside the cage. As many priests as like can watch them. I'd like the people of Narada to know that the tiger *is* being watched so there'll be no hocus-pocus. This here is going to be a big league miracle."

"If I were sure—"

"You seen me tame this elephant," Quorn answered, getting off Asoka's forefoot. "Up you get, two tails! Give his Highness your college yell. Salute him good."

Asoka threw his trunk in air, screamed, and thumped his forefoot in the dust. The rajah spun a coin in the air.

"Heads!" he exclaimed. "Heads it is. Very well, Mr. Quorn, Bamjee and Moses shall watch the tiger and you may go in to see him as often as you please. I will arrange that with the priests."

The tiger turned out to be worse than Quorn anticipated. He was in a big cage half hidden by creepers that climbed on the masonry in a corner of the temple courtyard, close to where a flight of ancient steps led up beside a high wall toward upper levels from which the bridge led toward the farther temple—that of Siva. This being the temple of Kali, the Bride of Siva, all the carvings were of skulls and

snakes and other dreadful symbols of the universal principle of death.

But there was nothing there more dreadful than the
brute that lurked behind those bars. Some animals are
maniacs. When Quorn approached the tiger sprang and
tried to tear the bars apart, wrenching at them with teeth
and claws—a mad, magnificent striped devil that would
kill for the love of killing. He was a pet well chosen for the
Goddess of Destruction.

THE PRIESTS WATCHED Quorn to make sure that he
threw no poisoned or drugged meat between the bars. They
were amused when shown the rajah's order permitting
Bamjee and Moses to keep watch in turns lest the tiger
should be interfered with. One of the priests, too proud to
speak to Quorn except through an interpreter, said:

"Doubtless your gods have told you how to tame that
animal, as undoubtedly they told you how to tame the
elephant. We will all be here to see you do it."

But the sarcasm escaped Quorn. He was far too interested in the cage.

There were two doors—one at the side, beneath an arch,
made fast with a padlock bigger than a man's fist, and the
other was in front. Ten of the bars formed part of it, and it
was fastened with a bolt that led into the masonry above.
There was a hole in the bolt through which a wooden peg
passed. If the peg was pulled out, the bolt would drop by its
own weight and the barred door would fall forward. That
peg, however, was high out of reach.

"But ain't that like a priest to fasten one door with a
padlock and the other with a peg!" Quorn muttered.

"This door, this other one under the arch, is that through

which the princess must enter to bring the tiger forth," a priest explained. "We have the key. We will unlock it for her." Quorn nodded.

Outside in the street, when he was sure that no one overheard, he instructed Bamjee:

"Get some sewing machine oil and a spool of good stout cobbler's thread. First chance you get, oil the hinges o' that front door of the cage, and mind you, oil 'em proper, but don't let anybody see you."

That night Quorn returned to the temple with a peg in his pocket. He pretended he wished to make sure that Bamjee was awake, but he took the spool of thread from Bamjee, tested its strength, and tied one end of it firmly to the peg. Then he walked up close to the cage. The tiger snarled and leaped against the bars. Quorn studied the bars and insisted that the peg at the top that fastened them, was loose. It was dark. Nobody could really see. After a lot of argument a priest agreed to bring a ladder and to let Quorn examine the peg. Quorn carefully replaced it with the other. On his way down he concealed the thread among the creepers, tucking away the spool into a crack in the masonry behind some leaves, where it could easily be reached by anybody standing on the ground. And whoever should pull that would pull out the peg, which would let the bars fall and release the tiger.

On the following day, in the elephant lines, he astonished the mahouts by drilling Bamjee in the art of throwing a certain weight a certain distance in the air.

"Remember now," he said, "I ain't no Babe Ruth and I'll be sitting on an earthquake. So take your time and aim careful. Try to hit me on the nose and make sure the bouquet don't hold any bricks."

And then, one moonlight night, rehearsal at the back of the elephant lines with the aid of four palace servants whom Quorn and Bamjee had decided they could trust—a coachman and three footmen. The princess was so excited and full of laughter that it was difficult to keep her mind on anything. Quorn had to speak to her almost sternly before he felt sure she knew her part.

"If we slip up, miss, we're done for. We've got to do this letter perfect. Now remember, you've a right to have ladies with you, and they've a right not to be seen in public, so in case anybody asks you, the carriage what comes behind you has some six, seven, eight o' your ladies in it. Nobody'll know you're prevaricating if only our tiger keeps quiet, and we'll have to trust to luck for that—luck and a fair to middling solid meal. There'll be two men up behind, and one up beside the driver, to make sure nobody peeks through the shutters. That part's up to you. You've got to send word to the priests that you're coming with a carriage full of *purdah* ladies; and if the priests raise any kick about it we'll have Bamjee do some propaganding so's the crowd'll shame 'em into letting the carriage go through the temple gate behind us. Now are you sure you've got that? Good. Then come on. Let me see you lead this tame pussy of ours into that carriage and feed him some scraps in there. Then lead him back into his cage and feed him a fine big belly full o' fresh meat what'll make him remember he had it. We've got to get him used to the idea that a carriage ride means something good now and lots more later on."

To lead even a tame tiger in the dark is no sinecure. It

is very different from leading the same animal in daylight. But a man went ahead, trailing a piece of meat along the ground. Quorn had an extra, loose line passed through the ring in the tiger's collar. Two men kept near with a net in case of accident. And all went well.

"The gods are with us," said the princess.

"Give the gods a back seat," Quorn retorted. "One more rehearsal tomorrow night, then me and you'll make a big league miracle or bust! It's lucky for us that the sun will be shining in his eyes and make this striped puss blind and lazy. That way, when you lead him along the parapet you'll be able to move reasonable slow and dignified."

THERE WAS NO law against crossing that ancient bridge. It was not closed, but deserted because men were superstitious. Quorn sent Moses with a piece of meat to be drawn at the end of a string along the full length of the yard wide parapet and leave its stench above the heads of the gods and goddesses on whose shoulders the doves cooed all day long. And Asoka spent the last night at his own picket, chained by both hind feet instead of only one, fidgeting and needing to be coaxed at intervals because he could smell and hear tiger just beyond the compound wall. All through the quiet night he plucked at the bright steel ankle rings.

At last the great day dawned and all Narada kept gay holiday. The streets were thronged from early morning with crowds on whose lips were the names of Gunga Sahib and the Princess Sankyamuni. There was no doubt. Nobody believed that such an ancient, thoroughly authenticated prophecy would not come true. Had not they all not long ago seen the Gunga Sahib tame the furious Asoka and bring back the Princess Sankyamuni, radiantly lovely, riding on him through the city streets?

They had seen it with their own eyes. So indubitably she would tame the tiger now in Kali's temple, and would lead him across the bridge as prophesied—especially, of course, because it was no secret that the Gunga Sahib was to take her to the temple on that self same elephant Asoka, who had had part in the former miracle. The thing was fore-destined.

There was nothing to do but wait, and watch, and be hot and excited, and lose the children in the crowd, and be good tempered and merry and behold how true the legends were.

"*Bande* Sankyamuni! *Bande* Gunga Sahib!"

The sweetmeat sellers and the sticky pink lemonade sellers did a roaring business. And the rajah, in the palace garden, chewed his finger nails, until he decided at last that the only sensible course for him was to take to his bed and pretend to be ill, so that nobody might blame him for whatever happened.

Asoka's nerves were so upset by the smell of tiger near his picket that Quorn had a hard time to get him polished up and harnessed with the silver plated howdah.

But it was accomplished at last, and then Quorn made a caste mark on his own forehead with the aid of a carmine lip stick borrowed from the princess. He put on a turban that Bamjee had given him, and wore a long, white cotton Indian shirt. He was a modest man and not even deadly danger could induce him to abandon trousers, so he looked like a medley of East and West when he mounted Asoka's neck and stuck his knees under the enormous ears, with a chief mahout's jeweled *ankus* in his hand.

But no native of Narada could possibly have mistaken him for anybody other than the Gunga Sahib, whose features, a thousand years ago, were carved in limestone on the end wall of the market place. Undoubtedly, the gods had sent him back into the world to help to fulfill the ancient prophecies.

A very large shuttered carriage, drawn by four horses that had been broken to elephant and every other kind of animal that one may meet in Indian streets, with two men on the driver's seat and two fierce looking, whiskered attendants standing on the little platform at the rear, followed Asoka into the palace grounds, where a screen was drawn, so that none might see the ladies as they stepped into the carriage. But numbers of impudent rascals, hidden amid the shrubbery, beheld the princess come forth from the palace, radiant and unveiled, to climb into the howdah by a ladder. And there were several of those who said afterward that no ladies followed her and none got into the carriage. Nevertheless, they said they heard strange noises coming through the shutters—noises that ceased unaccountably when somebody threw in what appeared to be meat.

But why should any one believe such nonsense? Did the crowd not see the shuttered carriage, with their own eyes, following Asoka through the streets? Everybody knew that a shuttered carriage is intended to hold *purdah* ladies. And if there were no ladies, why the fierce looking attendants scowling to the crowd to keep its distance?

ASOKA BEHAVED MAGNIFICENTLY in spite of that tiger smell that had so upset him. He was always manner perfect when he bore that silver howdah and had Quorn's knees under his ears. He was a beast of monumental dignity, who could sense a dramatic moment and live up to it, so the procession through the colorful, tree lined streets was solemn and as satisfying as even Narada, almost sated with splendid processions, could have wished. They had to pass through the midst of the enormous throng that packed the Pul-ke-nichi and swarmed on roofs and walls, whence they could see the parapet of the ancient bridge. It was along that parapet that legend said a princess had once led a tiger. Everybody, except the temple priests, implicitly believed that miracle was now about to be repeated. Had the priests not said it should be? And here was the Princess Sankyamuni, unveiled, lovelier than legend, riding on the very maharajah of all elephants, in a silver howdah, behind the Gunga Sahib with the he-goat's eyes. Anybody who might think there was not going to be a miracle was absolutely crazy.

The crowd roared encouragement until the limestone walls re-echoed and the narrow Pul-ke-nichi became a river of splendid sound. But Asoka began rumbling ominously. He smelt tiger again. As they made the turn into the temple courtyard gateway there were some who noticed that Asoka was beginning to be almost out of hand. There might have been a panic if the great wooden gate had not opened so swiftly, and closed again so swiftly behind the four horsed, shuttered carriage. There was silence then—an eager, breathless silence of anticipation as the entire crowd stared into the sun toward the parapet.

Asoka swung into the temple courtyard at a great pace, rumbling and swaying his trunk from side to side so ominously that a crowd of priests made way for him, forgetting dignity and taking refuge behind columns. There was almost a stampede. Even the chief priest had to step aside. He had taken his stand in full regalia before the tiger's cage, expecting to see the princess swoon at the sight of the dreadful brute. As a piece of exquisite sarcasm he had ordered a strip of carpet laid on the flight of stone steps, up which the princess was to lead the tiger in order to reach the bridge. But he was all ready with scornful words, at the first sign of her shrinking to order her home again and into life long *purdah*.

He had a speech ready, too, for the crowd outside, that should send them home with something else than miracles on which to meditate.

Asoka upset calculations by behaving like a bull just loosed in the arena, turning this way and that—for a victim. He could not endure that smell of tiger. It was scandalous. It aroused every fighting nerve in the whole five tons of him. And as he approached the cage the tiger leaped up at the iron bars, snarling with all the passionate fear and hatred that a tiger feels for an elephant. Asoka screamed. He trembled like a boiler before it explodes. But he paused for one second with his trunk held rigid and a forefoot raised in air, because he heard Quorn's quiet voice. And in that second Bamjee, crouching in the shadow of an arch, threw a bouquet of flowers, which Quorn caught. Nobody saw the dark, thin, strong thread tied to it. Quorn passed the flowers to the princess, jerked at the thread, and the peg dropped out that held the bolt that fastened the front of the tiger's cage. Ten bars fell forward with a crash. And like a flash of lightning out leaped the tiger, loose among priests in the temple courtyard.

There was pandemonium. Asoka thought he knew now what Quorn's voice had meant. He screamed again. The four horses went crazy and had to be loosed to prevent them from dragging the carriage all over the courtyard and upsetting it. A resourceful footman cut the traces. The horses galloped among the priests and scattered them. Asoka's little angry eyes blazed red and there began such a tiger hunt as only monkeys see in jungles when tiger has challenged elephant and there is a war to the death between them. Only now a silver howdah instead of a hunting saddle swayed and shook on Asoka's back—the fleeing animals were terror stricken priests—the trees were courtyard columns—and there was a quiet voiced man directing the terrific battle.

"Take your time, you sucker, or you'll scrape us off under the archway! Easy now, easy! What's your bean for? Use it! You've got to corner him first—you can't crush all out doors! You ain't no polo pony—save yourself a bit. There— now you've got him! Give her the gas now! Fire when you're ready, Gridley!"

BOTH SIDES FIRED together. The tiger had taken refuge down a short arched passageway that was closed by a door at the farther end. Asoka charged into the passage. The tiger leaped at the flailing trunk, that just escaped his claws, and landed on the broad head, snarling, his fangs gleaming within two feet of Quorn's face, his baleful eyes blazing in gloom as he struggled for foothold. The hollow arch rang with the battle, and then with thunder, as Asoka crashed into the great teak door at the end of the passage and crushed the tiger, shook him off—trampled—trod him into crimson pulp.

"There—there's a bully boy—king of elephants," said Quorn, examining the enormous head to see what damage the tiger's claws had done.

It was nothing much—nothing that could not be healed with washing, and lint and tape. He turned to the princess.

"Now, miss, do your stuff and make it snappy. Slide down by his tail while I keep him headed this way. He'll go crazy again—he'll spoil everything if he sees that other tiger."

He encouraged Asoka to knead his victim's carcass into red mash while the princess threw down over his rump a rope that had been tied fast to the howdah. With the aid of that and his tail, she reached the paving stones. She ran then—ran to the shuttered carriage, and while the four men held the horses she led out a big, sleek, sleepy tiger who had only had half his dinner and knew he would get the other half if he walked a little way beside this person with the vague, delicious scent on her gauzy garments. She had fed him twice thus, why not now, a third time?

One priest lost a lawn shirt, because Quorn tore it off him to dip in water and staunch Asoka's scratches, praising his charge the while and calling him pearl of elephants. Some of the priests had taken refuge in the chambers that gave on the cloistered courtyard. The others, including the chief priest, saw the princess lead her tiger up the ancient stairway, and saw Bamjee follow at a good safe distance, carrying a sack containing meat. And presently, from outside, from the street and from the roofs and walls, they heard the thunder of a crowd's voice welcoming a miracle and praising Mother Nature because the ancient tales were true. The crowd made such a noise as should have brought the sky down.

Those priests of Kali knew the meaning of defeat. They had presence of mind. They might still prevent disaster to themselves by snatching unmerited prestige. They urged their chief priest to ascend the stairs to the bridge, mount the parapet and give the multitude his blessing. Perhaps he was grateful that his temple tiger had not killed him and a few of his attendants. At any rate, he blessed the people beautifully; and that, of course, was accepted as official recognition of the miracle.

If anyone should tell the people ever any more, amen, that there are no such things as miracles they would stone him with stones from the dirtiest part of the street, and serve him right, the infidel.

Quorn calmed Asoka, patched him, hid the patches under an embroidered cloth that he took from a priest, and that made Asoka's ponderous head look more dignified than ever. Then he helped catch the terrified horses and sent the empty shuttered carriage home by quiet by-streets; after which he mounted Asoka again and rode him down the crowded Pul-ke-nichi to the courtyard entrance of the farther temple, receiving on his way such an ovation as surely even Akbar never had.

The crowd brought out bands and banners. And when the princess came forth presently, surrounded by Siva's priests, who pretended they were glad to have received the tiger and to have seen a prophecy fulfilled, and by Bamjee, who was smiling all over his face and rubbing his hands surreptitiously to get the smell of meat off them, there was such a glorious uproar as would have graced a base-ball game.

Asoka knelt. The princess, now for evermore unveiled and rapturously lovely, stepped into the howdah. Bamjee borrowed a horse and made haste to the palace to inform the rajah what had happened. The bands struck up, the streets reverberated to the din of jubilee, and a glorious procession flowed all through the city until it reached the palace gate, where the rajah, roused out of his bed, had to stand surrounded by his courtiers and greet with a royal smile his only daughter, heiress to his throne, who was henceforth free to choose a husband for herself, and ever to powder her nose in public if she wished.

THE RAJAH KNEW how to be gracious when there was no way out of it. He gave Asoka two whole pounds of sugar. And when Quorn got home that night to eat the goat chops prepared by Moses, he found a box of the rajah's fifty cent Perfectos waiting for him. He bit off the end of one and lit it. He gave one to Moses. Then he looked at himself in the mirror and thought of the taxicab he used to drive. He grinned. He nodded.

"Yes," he said, "it was a big league miracle all right."

ON THE ROAD TO
ALLAH'S HEAVEN

*Another exciting tale of Ben Quorn in
the whirlpool of India's mysteries*

MOHAMMED, SAYS THE legend, rode to heaven on a horse; but that, of course, is an allegory intended for Arabs, who prefer hints to hard specifications. Love the horse and cherish him; thus thou shalt know thyself and find the way to heaven—and many another hint the Prophet left them. Thou shalt not steal, for instance, is a hint that, unless you are a horse owner, may be said to have no reference to horses, any more than the embargo against wine prohibits whisky, which was not invented in Mohammed's day. Sayyid the Wahabi saw and—in the name of the Prophet—took the mare Dahura, who was in foal to Abu Zeyd, a stallion so famous that some men swore by the snort of him instead of by their own beards.

"No sin," said Sayyid to himself. "On the contrary, it would have been sin to neglect this opportunity provided by the All-wise, All-merciful—praise be to His Prophet! Should I have left this wind-bred wonder of a mare in the possession of a slothful fool who slept when such as I, who know horses, was awake and prowling? By the beard of my father's son, such a mare as this deserves a master such as me."

But he knew that opinions differ. Each man in the desert puts his own interpretation on the laws concerning property. Astride of an iron gray gelding, therefore, leading the

mare Dahura, he departed thence in stealth, by night, to
look for heaven. And because Arab vengeance is a patient
pastime, and life is sweet, and the world is large, there
began a wandering whose tale would fill ten books as bulky
as the Koran in the Mosque at El-Kalil.

It is a long way; there lie deserts, fierce tribes and a
stormy sea between the scant, wind scorched oases where
Ibn Saoud the Stern feeds iron discipline to lean Wahabis, and the lush, well watered rice fields of Narada, where
a one gun rajah then was tolerating lazy insolence from
two or three hundred thousand Hindus, who are mostly
fat from long siestas in the afternoon with no war nor any
foe except the moneylender.

To Narada came Sayyid, dry with fever, riding a dish
faced, lean bay mare and leading a stallion colt now nearly
three years old. Sayyid had little to say for himself, but his

eyes told of terrible hardship, and it was plain that he had not found as yet that paradise he looked for.

He had no money, but the man who can manage without it is rich as Midas. There was not enough money in all the world to have tempted him to sell mare or colt. He had proved that. He had resisted exquisite temptations. He had withstood threats guile and flattery. He had fled repeatedly from both legal and lawless violence. He had learned, too, that Allah plants seeds of compassion in unexpected places; so that it did not surprise him when he met Ben Quorn at the rear of the rajah's elephant lines and Quorn said—

"Peace to you."

When he answered "Peace!" Quorn bade him come under the *neem* tree and be seated on a clean felt *numnah*. Quorn gave him a glass of whisky and cool, effervescent water. Then Quorn offered tobacco, but Wahabis don't smoke.

IT WAS THE heat of the day. There was nothing much to do except sit or sleep and wait for the sun to burn less brassy in the pale blue sky. Sayyid watched four and thirty elephants all swaying at their pickets until, after twenty minutes' silence, his horseman's heart made him aware of a great contentment reigning among the beasts and he knew that Quorn had much to do with it. So he looked into Quorn's strange, goatish eyes and read in their depths a quality that was not on the surface.

"You were born among the elephants?" asked Sayyid.

"Hell, no! I was born in Philadelphia, Pennsylvania. I was sent here to be caretaker of some abandoned mission buildings. Luck changed. Things happened to me, same as they do in dreams. An elephant—Asoka—that's him—

that big one—ran away, with me on top. We crashed a wall and found a princess. She's a pippin—I mean a humdinger, if you know what that is. Brought her home. Folks saw me and said I'm Gunga come back to life—a Hindu guy whose face is carved on a stone wall in the market place. He croaked a thousand years ago, but these folks are so sure I'm him that I don't know who I am myself. Anyhow, the rajah put me in charge of all these elephants. Later I tamed a tiger for the princess and we worked a kind o' miracle in public—trick stuff, but the crowd fell for it good. So now they swear harder than ever I'm Gunga. Can't make 'em believe I ain't, and seems I'm everybody's friend—or most everybody's. I get presents—bits of sticky sweetmeat—fruit—all sorts o' things. Women bring babies for me to touch 'em. Me! I used to drive a taxicab back home and all I ever got for nothing was a ticket from a traffic cop."

"You know a horse?" asked Sayyid.

"No. They've hair on 'em. They kick and bite. I can tell one end from t'other. That's my limit."

Sayyid stared into his eyes again.

"But you knew an elephant before you came here?"

"No. I'd seen 'em—at the circus."

"But a tiger?"

"No."

"Then it is as I thought. It is Allah's doing—praise be to His Prophet. You have the eyes of understanding. Look! You behold a mare of the Kehilan Ajuz strain and her he-colt. There is not their equal under heaven."

"You don't say." Quorn lighted his pipe and cocked his head to one side, showing courteous interest.

"By the beard of God's Prophet, on whom be blessings, I swear it. Behold the Jibbah."

He pointed to a slight protrusion that extended downward from the colt's forehead to a point between his eyes. There was the same protrusion on the mare's head.

"Such horses are fit to ride to heaven on. That swelling means cleverness—sense—it is the mark of the hand of God. I have named the colt El Gamel."

"Don't that word mean camel? He don't look like one," Quorn hazarded.

"It means the perfect one. He is better than fifty thousand camels, lean and hungry though he is, aye, and the mare also."

"Haven't they et much recently?"

"Sahib, none of us has eaten more than kept life in us. We have come a long journey."

"Broke, eh? Well, that part's easy. Help yourself to corn and hay. You can sleep in that shed yonder. It's clean. There's a good bed. You may take your meals with me."

The Arab arose and bowed with the dignity that is only bred in deserts. Gratitude, he knew, does more for him who is grateful than for him who bestows the favor that aroused it. At that moment he wished to do more for Quorn than for himself; wherefore he bridled gratitude and praised only Allah, who was, after all, the source of all benevolence.

"May God continue to make use of you," he murmured.

AND SO QUORN and Sayyid became host and guest. They entertained each other with stories of West and East—of skyscrapers and subways—of horses and desert feuds—of buildings raised on steel frames, raw new, almost over night—of fabled cities buried beneath desert sand—

of Washington and Lincoln—of Haroun al-Raschid—
each man doubting, and yet credulous because of innate
courtesy. Daily Sayyid watched Quorn humoring his
elephants, his soul outpeering through his eyes because
he loved the beasts.

Quorn watched Sayyid train the bay colt. Admiration
crept in; each could recognise the other's genius. So friendship grew. They wore each other's spare shirt and there was
no thought of money between them.

"Haste," said Sayyid, "comes of Satan. The way of Allah
is wise slowness, always, but above all with a young horse.
Doubtless it is also so with elephants."

Quorn nodded.

"There's a woman I wish would learn that."

He told Sayyid about the only daughter of the rajah.

"She's prettier than daybreak, brighter than new money.
But she's hasty. There's more sense, and more nonsense in
an inch of her than in a mile of funny papers. She's full of
ancient heathen scripture and modern novels—nor I don't
know which is worse. She's one of these here new women.
She has earned the right to act any way she pleases, marry
any one she chooses. She don't have to wear a veil no longer.
It was like a dream, me taming an elephant and then a tiger,
helping her to gain her freedom, me not knowing what I
did—all accident, you might say."

"Allah," remarked Sayyid, "uses whom He chooses, nor
may any question Him. There is no such thing as accident.
All happenings are written in the Book of What Shall Be."

"And now," said Quorn, "because we had some luck, she
treats me as if I was the wisest guy in India. She comes to
me for advice on every kind o' matter. She's a young girt full

o'youth and high spirits, and me, I know less about women than horses, which leaves about all of it yet to find out. Yet she asks me questions such as Brigham Young couldn't have answered—no, nor your Prophet either. She'll get me killed, the way she carries on. The priests and her father, the rajah, blame me for the advice I give her, although she 'most always turns it hindside before and does the exact opposite."

"I was born of a woman," said Sayyid, "and without her I would not have been born. Therefore, when anger concerning women seizes me I hold my peace and think of horses."

BUT A COUNSEL of perfection such as that is easier in theory than practise. The princess Sankyamuni heard of Sayyid and came to see him under the pretense of feeding sweetmeats to the elephants and she was saluted by all the four and thirty elephants as she stepped forth; but that was her prerogative that no one challenged, so it hardly interested her. But, being a woman, she detected instantly that there was friendship between Quorn and Sayyid, Quorn being her own discovery, to whom she had neither right nor title, and for whom she would therefore fight at anybody's challenge.

She decided at once to try to make Quorn jealous. Never desert Arab lived who did not worship woman in his heart of hearts, though the Koran and the stern Wahabi teaching make him bury the truth beneath a mask that took a thousand years to make. There was fire in Sayyid's eyes as he beheld her, and she saw the fire. And he saw in hers a hidden motive, which had nothing whatever to do with jealousy, so he watched and waited.

She flattered Sayyid. She praised the mare Dahura and

the colt El Gamel, who could be turned loose to scamper around among the elephants, and make believe he was afraid of them, whereas he feared nothing whatever with Sayyid in sight. At the word of command he would jump over any obstacle without rein or rider. He would come when whistled. He would lay back his ears and snort and show his teeth as if about to kill a man, and at a word from Sayyid he would lay his soft velvety muzzle confidently against the same man's cheek. He had eyes such as nothing under heaven has except an Arab horse, and of Arab horses he was one among a million.

"I will buy them both," she said to Sayyid.

Quorn laughed. But he did not recognize that jealousy had crept into himself.

"There is but one price," answered Sayyid.

The princess raised her eyebrows ever so slightly. It is not good manners to talk about price to an heiress to an ancient throne.

"Babu Bamjee, my father's agent, will arrange about the money," she said, staring at him.

She knew she had met a man whose passion for freedom was as indomitable as her own. That, naturally, was a challenge, she being young and not yet grown to the full stature of her wisdom.

"But one price," he repeated. "My life or the buyer's."

"You may come with them," she retorted. "I will pay you wages."

Sayyid was careful not to smile, because strength is strong and needs no cheap discourtesy to lean on. He had no pride, only dignity. He could be gentle toward ignorance—gentle and firm, even as when he was training the colt.

"The Sahiba is pleased to rebuke me. What have I done that my name and the name of wages should be spoken with the same breath?"

Now Quorn knew that he was jealous and he fought against it for the sake of admiration of his friend. He had become almost a demigod in a superstitious crowd's opinion; he was superintendent of the rajah's elephants; he could talk familiarly with a rajah and a princess—he whose utmost pinnacle of fame at home had been his name on a cab driver's license.

He knew, of course, that some of that was creditable to himself, but he knew, too, that it was not in him to achieve such dignity as Sayyid's. Pride he could attain to. Dignity he could only recognize. So he was jealous, and ashamed of being jealous. He wiped his sunburned face with a bandanna handkerchief to hide embarrassment when the princess answered Sayyid almost as an equal. One does not challenge one's inferiors.

"I will have both the mare and the colt. I will not be refused. If you think you can resist me, I will have to show you."

Sayyid bowed, appraising her with eyes trained in the deserts where a man learns to distinguish between what is and what might be, or else dies before his time. The princess, only seventeen, and only having dealt with easy going Hindus, mainly women, maybe underestimated Sayyid. But Sayyid thought not. He was watching her.

"When you have changed your mind," she said, "you may

bring your animals and say so. I will give the market price and I will pay you wages."

SHE DISMISSED HIM, intimating she would speak with Quorn alone and frowning at her ladies, who were giggling through their veils in the carriage at what they considered Sayyid's discomfiture.

"Yes, miss?" said Quorn when Sayyid had moved away with stately dignity.

She preferred that he should call her miss because it sounded modern and she was under the delusion that she had discarded all ancient prejudices.

"You know I promised you should be my chief adviser, and indeed you have earned that."

"Then, missy, don't fight that Arab. He's a hot tamale. He's a wise guy with a gentle spirit in him and a heart like a Lewis machine gun, that can hand out bullets or bologny. I've seen him naked, miss; he's got more scars on him than a gray wild boar. He ain't the type that it's easy to put one over on. And besides, he's a friend of mine."

"You have only one friend in Narada who would be of the slightest use to you if the priests or anybody else should persuade my father to declare enmity against you," she answered. "You know very well you are only a foreigner here, and you have offended the priests by appearing in public twice as the reincarnation of Gunga sahib."

"That was your fault, missy."

"Never mind whose fault it was. If I should cease to be your protector you would last about five minutes."

Quorn did not lack common sense and he could smell a bargain half a mile away.

"Tell me, missy. I'll do anything in reason, but no more

tiger training! My price is peace for Sayyid. He's a good guy who's had some bad luck. Let him rest and take life easy for a while. What is it you want of me?"

"Bamjee shall tell you. I want you to understand that what Bamjee says to you the next time he sees you will be said at my request."

Quorn whistled softly to himself, so softly that the princess did not hear him, which was fortunate, because almost anywhere east of the Adriatic it is not polite to whistle, and bad manners have caused more wounds and death than ever malice did. The princess fed her sweetmeats to the elephants and drove away, with a lingering glance at the mare and colt and a long drawn stare at Sayyid, who saluted her with irritating calm.

Then Quorn made a generous gesture. He was perfectly aware that the princess would protect him as long as she believed him loyal to her; he could play his own hand best by leaving Sayyid to his fate, whatever that might be. But he had had no friends in all the world until he conquered the great elephant Asoka. Sayyid was the first man whom he had ever really trusted, though he did not know why he trusted him.

"The princess has it in for both of us," he lied. "I'll stand by you and we'll play this game together."

Sayyid stared, straight into Quorn's eyes. It appeared that again he could see in their depths what was not on the surface. He knew Quorn was lying. He recognized the generosity.

"Allah the All-merciful sends wisdom at the right time, and what the future holds none knoweth," he answered.

"But I have eaten your salt these many days. If I forget that, may Allah forget me also."

"Let's go and eat now," said Quorn.

He lighted his pipe to hide emotion, being unused to such revelation of an inner man. It was a long time before he could speak again because something choked him.

BAMJEE CAME WHILE the two men sat on the veranda of the mission gatehouse after *tiffin*. Bamjee was so hot that his silk suit oozed moisture and his cherry red turban looked like the flames of mental anguish. His spectacles kept sliding down his nose all slippery with sweat, and his efforts to appear calm only made him look more ridiculous.

"Quorn sahib," he exclaimed, "we are as good as dead men."

"Dead men's bad, not good," Quorn answered. "Sit down, sit easy, then spill the beans. Me and Sayyid are the two livest guys that ever listened to a line of hooey. Shoot it."

Bamjee gasped a moment, wiped his face, spat, crossed his legs, uncrossed them, fanned himself with his handkerchief, and presently commenced his tale of woe.

"Quorn sahib, women are worse than reptiles! They should be married at the age of ten to keep them out of mischief! There is no justice in this world. No sooner do we settle down to garner the fruits of industry than some damned woman puts her finger in the pie! So now there is something rotten in the state of Denmark, I assure you."

Bamjee had a B.A. degree, so it was natural that he should mix up quotations and metaphors in the bowl of his excitement, but Quorn did not know what a metaphor is, so it made no difference. He knew Bamjee was merely paving the way for some intrigue or other.

"Shut off the music and saw some wood," suggested Quorn, who also mixed them.

"Quorn sahib, the court astrologer says fur is about to fly. There is fat in the fire. The dogs of disaster are loose without leash or muzzle. Our princess is an Aquarian, which means she was born in February and has to manage all the universe! She is in love with a man who was born in Leo, which means he is impulsive and believes the wide world is his oyster. Nevertheless, he has nothing much yet except a pedigree and good looks. He is unmindful of cost or consequences because he has nothing to lose. He is a Rajput, meaning he would rather fight than eat. His name is Prince Rana Raj Singh. He is living in a group of tents ten miles away. He has with him a dozen or more followers, who have neither money nor prospects unless their master should marry money and so they are in favor of his marriage to our princess—very much so. He amuses himself by hunting wild boars with a spear on horseback. He has killed his best horse. So the princess wishes to present him with this Arab's horses."

"He may fight me for them," Sayyid interrupted. "By the beard of God's Prophet, if he is a man I would like to fight him."

"You and your prophet!" said Bamjee testily. "It would be simple to take your horses from you. There is poison. There are daggers, bullets, hundreds of thousands of ways of causing accident. Furthermore, if you should fight him and should have the luck to slay him, you would still have our princess to deal with afterwards. Did I not tell you she loves him? She would like to see him kill you because that would flatter her own judgment; but if you should kill him, she would think a sprouting bamboo shoot in your interior a much too easy death for you to die."

"Too much cackle and no egg yet," Quorn objected. "Where's the meat of this here argument? She wants the horses. She can't have 'em. What then?"

"The rajah, her father, and the priests also, wish her to marry a different prince."

"She's earned the right," said Quorn, "to marry any one she pleases."

"Yes, that is true. But it is considered ethical that she should please to marry that one whom her father and the priests select."

"I get you. Same as voting for President back home. You've one to choose from. Well? What of it? Why don't her father shift Prince Rana Raj Singh across the border into some one else's state?"

"How could it be managed? Have you seen our mountains and our jungles? We have an army of fifty men, who are paid double according to contract if required to do duty outside the city. Consequently they would make the campaign last as long as possible. Also they might desert and attach themselves to the service of Prince Rana Raj Singh, thus becoming dangerous outlaws."

"Why not appeal to the British government?"

"Because then the British government might charge our rajah with misrule and inability to govern. They might what is called accept his resignation. They might appoint some distant cousin in his place, whereas she—our princess—wishes to be ranee."

"And she his only daughter! Well, a spanking is all the girl needs," Quorn remarked. "She's all right. I'm for her.

She has some notions, though, that the backside of a hairbrush would remove first rate."

"Unfortunately, Mr. Quorn, imprisonment or violence would only arouse the indignation of Prince Rana Raj Singh."

"What of it? Ain't there all the jungle and the mountains to go gnash his teeth in?"

"Too many mountains. Too much jungle. There are also fierce villagers who live in the mountain foothills and who like Prince Rana Raj Singh. It would not be difficult for him to raise a revolution.

WELL? WHERE DO I come in? I've charge of four and thirty elephants. Am I to parade 'em? I've signed on with no army, nor no revolution. And I ain't neutral. Me for the princess. If she was my girl I'd spank her good. Seeing she ain't and I'm not responsible, my advice to her is to marry whom she pleases and then see what happens."

"But, Mr. Quorn, this is not America. A royal princess and a prince of the longest line of Rajputs can't just walk around the corner and be married. Their wedding should cost several crores of rupees. There should be at least a hundred elephants. The ceremonies should last at least a month. Remember, she is heiress to her father's throne. Narada, all Narada would be scandalized by an unconventional wedding. The people pay the taxes and submit themselves to many impositions, so they rightly feel they are entitled to a gorgeous spectacle now and then. Besides, the priests must be considered. They insist on ceremony."

Quorn scratched his forehead.

"Well," he said, "I don't see no solution. What do you say, Sayyid?"

"That prince may fight me for my horses," Sayyid answered. "By the breath of Allah, on the head of whose Prophet be blessings, that might be a good solution. For thus this land would be rid of a poverty stricken lover, than which there is no worse source of evil. Lo, I had a wife once, who had gold and sheep and camels. There was no peace until I had slain six needy lovers, and her also. It cost me all the gold and sheep and camels to make peace with the lovers' relatives. But, *insh'allah,* I will win another fortune. Let the prince come. I will show him the mare and the colt. Let him stake his life and all his goods against them. I will fight him."

Bamjee wiped his face again and muttered tense expletives. It was obvious that he had not yet delivered all his message. There was something that it hurt him to drag forth, something that he dreaded.

"Mr. Quorn, may I speak to you alone?" he said at last.

He looked pointedly at Sayyid, who took no notice.

"No," Quorn answered. "What you'd say to me alone I'd tell to Sayyid afterwards. You can save me all that trouble. If you can't trust him, then you can't trust me. Shoot or shut up, as you're minded."

Bamjee hesitated. He who hesitates gains nothing except time, for which he pays with mental tribulation.

"Sahib, the court astrologer has said that the Princess Sankyamuni will before long occupy the throne of this state. Her father, the rajah, in the meanwhile, when he is not poisoning his mind with too much drink, is poisoning her food in order to prove that the gods propose and man disposes. This will be a charnelhouse—like Hamlet—

everybody dead and nobody wiser—unless we do something. How shall I say the rest to you? I—"

"I'll say it," Quorn retorted. "You were sent here by the princess to suggest to me that she's thinking of booting her papa off the throne, and grabbing it herself, and marrying this Rana Raj Singh bozo. Am I right?"

"Those are not my words," said Bamjee. "You drew your own conclusions, Mr. Quorn. I have not breathed one word about deposing anybody."

"No, you're a very discreet young feller. How does she propose to go about it?"

"She will need those two horses, the mare and the colt."

Sayyid's eyes, that had been slumbrous, suddenly grew alert and brighter. The Princess Sankyamuni had appeared to him too intelligent to be merely childish. Perhaps she had wished to let him know that she knew the value of the mare and colt, and to fix his own attention on herself.

"It is Allah who hides and uncovers. Praise be to His Prophet," he remarked. "The horses are strong again from the good corn and the long rest."

"Will you do the princess' bidding?" Bamjee asked him.

"I will do what my brother agrees with me to do," said Sayyid, watching Quorn's face with the corner of his eye.

"Better leave us and come back later," Quorn suggested. "Meet us near sunset in the elephant compound."

BAMJEE LEFT THEM. Quorn and Sayyid talked until it was time to go and watch the corn weighed for the elephants' evening meal. Strangely enough, they talked of heaven and the road by which to reach it, that being Sayyid's way of opening his mind to inspiration.

"One thing is sure," said Sayyid, "as we teach a horse to

look to his master, and the horse thus learns to find the breath of Allah in himself, so Allah teaches us. What shall be is already written. Let us wait and see. As Isa saith: 'This world is a bridge. Let us cross, but build no houses on it.'"

Sayyid put the colt through his routine lesson in the evening cool, until Bamjee came and the mare and colt were fed and picketed.

"The outlook is very bad indeed," said Bamjee. "His Highness, the rajah, has been drinking too much whisky and is *hokee mut.* He is irate. He has whipped the court astrologer. He has sworn to have me dismissed from my post of purchasing agent, and he has hinted less than vaguely that it would be no accident if an elephant should crack my skull like an egg. No argument can persuade him that I have not carried letters between our princess and Prince Rana Raj Singh."

"Well, you have, haven't you?" Quorn demanded.

"No, sahib. I never carried them. They lay between the saddle and *numnah.* And now it is more than my life is worth to leave Narada. I am watched. They have even lamed my pony."

"Where's her letter?" Quorn demanded.

Bamjee touched his turban, where a letter written on extremely thin paper lay between the folds of silk. Quorn glanced at Sayyid.

"It is time the horses had night exercise," said Sayyid. "Unless used to it they may grow fearful in the dark. A horse should be dependable at all times."

Bamjee gave the letter into Quorn's hand, blinking at him gratefully from behind the gold rimmed spectacles.

"Tigers!" he whispered. "Panthers! Leopards! Cheetahs!"

He did not want Quorn to lose the letter in the jungle, where it might be found and used as evidence against himself.

"Be careful, sahib! It would break my heart if evil should befall you."

"Yeh. They'd break your head under Asoka's foot," Quorn answered. "Which way lies the prince's camp?"

Bamjee gave intricate directions.

"And at the river, which is full of alligators, it is best not to use the bridge, because our rajah has his spies there. Two miles higher up there is a ford, which is full of boulders. The ford has not been used, except by robbers, since they built the bridge a hundred years ago, so the pool above the ford, being lonely and having jungle all around it, has become the tigers' favorite place to drink. Be very careful when you come to that place."

Bamjee moved out of hearing while Quorn spoke with Sayyid by flickering firelight near where *mahouts'* wives were cooking supper.

"The inspiration of the Almighty is good," said Sayyid, "and it is no mean sport to tilt a drunken rajah off his throne. But we should judge with our own eyes whether Allah has sent us a man in place of him, or whether the Pit has spewed forth another fool to be worse than the first. So I think we will carry that letter. But shall we not first read it? There is no seal. I have learned the trick of opening and closing envelopes."

"But we can't read the language it's written in."

"Bamjee can," said Sayyid. "He is afraid of elephants. Let us hold him close to that big one's forefoot. Let us

warn him there will be an accident unless he reads to us
what is written."

THEY LED BAMJEE aside to where Asoka munched hay in
darkness. There they laid violent hands on him and uttered
marrow curdling threats with voices so devoid of emphasis
that Bamjee could not doubt them. At Quorn's command
the elephant Asoka raised his enormous forefoot. Consequently Bamjee told the truth in hurried whispers, adding
protests for the sake of self-esteem.

"Sahibs, what need of this violence? You are my friend,
Mr. Quorn; I am your friend. I would have told you for the
asking. I am always ready to have no secrets from you. Why
did you not simply ask me? The truth is that the princess
read that letter to me and though I urged her to make some
changes, she refused. I have read the letter at least six times,
so I know it by heart. There is no need to open it."

But Sayyid did open it because he mistrusted Bamjee's
memory. And since Bamjee still had to translate into a
language that they could understand Quorn continued
to hold him close to Asoka's forefoot, while Sayyid held
a lantern. Sayyid's eyes glowed as he listened to honeyed
phrases of royal love.

"If Allah wills, this prince shall have a chance to prove
himself! It were a shame to let a man be called by such
starlight names and not provide him with darkness in
which to shine! Surely her words should set him burning
for the dust of battle and the noise of fighting! Should a
woman call me one of those names, I would kill a king for
her before tomorrow's dawn."

It was the middle page of the letter that contained the
important part. Bamjee undoubtedly would have omit-

ted the incriminating references to himself if he had been lying. As he recited the whole letter parrot fashion it became clear that Bamjee was the real originator of a plan to depose the reigning rajah in favor of his only daughter, who might then marry Prince Rana Raj Singh, who would become prince consort. Bamjee's motive was equally clear, just as it was clear that the Princess Sankyamuni understood his motive. The reading of the letter was as follows: **"WE CAN DEPEND** on Bamjee" (wrote the princess) "because he has not yet had time to grow rich, but is growing rich. He is therefore afraid to lose his position as purchasing agent. But he is quite sure that he will lose it unless there is a change of government soon, because my father has begun to detest him and to suspect him. Therefore he has suggested to me that my father might be deposed. Bamjee feels that if I should become Ranee I would then be grateful to him and would confirm him in his position; and this, indeed, I would certainly do if Bamjee should deserve it by being absolutely faithful to me and to my cause.

"But we have a difficult problem before us, my beloved; because, although I have money, we have no soldiers. And even if we did have soldiers it would be very dangerous to employ them, because the British would immediately send their army and our little revolution in a teacup would be very swiftly spilled, so that only the British would be the gainers. And they have too much power already.

"The greatest difficulty is Colonel Max, the British resident who, as you know, is supposed to keep watch over us all and to report our doings to the viceroy and his council. But he is not a very astute person. He is fat. He enjoys his

meals too much, and he drinks bottled beer, which is bad
for his liver. I think sometimes he thinks with his liver. He
is also much impoverished through having betted on his
own misjudgment of horses, and his judgment in all other
respects is of equal consequence.

"It should therefore be possible to cause him to misjudge
this situation and to send a report to the viceroy concerning
us and our doings that shall cause our indiscretions to be
overlooked. I do not wish him to know that my father has
tried repeatedly to poison me. I do not wish to appear to
the eyes of the British as a helpless victim. I wish to appear
to them perhaps less capable than you, my beloved, believe
I am, but nevertheless quite capable of grasping the reins
of government.

"Above all, although it would be difficult to say exactly
why, I am depending on a man named Ben Quorn. Perhaps
I am depending on him because it is illogical to do so. The
gods are almost never logical, and Ben Quorn seems to me
to have been sent by the gods to Narada. He is a person
of very humble origin, but he seems to have a faculty for
fitting like a cog into the wheels of destiny. For the present
he knows nothing about our plans.

"I had hoped to send you two beautiful horses, a mare
and a colt. But the Arab who owns them has not yet realized how surely obstinacy will lead him into difficulties; so
the horses are still in his possession."

THERE WAS ANOTHER page, so loaded with lovers'
phrases that it sounded like a poem of the period when
passion was considered godlike and men and women were
not ashamed to praise each other. Sayyid's eyes glowed in
the dark like hot coals as he listened to it. So, with such

words, could he love hotly and wholly and without fear of consequences. But because of the zeal of many generations of reformers the desert Arab has transferred his flood tides of romanticism to the horse, so the actual effect was to send him striding away into darkness to stand by the mare Dahura and to call her colt "Son of the Wind". Then, nasally and low, he sang a song in Arabic about the horse "who heareth the sound of the battle afar off, who snorteth, who paweth the earth, who layeth long leagues underfoot." It was a good song. Even the *mahouts,* who could not understand a word, enjoyed it.

"We'll take an elephant," said Quorn to Sayyid presently. "Yes, horses 'ud go faster, but you'd have to tie my legs beneath his belly or I'd fall off. And besides, there's tigers. You can gallop away from such by daylight, but in the dark they git yer."

ASOKA, A GREAT gray swaying shadow, melted into darkness with two men seated one behind the other on his neck. He moved as silently as smoke, and because things were always interesting when he went with Quorn, and the jungle was full of appealing smells, and he was curious, and dignified, and eager to please, he put his best foot foremost. Fortunately there were no tigers drinking at the pool by the ford, or there might have been trouble; the very smell of tiger always made Asoka fighting mad; and if there were alligators they must have fled from the monstrous splashing. So a long time before midnight and before the moon rose, talking together in low tones in blinding darkness as they followed an easy jungle lane that was as a lighted high road to the elephant, they came within sight of campfires. There they halted, because Sayyid said it is unwise to risk too lightly the life that Allah gave into our keeping for an appointed time.

"There are dangers enough that only Allah can foresee," said Sayyid. "Let us use such wisdom as we have."

So they waited in the shadow of a great tree until the moon rose and they could show themselves within bullet range as the peaceful messengers they were. And even so they found themselves surrounded, receiving the first warning of it from Asoka, who could read every sound in the jungle, and every smell. The first challenge came from a shadow less than fifty feet away.

They were not admitted within the circle of camp-fires. There was much gruff talking before a tall young man with a black beard strode out of a tent and stood as straight as a lance in the moonlight, until Asoka raised a forefoot for a step and Quorn and Sayyid scrambled to the ground. Here was some one who knew what was due to him; he did not talk from beneath to a mounted messenger. On the earth then, eye to eye, they sized up one another—a lithe, steel-sinewed scion of a line of warrior kings, and two men such as he had never seen before, each of whom came from a land where aristocrats are self-made and not taken at face value. He had judgment; even in the moonlight he could tell that both men were governed by self-respect, although in different ways.

HE SPOKE TO Sayyid first:

"I am Rana Raj Singh. You have a letter for me?"

"Peace to you," said Sayyid. "I am here to behold your face and to learn what sort of spirit Allah breathed into your clay. This one has the letter."

"I am waiting," said Rana Raj Singh, studying Quorn's goatish eyes, on which the moonlight shone.

Quorn handed him the letter, he hardly glancing at it. He appeared puzzled.

"Why did Bamjee not come?" he demanded.

"Bamjee is being watched. I am Ben Quorn. My name is written in the letter. This man is Sayyid, who owns the horses that are mentioned."

"Wait," said Rana Raj Singh, turning toward his tent.

He went to read the letter by the light of a kerosene lamp; and meanwhile three of his followers tried to draw Quorn and Sayyid into conversation. They were well bred, plainly reckless gentlemen, one of them middle aged and bearded, all three adepts in the art of probing for information for their master. But art needs its proper medium— material to work on.

"Why not ask the elephant?" suggested Quorn. "He's talkative."

"What is written is written," said Sayyid. "If it shall be added to, let Allah do that in His own time. Who am I? By Allah's grace, I am the friend of him who brought a letter to your master."

So there was silence, broken only by the sound of Asoka crunching the branch of a tree, and by the night wind breathing through the treetops, until Rana Raj Singh strode out of the tent at last and put his answer to the letter into Quorn's hand.

"For the princess."

Then he turned to Sayyid.

"I, too, had a mare I would not sell. She fell at a water-course. A wild boar ripped her. I was forced to slay her with

my own hand. I have written in this letter that I would not
accept your horses as a gift except from you, who would
never give them. Nor will I buy them, since I know you
will never wish to sell."

"Allah!"

Sayyid wondered whether this was soft speech set within
a trap as bait for the unwary. His eyes narrowed slightly,
wrinkling at the corners.

"But I would accept your services, if you should offer
them."

"As Allah is my witness I am no man's servant," Sayyid
answered. "But I have eaten this man's salt and we follow
the Princess Sankyamuni in all such ways as a man may
keep without offending God."

"Then one and the same star guides us," answered Rana
Raj Singh, nodding.

He turned to Quorn again:

"Pray accept thanks. Should I offer you money?"

"Not if you look to see me here again," Quorn answered.

THEY RODE BACK through the jungle faster than they
came. Asoka was a beast who always seemed to think that
home might have vanished in his absence; homeless by
nature, he had adopted a human view of things, which
included worry and much gurgling. Doubtless they were
a strange sight when the moon discovered them from
between the treetops, and when they crossed the ford,
where Asoka paused to drink and they were reflected in
the midnight mirror. But they loomed into the compound
finally like any other shadow and the clink of Asoka's
picket ring aroused no sleepers. All was quiet. But there
was disaster and a muttered streak of verbal dynamite from

Sayyid. The horses were gone. There was not a sign of them. If the blast of Judgment Day had sounded amid the stars, Sayyid could not have been more disturbed or astonished.

"And now what?" Quorn looked wonderingly at Sayyid by fitful matchlight shielded between his hands as he sought the comfort of his pipe. Sayyid swore—long, comprehensive oaths in Arabic and his eyes grew harder than golden quartz. Quorn, guessing shrewdly who had done the mischief, wondered how to reach the princess. He imagined her sleeping on a gilded bedstead, perhaps on the palace roof, surrounded by her women and guarded by armed attendants. He supposed it was quite impossible to reach her.

"Some folks need spanking worse 'n hell," he muttered.

He had forgotten Bamjee. Suddenly Bamjee's servant stepped out of the darkness, proffering a sheet of white paper, folded and heavily sealed. Sayyid struck match after match while Quorn swore at the spidery handwriting.

Sahib—please destroy this after you have read it. It is best to burn it. Please become the Gunga sahib; this my servant brings a bundle with turban and native clothing, also coloring for caste mark. Please make haste to the small back gate of the palace garden, where you will be admitted to the smallest summer house behind the bamboos and the lotus pond. Kindly be very discreet.

Your obedient servant,

—YOU-KNOW-WHO.

There was only one turban, one suit of clothing, but the servant was fully clothed. He could be stripped.

He was stripped, without as much as by your leave.

Quorn and Sayyid dressed themselves as natives in the

shed where Sayyid usually slept. Within twenty minutes they were close enough to the back gate of the palace garden to be seen by somebody on watch.

A face half hidden by a white cloth peered out of a shadow.

"Gunga sahib? Softly, sahib—very softly! Who is this other?"

"He's along o' me. You lead the way and mind your own business."

The gate creaked and they saw fairyland. Soft colored lights among the bushes indicated rather than revealed a kiosk, glowing dimly rosy on its marble wall. There was scent of musk and jasmine—a muted instrument—low women's voices—and then silence as sudden as when the frogs cease at the sound of footsteps. They were led by a winding path around a lotus pond and up stone steps into a cushioned chamber that stunned Quorn's imagination. Sayyid was less stunned; he was almost critical, having heard the *mullahs* speak of paradise, to which he knew he would be going some day.

THE PRINCESS AND six of her ladies lay like *houris* clothed in color of sunset silk that glistened in the lamp-light against a background of polished rose wood. She, the youngest, was the only one unveiled; the others were merely eyes that peered above silken *saris;* she, with her *sari* draped over her shoulder and her hair, like woven jet, adorned with one scarlet flower, read the desert bred passion in Sayyid's eyes and laughed at it—laughed gaily. Then she ignored him as the way of woman is.

"You have seen him, Mr. Quorn? You have seen Prince Rana Raj Singh? Isn't he wonderful?"

"I have seen much worse looking men, miss."

She frowned and stared, then realized that that was praise as Ben Quorn measured it, so she laughed again. Quorn handed her the letter. She read it leisurely, her bright eyes smiling.

"And now do you know why I wanted the horses?" she asked Sayyid.

It was clear that she had taken his measure, understood him, and knew from now on she could manage him as subtly as he managed the bay colt.

"None, sahiba, knows a woman's answer to a riddle. But by favor of Allah those horses are mine."

"Whose corn have they eaten?" she demanded.

Sayyid stared at her. There was long uncomfortable silence. It was Quorn who answered—

"They've et the rajah's corn, but it amounts to nothing that I can't pay for, miss."

She chuckled.

"After you were gone tonight I sent my servants to take those horses to keep my father from taking them. He has been told they have been fed at his expense without his leave. That is why I told you I will have them and will take you also, Sayyid. And that is why I wish to send the horses to Prince Rana Raj Singh, and why I wish you to go to him also. Those horses are well trained, are they not?"

"They are fit to ride to heaven on," said Sayyid.

"We are all on the way to heaven, and each to his own," she answered. "But they shall carry me to the throne first. Afterwards you shall have them back to ride on them to any kind of paradise you fancy."

"The throne?" said Sayyid. "Is there then to be a killing?

This man my brother Quorn and I were born to trouble as sand that is blown by the wind and by Allah we have grief enough without seeking it. As Allah is my witness, I will have no part in any killing, saving only if some one keeps my horses."

"Listen," said the princess. "I will speak without guile. I speak truly, in the name of our gods and in the name of whatever god you worship. My father, his Highness, the rajah, has tried to poison me. I have unanswerable proof of it—in writing—a signed confession from his servant and from my servant, who were in league with him to kill me. And I have the poison in the cup that they had given me to drink."

"Sahiba, if you speak truth I will eat my words. There shall be a killing. I myself will slay your father," answered Sayyid.

"Too easy. Let him be made ridiculous. I might appeal to the British, who would investigate and depose and punish him. But his wives would lose their husband, and I bear them no grudge. And the British would patronize me, which would be loathsome. No, let him be made to abdicate. Then I will become Ranee and may marry whom I choose."

"God knows, you lack no leave of mine to marry any one you please," said Sayyid, "but if Rana Raj Singh takes my horses, he shall fight me. I have spoken."

"Speak again then. When my father learns that those horses have been sent to Prince Rana Raj Singh's camp, he will try at once to seize them, because he is angry and ashamed and must vent his spite on some one. He believes I am too ignorant to complain against him to the British government. He does not understand that I am too proud to do it. He would very much like an excuse to treat my prince high-handedly. And he will make a mistake, because men who use poison have neither dignity nor wisdom. You, too, will make a mistake unless you fall in with my plan; because, if I should let my father seize the horses, you would never get them back. He would be mean enough to kill them rather than return them to you."

"Where are they?" Sayyid asked her.

"I will tell you where they are if you will first agree to do my will in this matter. Afterwards, when my father no longer has power, I will return the horses to you. But you must promise."

"Insh'allah."

"What does that mean?"

"If God wills."

"But I want to hear what *your* will is."

"Very well, I will do it."

"They are in my stable. Two of my own horses are in Bamjee's stable, a horse and a mare, not bad ones, although they are as asses compared to yours. Nevertheless, they are of the same color."

"But who is handling my mare and colt? In Allah's name, if a *sais* should harm them I would kill that *sais* as if he were a cockroach!"

"Go you and handle them. But go dressed as you are. And when dawn comes ride with them to Prince Rana Raj Singh's camp. Bamjee at this very minute is taking my horse and mare to the elephant lines for my father's men to seize. My father will be so angry when he discovers the ruse that he will scour the country for news of yours; so make haste. You may trust Prince Rana Raj Singh, even though you do not trust me."

"By the beard of God's Prophet, he who trusts a woman is in need of counsel. Nevertheless, what else is there to do?" said Sayyid.

"Go then. You have my leave to go."

SHE KEPT QUORN standing before that semicircle of lustrous eyes, he less embarrassed than he might have been, because he was dressed in native clothes. There is nothing like western clothes to make a man feel foolish in the presence of mystery and women. There was mystery still to unfold, beyond a doubt of it, a mystery that made Quorn scratch his forehead, wondering.

"My father will order the elephants out tomorrow," she said at last. "He will put soldiers on the elephants. He will invite the British resident to come with him on the pretense of hunting tigers, because he will wish for an important witness that he acts within his legal right. And that witness shall be his undoing. He will want cow elephants, of course. But can you think of an excuse for not taking Asoka, should he ask for him?"

"Sure, miss. Asoka did twenty miles last night. He'll figure he needs a rest. Unless I talk to him good and plenty he'll act ugly when they try to put a saddle on him. Trust Asoka! He won't be put upon by nobody but Ben Quorn."

"Good," she answered. "But you can manage him afterwards? He is fit to travel?"

"Sure. He's as fit as a fiddle. He'll do anything I ask him. Only he's fussy, that's all; he likes humoring. He's apt to get sore at the other elephants and tusk 'em all over the place if he thinks he's slighted. Acts jealous like."

"Good. Then have him saddled, when the rest have started. Use a hooded howdah. Do you think I can trust Sayyid?"

"Dunno. Me, I trust him," Quorn answered. "But some folks think I'm crazy."

"You are Gunga sahib. You are a special sending from the gods. I value your advice more highly than any one's, and because you think so well of my plan I feel quite sure of success."

It was not until he was outside, with the small gate shut behind him, that Quorn realized the irony of that last statement. He wondered whether all women were like that.

"Do they all tell you half o' nothing, and then kid you how smart you are for having said what you didn't say and thought what you didn't think? Me? If she'd listen to my advice she'd appeal to the British and act sensible. But there ain't no sense in India. We're all crazy—the rajah, me, her, Sayyid, everybody!"

But Asoka was not crazy. Quorn could always get comfort from him. Instead of going home to bed he set a chair close to where the great brute lay asleep and sat smoking pipe after pipe, wondering why Asoka was not leader of the herd, he being a bull, and the biggest, oldest, strongest, most intelligent. But even Asoka appeared to recognize the female Beegum as leader. Is that the way the world is run? Do females always rule the herd in spite of appearances? He wondered. Asoka awoke long before dawn.

Then Quorn himself dozed off, with the elephant's trunk fooling at his clothes and pushing his turban down over his eyes; they were friends, they two, whatever else might happen. He was awakened by the rajah's men, who came and took away two horses, a mare and a colt, that stood where Sayyid's horses had been picketed the evening before. Quorn was offended by the discourtesy with which they took them without asking his permission, he being superintendent and in lawful charge of all that compound.

" 'Tis little things," he admitted to himself, "that make a man's mind up for him. Now if they'd not been so snooty I'd have maybe wondered whether I'd got this story right. I'd have thought maybe the rajah might have something worth saying on his side. But a man don't act discourteous, nor his servants neither, when he's doing what's right and decent. No. I'll see this business through. I'll play my hunch—or is it *her* hunch? Well, who cares? I'll play it anyhow."

HE FED THE elephants, then changed into his ordinary clothes. It was eight o'clock before a man came hurrying from the palace to demand where Sayyid's horses were and why two others had been substituted. By that time all Quorn's native obstinacy was uppermost. He knew nothing, had seen nothing, had no idea what horses were referred to, knew nothing about Sayyid, nor where he had gone, nor anything else except that it was breakfast time. Questioning only increased his conviction that his paymaster, the rajah, was up to devil's work, and a kind of cold frenzy seized him at the thought of having been trapped into working for a heartless rogue.

"Taking his pay is as good as me condoning him," he muttered. "Feels like taking dirty money. Well, I've took it, and I've given money's worth. And maybe I'll be fired before the night's out. Who knows? Sayyid 'ud say Allah knows, but that don't git yer much."

He was at breakfast when the order came to get all the cow elephants ready at once for a tiger hunt. It was plain enough even to Quorn, who knew less about palace intrigues than a *mahout* knows of mathematics, that the princess had planned every move in advance in this intricate game.

"She needs a spanking, she sure does, but 'tain't my job; and me, I like her. I'll bet it was she who tipped off the rajah that Sayyid's horses were eating his corn. I'll bet she's figured out some way to make the rajah think this tiger hunt is his very own bright idee. I'll bet he thinks he's going to find those horses in Rana Raj Singh's camp and accuse him of having stolen 'em. I'll bet he plans to order the prince out of his territory, in the presence of the British resident as witness. I'll bet he means to smash the prince's camp and have the elephants trample it all to pieces. If the prince puts up an argument he'll have the soldiers kill him, and the British resident can swear the rajah was attacked and had to be defended. Weil, I wonder what *her* game is. One thing's sure, she'll blame me if it goes wrong. And if it goes right she'll say the gods did it. And either way, she'll know she done it all herself. Maybe I'll get so I understand a woman 'fore I'm through!"

There was an hour of shouting and confusion while the elephants were saddled and loaded. There had to be a special elephant for Colonel Max because he was obese and nervous, failings that were masked beneath pompous assertion of dignity due to a viceroy's representative; the howdah had to be large enough to hold a case of beer with

lots of ice, as well as Colonel Max, his servant and a battery
of guns. And there were elephants with tents, elephants
with pots and pans, elephants with cooks and cooks' assistants: preparations for a three days' jaunt, at any rate, with
an important looking guard of twelve bewhiskered sepoys
and a sergeant, loaded on throe cow elephants, to bring up
the rear in the dust and to do all the dirty work around the
camp at night—presumably. Or perhaps they were there
to salute Colonel Max when he sneezed.

Quorn did not saddle Beegum, the herd leader. He left
her swaying and dusting herself at her picket. His excuse
was that her feet needed attention, but the fact was that he
knew elephants and his hunch was working over the head
of argument and reason.

THERE WAS NO hurry as far as Quorn was concerned. Two
of the elephants had to go to the palace to pick up the rajah
and his attendants. But Colonel Max came down to see
his guns and beer packed properly, and for the first time
since Quorn came to Narada they two had words together.

"I am not at all sure, Mr. Quorn, that I approve of a white
man taking service in a native state. Have you a contract? I
am not sure I shall not advise his Highness to replace you
with one of his own countrymen."

"Are you an Indian? You're working in India, ain't you?
Drawing pay for it?" Quorn asked him.

"Confound your impudence!" said Max. They did not
love each other.

An hour after the procession had left the compound,
and while Quorn was busy saddling Asoka, the princess
arrived, all alone, on a milk white pony. At first he did not
recognize her, which was hardly be to wondered at; nobody

else had recognized her, though she had ridden all through the city from the palace. Quorn wondered where and how she had learned to ride so beautifully.

She was dressed in man's clothes—turban, silk shirt, breeches, riding boots, a flannel jacket thrown across in front of the saddle—sitting her cantering pony as easily and gracefully as any youth in India, where well bred youth rides as if born in the saddle. She looked like a boy of fourteen rather than a seventeen year old girl. Her white teeth flashed amusement. She was excited. She exuded contagious liveliness and mischief. Even Quorn, who had reason to dread her delight in novelty and danger, began to feel enthusiastic, though he did his utmost not to show it.

"Asoka may make trouble," he told her. "He's as jealous as an old granddaddy because the rest of the herd went off and left him."

"He jealous and you scandalized," she laughed. "But you should see my women. They are all hysterical."

She made Quorn dress again in native costume, and she laughed at the notion of taking along a tent or provisions.

"I am Sherman marching to the sea," she chuckled. "I will live off the enemy's country. You see, I know the American theory. It remains to practise it. Let us begin by a short cut. I will show the way."

They left the pony tethered and she lay at full length in the howdah, hidden by the folded top, whose shadow protected her from the sun; and it appeared that she not only knew of a short cut but had sent her servants in advance to show where it turned off into the jungle, so that they wasted no time hunting for it. And because Asoka was lightly loaded and the jungle path was soft and pleasant to his feet, they made such good speed that they reached the river, unseen and unsuspected, more than a mile in advance of the rajah's cumbersome procession, and were able to cross by the bridge, thus saving time again. Then they plunged once more into the jungle by an unfrequented path, taking care to leave no footprints on soft earth where they turned off from the main track.

"And now I know I will win!" the princess laughed. "The gods are working with us."

She began to sing, sitting upright in the howdah, her young face looking hardly human because of the golden green of sunlight streaming through the branches over-head. She was as full of mischief as one of those elemental sprites with which superstition peoples all the jungle, as pleased with wearing man's clothes, and with outraging propriety by visiting her lover without a mystery of awnings and scores of armed attendants, as with the thought of vanquishing her father.

Apparently the spirit of revenge made no appeal to her. She proposed to defeat him, to make him confess defeat, to ascend his throne as Ranee in her own right, and then to let him live in dignified retirement.

"Should I be as mean as he is?" she protested. "Should I waste my soul on vengeance just because he poisoned his by trying to poison me?"

But Quorn could not talk in terms of Oriental mysticism.

"Let him roast in hell, you mean, miss? Why not send him there? They'd 'lectrocute him in the States."

But she could not think in terms of Western ethics, so the conversation dwindled into silence, until they swayed out of the jungle at last into dazzling sunshine and saw Prince Rana Raj Singh's tents.

It was a sumptuous looking camp by daylight—a *marquee* and a group of smaller tents, all backed against a big volcanic rock and flanked on either hand by smaller rocks that made a sort of horseshoe shaped redoubt; but from in front the camp was readily accessible; the rolling ground sloped gently up toward it. No horses, no Sayyid, no smoke, nobody in sight.

THEY APPROACHED THE camp, Asoka snooting at things curiously with his trunk. They cried out, but there was no answer. It was not until Asoka loomed around the great *marquee* that they saw Prince Rana Raj Singh standing there, and Sayyid and the horses hard beside him. The prince smiled, but his eyes looked troubled when the princess leaned out of the howdah to greet him and call him by name. He set his teeth. It appeared he was not yet used to the thought of his royal lady love in riding breeches and without veil or attendants. Nevertheless, he came of a race whose women have commanded armies in the days when Rajputs held their hills against the Moslem; he had only to fall back on ancient tradition, which is easier than to leap forward.

So the mood passed; he caught her spirit of enthusiasm and of daring. But he was still the slave of custom; he could not act the way a Western lover would have done and take her in his arms, not though she jumped down by Asoka's trunk and knee and stood before him.

Quorn felt vaguely annoyed.

"Ain't going to be no petting?" he wondered.

As a friend of the family, so to speak, he thought he had a

right to see at least an exchange of kisses; and as for Sayyid, who should mind an Arab from the wastes of far Arabia? But kisses there were none. The prince and princess stood a yard apart and talked in low tones without emphasis, until Quorn grew tired of watching. Then, when he listened, he could hear the sound of bits and stirrups clinking behind the great rock that formed the background of the camp.

"There'll be doings," he muttered, "impossible darned crazy things that she's thought up to blame on the gods and me. Wish she'd spill the beans a bit, so I'd know what next."

It was no use trying to talk to Sayyid, who kept his distance, fussing with the mare and colt, as if he knew something important but was determined not to tell. So Quorn began to pay attention to Asoka, talking to him and by a patient familiar process getting him to understand that business might begin at any time.

And at last came the rajah, leading his procession from the hunting howdah of a staid and steady old cow elephant. They swung out of the jungle, one behind the other, like symbols of the stately procession of epochs—fragments of eternity, unhurried. It was almost a shock when they halted in the open; it seemed as if the years had hesitated and that time had almost ceased. Quorn, seated on Asoka's neck, could just see them over the corner of the *marquee*. The prince and princess watched them from the shadow of a tent, unseen but able to see every move the rajah made.

FOR SEVERAL MINUTES the rajah talked to Colonel Max, who was on the elephant behind him. Then he rode forward and shouted:

"Whose encampment is this? And by whose leave is it here?"

For about thirty seconds there was no answer. Then a turbaned head appeared above the big rock at the rear and one of the prince's followers answered in a ringing voice that the tents were those of Rana Raj Singh, Rajput, prince of the clan of Kotah.

"He is without right here," the rajah shouted. "This is my territory. Take those tents down and remove them."

He was answered by shouts of laughter and by a man who made ribald gestures from the summit of the rock. They were gestures such as no one in the East could misinterpret and they did not suggest obedience or respect. The rajah's face grew black with indignation.

"Trample those tents down!" he commanded, standing in the howdah to shout to the soldiers, who were on three cow elephants at the rear. So the soldiers spoke ungently to the *mahouts,* and three elephants moved forward.

"Now I understand," said Quorn to himself, "why I left old Beegum at her picket in the lines."

The rajah began to marshal all the other elephants to follow the first three and do a good job of destruction. If Beegum had been among them it would have been useless to ask Asoka to protect the camp; if he had not done what Beegum did, at least he would have done nothing to prevent her.

"Gunga sahib," cried the Princess, "will you and Asoka not protect us?"

So Asoka circled the *marquee* and stood grumbling and extremely businesslike in the center of the fifty foot wide opening of the horseshoe. There was plenty of room on either side of him, but there was not an elephant of all the rajah's herd that could be induced to try conclusions with

him, not though their *mahouts* used the ankus freely and
tried shouting to Asoka to make him disobey Quorn. He
was listening to Quorn's low voice and studying the pressure of Quorn's knees.

"Who is that?" the rajah roared in English. "Is that you,
Ben Quorn? What the devil do you mean by taking that
elephant out without my leave? I sack you, I fire you, I
dismiss you! You are no longer superintendent! Take that
elephant back to the lines and draw your pay and get to
the devil out of Narada!"

"Neck or nothing now," Quorn muttered to himself. "I'd
a hunch I'd lose my job. What shall I answer him, miss?"
he called to the princess over his shoulder.

There were plenty of retorts that it occurred to him to
make, but as a conspirator he was anxious not to spoil her
plan, whatever that might be. But she was nearer than he
thought; she and her prince were already standing there
beside Asoka, and in another moment Sayyid was beside
them, riding the mare Dahura and leading the colt, who
was saddled.

The rajah did not recognize the princess, but he knew the
prince by sight. Somebody told him who Sayyid was and
that those were the mare and colt he wished to seize. He
swore like a rumbling thunderstorm when he saw Sayyid
leap to earth to let the prince and princess mount the mare
and colt. Sayyid demanded a lift on to Asoka's neck and
at Quorn's command the great brute picked up the Arab
and swung him into place. Colonel Max, who had drunk
beer enough to make him feel important, urged his *mahout*
forward and, after a moment's low voiced consultation with
the rajah, came on alone, kneeling in the howdah, red faced,

almost apoplectic, passionately striving to be dignified ana stem and diplomatic all at the same time. But beer and the Indian sun and those don't go together.

"Come, my man," he said, addressing Quorn. "If you want to save yourself serious trouble you'll do as you're ordered and ride home."

"Trouble?" Quorn answered. "I'm used to it."

"Move that elephant away then. Hurry up now."

"Suppose you come and try and move him," Quorn retorted. "Maybe he's *musth*. He ain't acting reasonable."

Under heaven there is nothing more murderous and uncontrollable than a *musth* elephant and Asoka was a tusker who could pierce as well as trample. The suggestion, false as it was opportune, gave Max his excuse to retire.

"Musth?" he exclaimed. "The brute's deadly! Why didn't you warn us?"

He ordered his elephant out of range, to the rear of the herd where he felt protected and could take a little something for his nerves.

THE RAJAH'S ELEPHANT was made to kneel and the rajah came to earth. The rajah was passionate now beyond all hope of self-control, the lees of whisky fuming in his brain exciting him to prove to Max that he was master of the situation. He had not brought his soldiers for nothing. But before he could turn to order them to come down from their elephants the princess gave Quorn his orders.

"Gunga sahib, quickly now—stampede the whole herd!"

That job was easy. Any one can stampede elephants if he knows the fussy-old-lady side of their character, and particularly if the leader of the herd is absent. It was merely a matter of making Asoka act up and then sending him at full speed into the midst of them; and it was as easy to make Asoka do that as to arouse the fighting frenzy of a dog. Asoka charged, screaming, Quorn and Sayyid clinging on for dear life, and in a moment two and twenty elephants were scattering across the landscape, heading in any direction for the jungle where they might hide from whatever it was that had terrified their big bull.

It was not nearly so easy to bring Asoka back under control, but Quorn did it at last, after he and Sayyid had escaped a dozen times from being brained by overhanging branches. The only elephant in sight when they emerged into the open was the one that carried Colonel Max; he and the *mahout* between them had restored her to a state of calm. She had been given beer that morning and supposed she might be given more of it if she behaved. So she followed Asoka back toward the prince's camp and the two of them arrived in front of the *marquee* within a minute of each other.

"Hi, you!" Max shouted. "Keep that big brute of yours away from here!"

Max was struggling between fear and the sense of his own importance. Quorn simplified that issue for him. At the touch of Quorn's knee Asoka turned as a ship turns in a tideway and the cow elephant on which Max was mounted instantly betrayed anxiety. Max had had plenty of stampede for one day; with surprising activity for a man of his build and condition he climbed out of the howdah and let himself down by the crupper and tail. He attempted to land on his feet with dignity, with the agility of younger days in the gymnasium at Sandhurst; but unfortunately the cow elephant chose that moment to turn and run before Asoka's onslaught.

Max sat down so hard on the kiln dry earth that his false teeth bit his tongue and his helmet fell over his eyes. He swore and spluttered and, unfortunately for the rajah of Narada, twenty voices laughed. Max was so explosively indignant that he smashed his spectacles, and that was the end of all logic, dignity or even sanity so far as they concerned him. He was in the sort of mood in which a man thrashes his native servant on suspicion.

"Damn and blast!" he shouted at the rajah. "Curse you and your elephants! They're like your lousy subjects; they have no more respect for common decency than you have!"

Twenty people heard that. There was the princess, whom no one had yet recognized; there was Prince Rana Raj Singh; there were Quorn and Sayyid; and there were sixteen of Prince Rana Raj Singh's men, who had appeared on horseback from behind the big rock at the rear of the camp. The rajah was already in a state of frenzy; he had demanded the mare and colt from Rana Raj Singh and had been rather politely but stingingly refused. This last affront was altogether too much. He strode toward Max and, as the latter struggled to his feet, he smote him across the face, back handed, sending him sprawling again.

"I win!" the princess shouted, then clapped her hand to her mouth and cantered away behind the tents, lest any one should recognize her too soon.

For a moment it looked as if Max and the rajah would fight. Nobody seemed interested to prevent them.

"You swine!" growled Max. "You shall pay for this."

"You beer swilling rogue!" sneered the rajah, which was

hardly diplomatic as between a ruling prince and the representative of British overlordship.

There were too many witnesses. It meant that either
Max must quit the service in disgrace or else the rajah must
submit to drastic humiliation, from the British government. The only possible other alternative was that the story
should be hushed up.

But there was a throne at stake, so not much chance of
hushing things.

IT WAS THE princess and Prince Rana Raj Singh who
cantered up to where Max sat spluttering on the ground,
dismounted and, between them, raised Max to his feet. He
stared. He stared again.

"My God!" he exclaimed. "Who are you? You're not
Princess Sankyamuni?"

"Hi-yi-heh!" yelled Sayyid from behind Quorn's back.
He began to shout excitedly at Quorn in Arabic, then
broke into English:

"Allah! Quickly, quickly! Spur this elephant!"

The rajah had seized the mare Dahura by the bridle. He
had tried to mount her. She had wheeled away from him.
He backed her against the colt and as she sprang away he
swung into the saddle. He had no spurs, no whip; he lashed
her shoulders with the reins, and he tried to lead the colt
away, but the colt escaped him. Sayyid whistled to the colt
who came cantering back. Heading straight for the gap in
the jungle where the homeward road began, the rajah sent
the mare as fast as he could make her gallop.

But Sayyid cried and whistled; the mare heard him and
stubbornly refused to extend herself. Quorn urged Asoka
straight for the same jungle gap that the rajah was head-

ing for; and for a short spurt a determined elephant is not much slower than the fastest horse; he is faster than a horse that runs unwillingly or is badly ridden.

Prince Rajah Raj Singh caught the colt, mounted him and gave chase. A race was on, with Sayyid acting from a moving point of vantage as the old Greek gods did when they rigged the fortunes of the Greeks and Trojans at the siege of Troy. He cried out, making both mare and colt move sluggishly, until Asoka had gained the gap ahead of both of them and stood panting, half hysterical, ready for anything and wondering what next.

Sayyid shouted; the mare swerved and went like the wind along the edge of the jungle, with the colt hard after her.

"Now let them race!" said Sayyid. "By Allah, it will do them all good. The mare is faster than her colt as yet, but the prince is lighter. He has drunk less; he has lived more manly. Let us hope one slays the other."

Those Arab horses moved with the rippling melody of motion of the wind on grass. It was less than a mile around that jungle clearing, but the pace soon told on the mare because of the rajah's weight. The colt kept gaining on her, partly, too, because the prince was the better horseman. The rajah turned and shouted at the prince, his voice ringing clear and echoing among the trees—

"Keep away from me or I'll kill you!"

There was no answer except the thundering of hoofs; and what the prince intended if he caught the rajah no man knew.

The prince's followers rode forward, better to watch the race, and the rajah appeared to think they meant to cut him off. He turned the mare and came diagonally down the middle of the clearing, straight for the gap in the jungle again, and as he neared it he drew a repeating pistol, pointed it at Quorn and shouted; but his words were indistinct. He shouted again—

"Get out of the way or I'll kill you!"

Quorn did not believe the threat, so he did not move. The rajah fired three times, missing wide with all three shots, then turned and fired point blank at Rana Raj Singh.

The firing scared Asoka, but the mare and the colt were used to it. Asoka swung, flank on, across the jungle path, completely blocking it, and Sayyid shouted as a man shouts in the heat of battle, loud and shrill. Both mare and colt put all four feet together and came snorting, sliding, scrambling to a standstill. It was so, in that second, that Rana Raj Singh caught the rajah by the throat and wrenching at him hurled him to the ground.

Sayyid scrambled the earth with the aid of Asoka's tail and caught the mare. He mounted. He and Rana Raj Singh wheeled away and rode toward the tents. Quorn followed on Asoka and they left the rajah lying there, fuming and stuffing his pistol back into a holster inside his shirt, watched by the *mahouts* of many elephants that peered nervously through the trees around the jungle fringe.

The rajah got up after a minute or two, feeling his bruises, and walked toward the camp, glowering.

Glancing at him over his shoulder, Quorn decided he was either desperate and ready to do murder or else so humiliated that he did not care what happened. Either way the man was more dangerous than a cobra; Quorn wondered whether or not he ought to turn about and make

Asoka chase him. He decided at last to keep close to him, to watch him, and to rush him if he saw him move to draw his pistol.

IN THE MOUTH of the camp stood Colonel Max, with the prince on the mare and the princess on the colt beside him. Sayyid stood by with the air of a wolf who sniffs the wind. There were sixteen of the prince's followers on foot at their horses' heads, the horses snorting at the smell of elephant; they lined the horseshoe shaped redoubt on either hand and it called for nerve to face that wasps' nest if a man meant making trouble. Nevertheless, the rajah strode on past them, taking no notice of Quorn, who had waited for him near the camp mouth and now followed along behind him on Asoka.

Even now the rajah did not recognize the princess. He was not looking for her; he probably supposed she was one of Rana Raj Singh's followers; his eyes were on Colonel Max.

"Have you come to apologize for striking me?" Max asked him in the haughty tone of voice with which some people speak to their inferiors.

The rajah winced.

"I am glad I licked you," he answered. "You deserved it."

That was so true that it drew a grin from Quorn and half a smile from Sayyid. The princess laid a hand over her mouth, again postponing recognition. All the prince's men made movements to disguise the fact that they were grinning. Evidently somebody had dropped a quiet hint that Max was not to be further offended, so Quorn straightened his face.

"Lord pity him, I guess the rajah's in a trap," he muttered.

"Well, he walked in. His fault. Looking for a road to heaven like the rest of us, I guess. He's missed it by a mile."

Max had a terrible time inventing a retort. He was lost between indignation and a craving to recover dignity with haughty words. In the end he compromised.

"As a gentleman I can't answer you in the presence of these people," he said, "but in my official capacity I will have a great deal to say at the proper time."

"Then say it in the proper place—in the beer barrel where you belong!" the rajah retorted. He appeared to believe that he still had an even break with Colonel Max. "I know about your drunkenness and betting debts," he added.

"Break me and I'll break you, eh?" said Quorn to himself. "Well, neither of 'em's daisies."

"Those are my horses," said the rajah. "Give me one of them—I don't care which. I need it to ride home on."

The princess rode toward him.

"Are you sure they are your horses?" she asked, steadying her voice and looking straight into his eyes.

He stared. His mouth moved.

"You?" he said.

He turned his back on her and walked away. And all the prince's followers saluted her, not him.

"I will take that elephant. Make him kneel," he ordered, glowering at Quorn.

"Meaning you're coming along with me—you and your pistol, and me sitting with my back toward you? Nothing doing!"

But the prince spoke hurriedly to Sayyid. He and the princess would ride the mare and colt into Narada. One of the prince's followers would lend a horse to Colonel Max. Let Sayyid ride the elephant for Quorn's sake. So Sayyid helped the rajah climb into the howdah when Asoka knelt, and himself sat astride of the elephant's rump with his hands on the howdah rail, so that the rajah sulked and sprawled, as it were between two poles of cold contempt.

"By Allah, if we had you in the desert we would make short work of such a poisoner as you," said Sayyid.

At the word poisoner the rajah winced and looked scared but he said nothing.

"And as for a horsethief…" Sayyid added—and then grew silent; too.

There had been something rather personal about that thought—a trifle two edged. He dismissed it.

"Oh, well," he remarked, "the road to Allah's heaven is a long way. There are many turnings."

NOT ANOTHER WORD was spoken until they came to the ford, where Asoka stopped to drink and cool his hot feet.

"Too bad more of us don't drink this same stuff," Quorn remarked at last, using his knees and heels to keep Asoka from lying down and wallowing. "Give this old fool a gallon of the stuff you drink, sir, and he'll beat you to it! He'll act crazier than you did. Me, I like my liquor, but—"

"You've lost your job," the rajah interrupted.

"No, sir, I believe not, and that's why I'm talking friendly. You fired me all right, but the princess, she promised—"

"I intend to disown her."

"Mebbe. But she's more generous than what you are. Me and Sayyid know all about it. We was on in this piece from the second act. You tried to poison her in Act One. You slapped Max in Act Two, for I seen you and so did a dozen others. I've seen 'em slap a cop in Philadelphia and get away with it. But if a member of the U.S. Senate was to slap an ambassador I reckon we'd be shy a Senator until his State sent some one in his place. And you done worse than that; you're like a governor of a State who slapped the U.S. President. This State will be shy one rajah by tomorrow afternoon or I'll eat this elephant. So Act Three's easy. You resign by telegram before they beat you to it. You'll—what d'ye call it?—abdicate. And being sensible at last, you'll do it handsome, same as me and Sayyid would if we was ashamed of acting worse'n a hyena. Being sensible, you'll abdicate in favor of the Princess Sankyamuni; and she'll treat you handsome, 'cause there ain't a yellow inch in her whole body. Heh! Get on there! Get on home, Asoka, and no wallering— I've said my say. Quorn also is among the prophets."

"Wallah! Wallahi! It is a long, hard way to heaven," remarked Sayyid, "and there are no kings there—only peace and whom Allah loves. Allah! Blessings on His Prophet! They whom He loves—and their horses!"

GOLDEN RIVER

*A novelette of Ben Quorn in India
and the elephant who refused to be
neutral in a fight for a throne*

MARMADUKE BRAZENOSE BLAKE is a terrible name, but Blake endured it without breaking anybody's head too badly, or becoming morbid. He was the younger son of a rather moth eaten ancient family, who kept himself happy and broke in India by spending twice his salary most of the time, and economizing now and then. It had become a sort of after dinner platitude to say that Blake was capable of any heights, *if only*— Two horrible words.

"If only" is the death knell of ambition. However, Blake's ambition died unregretted; he preferred that his friends should be glad to see him, and that his enemies should instinctively not trouble themselves to guard below the belt.

Blake took himself no more seriously than he did the money he won on fast horses or lost on slow ones. For six rounds, with eight ounce gloves, he was the deadliest philosopher who ever took honors in ancient Greek and mathematics. He could speak nine languages with such fluency that they who had to talk those languages because they knew no other, thought him wiser than themselves; and as men think, they act, so he became an influence, which is a dreadful thing to be unless you have a saving sense of humor. But Blake did have. And he was the handsomest bachelor who ever learned the knack of saying no to

women armed with inno-
cence and good looks, so
that he was hugely to
be envied, even though
bachelorhood excluded
him from such important
jobs as only may be had
through married women's
wiles—of which there are
many, and more in India
than elsewhere.

Nevertheless, Blake
had his handicaps. He was much too heavy to play polo
in fast company, and too intelligent and too well read to
enjoy the society of pompous and officious nobodies, who
therefore regarded him with pious horror, that being their
only means of retaining a sense of superiority, without
which some folk are unable to exist and justify themselves.

So it was thought advisable in certain quarters, always to
send Blake to unimportant places, where his lack of dignity
and reverence might do less harm than they would at the
crowded heart of India's complex government. Those men
who understood his worth were outnumbered, but not
outmaneuvered—they, too, being men of talent.

Accordingly, Blake's luck became proverbial. He
was always sent to out of the way and half forgotten
places. Something in those places always provided him
with opportunity, to which he lent himself with cheerful common sense, which was regarded by his critics as
undignified opportunism, if not worse. And in a subse-
quent *Gazette*, Blake would be once more relegated to

some district where there was neither club nor daily paper, and where it was presumed that there was neither luck nor joy of living.

"Nobody," said Blake, "can hold his pants up and win at anything."

So he never worried. When they sent him to Narada, he did not even know that there would be nobody with whom to box of sultry evenings to keep his weight from turning into fat. He took along a crate of books, two favorite horses strong enough to have borne a man in armor, Abdul, his servant, several boxes of cigars, some forty year old whisky and his credentials as resident agent of his Britannic Majesty's government at the court of her Highness, the reigning ranee of Narada.

"This time, this time of a certainty we go to hell," said Abdul. "At Narada there is neither play nor profit. It is a land of Hindus, displeasing to Allah, the provider of blessings, by the beard of Whose Prophet I swear, your honor is too good for such a dung heap."

"Give the girl some silver and forget her," Blake advised. "She'll forget you anyhow, and there'll be others where we're going. Two or three hundred thousand people, Abdul. Something always happens in a place of that size. Did you pack the corkscrew and my riding boots?"

NO RAILWAY RUNS into Narada, partly because of the hills of dynamite resisting rock that hedge the tiny state, and partly because of ancient treaties drawn in good faith by devout and conservative men who hoped to preserve a piece of India for Indians, and to avoid for all time such obscenities as commerce and the tourists stir up in their wake. So you leave the railway and travel for two days, if you are nobody, by tonga—which is an instrument of torture that the Middle Ages overlooked—but if you are somebody you ride an elephant. A resident is more than somebody; he is the shadow of the Anglo-Indian raj. So the biggest of all the ranee's elephants was sent to carry Blake, and because Asoka, which was the great beast's name, had traits that needed humoring, Ben Quorn, super-intendent of the elephants, came also, perched on the great contemplative head, himself dressed native style in cotton clothes and turban.

It was no part of Blake's method to be aloof or distant—no part of his nature. He enjoyed the conversation of whomever knew whereof he spoke; and such people are as rare as oases in the desert.

As they threaded their way through jungle, and swayed upward toward the pass that shuts Narada from all contact with such as book orders and write guide books, Blake, who knew what the official archives had to say, sat, as it were, at the feet of Quorn, who knew things from the point of view of stables, horse lines and the palace back door.

"Don't tell anything you shouldn't," Blake advised. "I hate a man who cackles about other people's eggs."

"I thought you was a sort of fancy watchman, sir, supposed to keep an eye on things, like a Pinkerton watching a bank."

"No, I'm more like a referee," said Blake. "I stop 'em from hitting each other below the belt or in clinches—at least I try to. And you know, Mr. Quorn, a referee who has seen the family linen hanging on the line might want to get into the fight himself and slap both contestants into kingdom come. Tell me what you'd tell about your mother, neither more nor less."

"My mother," said Quorn, "was an ignorant woman with a heart o' gold, though heavy handed. 'Twas from her, I reckon, I learned the trick of elephants, though I doubt she ever saw one. There ain't no least resemblance between her and this place, or the folks who live here."

"But you liked her and you like them? Good. Go on, tell me. Only leave out all the linen on the line."

Blake, who had the knack of being comfortable anywhere, settled down in the howdah behind Quorn's back to smoke and listen. Quorn, who was only comfortable when he felt that his beast, his boss or his guest were getting their full due, shifted a quid of tobacco to his left cheek and spat meditatively.

"LEGENDS," HE SAID at last, "is true and untrue. But if you was to ask me, sir, I'd say they're like superstition, which is a sort of skin to common sense, same as a man's body hides his soul—or an elephant's either. Elephants has souls, and nobody can't kid me they haven't. But that ain't the point. There's legends in Narada as 'd make you crazy until you've had to listen. There's nothing much else to hear, no daily paper, no movie to go to. And then you sort of look into 'em, because there's not much else to do after your work's done and it's too hot to act sensible.

"By and by you come to figure legends ain't much wider of the mark than what the papers print at home and call it up to the minute news. You get so you can read 'em proper, same as when the sporting page says that Young Tiger Sullivan the near champeen middleweight is the Abe Lincoln of the ring. There's something to it. His legs do reach the floor. And so there's something to a legend. Only you have to listen to it right.

"And it's the same with superstition. If they tell you a cobra is the incarnation of a spiteful feller what pisened hisself so powerful that all hell couldn't hold him, you're missing with half your cylinders if you think there ain't something back of it. Cobras is as spiteful as the sweetest Christian when a heathen can't pay the mortgage interest. And if they tell you woman is mischief, that's less than half of it."

He glanced backward shyly. It was an everlasting mystery to Quorn that any educated man should be interested in what he thought about. And yet he was too shrewd a judge of character to be mistaken. Having driven taxicabs in Philadelphia, he understood almost any kind of man except a traffic cop, and possibly himself. He knew that Blake was interested. Blake made haste to banish the last lees of doubt.

"I expect you and I are bachelors for one and the same reason, Mr. Quorn. We cherish our illusions."

"Sir to you. You get me. A man makes a picture of a woman in his mind. He knows she can't never live up to it, so he stays single. And they tell me some governments tax him special. But there ain't much justice in the world. And if there was, they'd tax the women for the benefit of you and me what keeps a lot of cheerio illusions going full blast. Me, I'm full of 'em. I wouldn't swap 'em for all the honey in the hymn books. F'rinstance, I like to kid myself this elephant holds me sort o' high in his affections. I've had what I'd call proof of it and what the scientists would say is stupid. But the scientists are guys who like to prove a man ain't happy 'cause you can't put happiness inside a tube and label it with no doggone formula. And this here elephant kids himself he likes me first rate. So we hit it, and that beats quarreling. You'll pardon my being so talkative, sir—I'm kind of reaching out for what I want to say.

"Our princess—what they call the ranee nowadays—is a cross between the cat's pajamas, Houdini and Fifth Avenue. She's *it*. My money's up. I wouldn't give you five cents for the good looks of the guy who said a word to me ag'in' her. Providence'd let me hit him once."

"I've heard she's quite a modern woman," Blake suggested.

"Modern? No, sir. Not unless the Milky Way is modern—Milky Way and Eve and Mother Nature. She's a Jennypippin—sassy as sacrilege and easier on the eye than thousand dollar bills—wiser than the old Sam Hill and foolisher than any flapper you ever set eyes on, except, that she has idees—snorters—humdingers.

"She's been reading about Queen Elizabeth of England and Catherine the Great and George Washington and Cleopatra. There was a guy called Machiavelli who wrote some dope she thinks is No. 1.

"And what she don't know about Napoleon hasn't been printed, I reckon. She can make a man like me, and maybe you, sir, feel as ignorant as a backwoods Congressman serving his first sentence in the lower house. The trouble is, her *idees* may be practical, but, take her on the whole, *she* ain't. What ought to be, is. That's her motto. She don't make no allowance for the ignoramuses who don't know what ought to be, and wouldn't like it if it was."

"She and my predecessor, Colonel Max, appear to have had some differences," Blake remarked, thoughtfully lighting a fresh cigar.

"I SEE, SIR, you're a man who likes to say things through a microscope. Mebbe the battle of Bunker Hill was just a difference of opinion. Colonel Max hated the sight of her because she laughed at his airs and his fat stomach. He hated her more after she tricked him into a stand up fist fight with the rajah. He could see clearly it was all her doing. But there he was, down on his back with a bloody nose in front of thirty witnesses—him, as you might say, an ambassador with his pants kicked by a one gun nabob.

"Of course, if Colonel Max had had sense, and had drunk less beer, there wouldn't have been no fight in the first place. But granting he wasn't smart enough to match wits with the princess, he might still have had sense enough to switch his bets and back the winner. There was nothing for it but for the rajah to abdicate damn' quick by telegram. And of course that put the princess on the throne, which was what the little bag o' mischief had been aiming at. If Max had took her part from that minute he'd have made himself a reputation, mebbe, instead of being sent home on a pension. But he was spiteful. Spiteful men, sir, are like safety razor blades; they're no use to themselves or anybody else once they've cut their crop o' whiskers. Max, he was long on pride and short on dignity. He looked up precedents and lord knows what else. He took counsel o' the Hindu priests, and he had a lawyer come from Delhi—a long nosed, thin lipped spellbinder with half o' the alphabet after his name. And between 'em they fixed it so that the abdicating rajah took all the money, leaving her with the throne, hard times, reduced taxes, and most o' the rajah's debts to pay—though how they managed that part of it'd take better brains than mine to guess.

"Then Max starts in to bully her and tell her she shall do this, and she shan't do that. But she's smart, and he isn't. She has the goods on him. She has his number. She jockeys him into the jaws of a dilemma, if you get my meaning, sir. And Max is yellow. Max quits. He claims his liver can't stand the climate."

"I have heard that the dilemma was rather an awkward one," Blake suggested.

"No worse than me or you could smile our way through any day," Quorn answered.

"She says she will marry Prince Rana Raj Singh, who is a Rajput—all bravery and good looks, with about a hundred thousand ancestors who came from the moon, on the Mayflower o' them days, mebbe, but without a dollar to his name. He has some fine horses and a following of more than a dozen courteous cutthroats with fine black beards.

They're all too full o' their own dignity to be rude to you or me or anybody else. They feel they can afford to be kind o' tolerant of our ignorance, and even to see a virtue in us here or there. But there ain't one of 'em can pay his board bill."

"Trouble about that?" asked Blake.

"No, sir. Creditors is patient, betting on the long shot. But the betrothal ceremony and the marriage ceremony is to cost something awful, and Max says the princess isn't to take it out o' the taxes. So she says she'll go into business and raise lots o' money that way. Max says no to that, too. Says it's infradig. No mixing up thrones and commerce. He tells her about Charles the First and pepper. And about the king o' Belgium and the Congo. And he remarks how every government official has to keep his hands clean.

"But she catches him staking a man named Bamjee in a speculation to buy up a few of the ex-rajah's debts. It weren't nothing real scandalous—not when you think o' what they call big business, or little business either. Me, I used to drive a taxicab. I know what graft is—both sorts. But she threw a scare into Max, so he let on that his liver needed London fog. I took him through to the station on this very elephant and his last words to me was—'Put not your faith in any woman, Mr. Quorn.'

" 'Tweren't till after he was gone, and the train belching smoke down the valley, that I thought of what I might have answered. But that's the way of it, and it's the same with legends, sir, and superstition, which are things men think of afterwards, either to flatter 'emselves or else to account for something they can't rightly understand."

THEY CAMPED THAT night at the halfway bungalow, Asoka swaying like a symbol of gray history against a honey colored moon, and the horses that had brought Blake's luggage snorting at their picket near a bonfire because leopards were on the prowl near by. Blake won the last of Quorn's respect by inviting him to share the evening meal at the big teak table near the open window, where they could use the moonlight, setting the lantern elsewhere to attract the myriads of moths.

"Now if I was you, sir, I wouldn't tell our young ranee what she can't do, because everybody has to find that out for himself, and the wisest learn the quickest. I'd tell her *how* to do what she *can* do. That'll keep her kind o' busy, since she's capable of more than any ten young women you and me ever set eyes on.

"She has sort o' Chinese looking eyes—dark brown they are, and as full of laughter as a pipe is o' comfort. Say to her seven times seven, and you can almost feel her figuring in multiples o' forty-nine. And she can see the light where other folks see nothing but the shadow. She can laugh at herself, and that's priceless. What's better, she can make us laugh at ourselves if we've got it in us. And she knows every legend in all Narada, so that she can usually put one over on the priests if they try to manage her too much.

"Between you and me, she has it in for the priests, on account of their helping her father to abdicate with all the family money. You see, sir, the family is rich. They've never had to live off the taxes. It goes against the grain of her dignity to have to argue about expenses with state ministers whose wives don't know the meaning of Paris underwear."

"Extravagant?" suggested Blake.

"I'll say so. By nature and by philosophy. She says the

sun's extravagant. Should she insult the sun, or whoever
made the sun, by acting otherwise? And generous—she
could get all her father's money now by having him jailed
for trying to poison her. She has positive proof. I've seen
it. But no, she don't grudge him money. She's only sore
with the priests and politicians who pouched fat bribes
for helping him to get away with all of it. She's reasonable. Left to herself she'd have gypped him out of all the
money and then slipped him half of it for having showed
her all that sport. Maybe I'm prejudiced. I'm only superintendent of elephants, but she uses me as if I was grand
panjandrum-diwan-vizier. Asks my advice on all sorts o'
subjects. Uses some of it, too—about once in ten times."

"About once in ten times I can take advice myself. How
would you suggest that I should manage her?" Blake asked.
"My business is to point out pitfalls and to steer her clear
of them. Narada, you know, is an independent state."

"And she's an independent female," Quorn assured him.
"My guess is that she'll try you out, and if she finds you're
a good sportsman you'll have no more trouble with her.
If not, you'll follow Max into the discard—meaning no
offense, sir. I was merely answering your question."

"You've mentioned legends several times," said Blake.
"Had you any special one in mind?"

"Why, yes, sir. She has a way of digging 'em up one after
another as she needs 'em, same as a conjurer takes rabbits
out of a hat. She's found a pippin this time. You see, sir,
things don't go good when the court hasn't money to spend.
Her father is spending plenty and he's living less than
twenty miles away. So there was a heap of talk at first about
getting rid of her—by accident, of course, and then rein-

stating her father, either by petition or public demonstra-
tion. Failing him, they might get the British government
to find 'em a wealthy ruler from some other state. Surrep-
titious, it was even said to me I might make lots o' money
for myself by dumping her off this elephant. I told her
what was being said, but it was no news to her. She acted
like a born lady."

"Raised your pay, I don't doubt," Blake said, watching
Quorn's face in the moonlight. Undoubtedly the man had
not a drop of anything but white blood in his veins; yet
his features were strangely oriental, and his eyes were like
those of a goat, or of one of Rustum's warriors.

"NO, SIR. I haven't seen my pay since the rajah abdicated.
I'm in debt for groceries. I'm lucky to get the corn to feed
my elephants. No, there weren't no conversation about
money. She always calls me Mr. Quorn and I always call
her miss, because she likes that. I says, 'Miss, they mean to
get you. They're like the gangsters back home. They'll try
every means.' And she says, 'If they get me, Mr. Quorn,
I shall have at least one good friend in the next world,
because I know they will have to get you also.' Wasn't that
a nice speech? Would you rather have a good girl think
that of you, or would you rather be John D. Crœsus with
a di'mond cigar holder and your feet on a golden desk?"

"But the legend? You spoke of a legend."

"Well, sir, there's more legends to the square inch in
Narada than in any other place on earth, I reckon. The
Hindu priests make use of 'em for propaganda purposes,
like party slogans at election time, to keep every one toeing
the line and voting the straight ticket, so to speak. Our
ranee uses 'em for debunking purposes. It's like a game

o' cards, and everybody with a spare pack up his sleeve or
in his pocket. The priests spank down a legend, face up,
and their own interpretation of it. Quicker 'n thought she
covers theirs with a better one and a better interpretation—'cause hers is honest.

"Mind you, the priests don't like her—no more than
mice like a cat. She's too smart for 'em, and she don't make
nice fat contributions to the temple like her father did.
They'd like to see her die o' something painful and just
lingering enough, but not too lingering for fear she'd
trump 'em afore she died. Their game is to make the people
discontented with her. So they dig up a legend about how
some guy a thousand years ago said there would be earthquakes in Narada, and the pestilence and famine if ever a
woman should rule who didn't worship the gods five times
a day and have a high priest for her chief adviser. Do you
see the slyness? They was offering a loophole. Let her put
herself in their hands and they'd let her keep the one gun
salute and a palace to live in.

"But she went 'em one better. She dug up a legend *two*
thousand years old, and a carving on stone to prove it. And
her legend weren't anonymous. According to the writing
on the stone a guy named Gunga had it from the gods
direct. And the legend was that a river of gold should pour
into Narada and make the whole state prosperous whenever a queen should rule who discarded *purdah* and married
a man of her own choosing. She discarded *purdah* long
ago. She goes unveiled in public and talks with any one she
chooses. She has told the whole wide world she means to
marry Rana Raj Singh. But that's not the half of it.

"There's a superstition here that this guy Gunga is reborn

once every thousand years, and every time he comes into the world he not only spills a prophecy or two but he has some service to perform for a woman named Sankyamuni. Now it happens *her* name is Sankyamuni. And there's a portrait of this guy Gunga carved on the old stone wall of the market place. He looks like me—the spittin' image of me. And as luck would have it I've been mighty useful to her more than once. It was thanks to this ugly mug o' mine, and me being by nature capable with elephants, that she made her break out o' seclusion and was saved from being married to a maharajah who had about a million wives already. And because the folks all know that, they're inclined to think her legend is the one to vote for.

"You see, the priests lie pretty free and frequent, though they're awful experts with an alibi when they're found out. But nobody has ever caught *her* lying. So she has the edge. And besides, a river o' gold sounds better than the pestilence and famine, and it's natural to believe what you'd rather believe. So her stock stands high in spite of her having no money. But where in hell she'll find her golden river'd beat Houdini and Scotland Yard and Christopher Columbus. Yet she's confident. You'd think to see her that she'd got the gold invested and was wearing out scissors clipping coupons. Me, I'm betting on her. But I'm betting blind, on a crazy blind hunch."

"Hunches are a sort of spiritual information," Blake assured him. "They're a sort of private secret service."

"Speaking of which," said Quorn, "there's nothing goes on hereabouts that ain't reported by spies to somebody. Just general principles—they don't mean nothing by it. They use each other the way an elephant uses his trunk. Morning, and he walks down for his water snooting this and that way; he gets the smell of all that's happened in the night and knows the inside story of it. Maybe he gets most of it wrong, and it's none of his dam fool business, but he likes it and it don't hurt nobody. We're being watched, us two. Tomorrow morning in Narada they'll know just how far into the night we talked and how many drinks you had. They'll know I refused a second drink, and they'll lay that to suspicion on my part; they'll deduce that you're an exacting kind o' man, sir, before whom I'd be afraid to appear worse for liquor. That may ease things for you."

"Till they find me out," Blake added. "Eh, what? River of gold—river of gold—that sounds like a well known formula. It's a strange thing, Quorn, how the human race—black, white and yellow—always imagines its ultimate bliss in the form of a river of gold. Well, let's to bed and dream about it."

BUT BLAKE DID not sleep long; and Quorn almost never slept, away from home at night, when he had Asoka to nurse and humor. The great beast could be as silly and hysterical as he could be steadfast and affectionate. The problem was to flatter him enough, but not too much, and never to let him even half believe that his affection was not fully returned.

A half belief of that sort, and tigers prowling in the dark, could let in panic just as swiftly as a dam goes down when water seeps in through a crack. So Quorn smoked on; and when the elephant lay down at last he set his back against him, timing the puffs at his pipe to the titan, tide-like breathing, watching the bats weave patterns, shuttle swift, in the purple darkness.

And so Quorn knew what was happening long before Blake awoke. And because he knew that he himself was seen he knew there was no danger—or not yet, at all events. Dark figure after figure, shrouded in flowing clothes that smelt of sandalwood, passed silently between him and the low moon that was dipping beneath earth's rim into a lake of liquid amber. When they had passed he knew the five were women, though they tried to walk like men, and then he began to feel rather more afraid.

"Women—who never carried water jars—and scent worth a dollar a sniff— They're either ladies—or else up to no good. And what are ladies doing here at this hour? Maybe Blake's a sport—he sort o' looks it. His sort—old fashioned religion, I take it, and courtesy toward inferiors, and kind o' mystic minded crossed with muscle and a heap o' hard sense— I've seen 'em play hell with the women. But he can't have made no dates with any one, 'cause he hasn't been out o' my sight. And why ain't they skeered o' me? They seen me."

One by one he watched them pass on to the tiled veranda and then vanish through the screen door into the silent, lampless bungalow.

"Five of 'em?" he wondered. "Five? If it had been murder they'd have given me mine first to save argyments later on. Mebbe it's some o' this here secret service he was speaking of. Perhaps old Max's stable's come here to report for duty. Well, I'm curious. Here goes Pinkerton, Sherlock, Burns, Flynn, Pussyfoot Quorn—and to hell with guesswork."

He knocked out his pipe against Asoka's backbone, rubbed the edge of one of the great ears a minute to suggest that all was well and he would come back presently, then kicked off his slippers and approached the bungalow by way of the deep shadow on the far side from the moon. There was a bathroom door that opened outward from that corner. It moved easily. The inner bathroom door had been left ajar and was hung so lightly on its hinges that the sudden draught opened it wider. Quorn passed through into the utter darkness of the guest room and, to avoid stumbling that might discover him too soon, sat down in the nearest corner.

For a while he heard nothing, except what sounded like a gnawing rat and the regular breathing of Blake, who slept as deeply as a healthy child. Nevertheless, he was conscious of other beings in the room, and he guessed he had been heard; they were keeping stock still, hardly breathing, listening. He could keep as still as they. At last he heard a whisper in Hindustanee.

"It was the night wind changing. It made the door creak. It is nothing."

There was more whispering, too low for him to catch the words, and movement, unmistakably betrayed by a stirring of the sandal scented air. Then a light such as he had never seen used—fireflies imprisoned in a glass tube—intermittent, cold, blue, just sufficient to show the faces of five women close together. He almost whistled. His thought became cameo clear. No words were needed. Elephants, tigers, temples, palaces, burning *ghats,* great, glowing jewels, daggers, poison, an astrologer, a moving panorama of intriguing men, then a river of gold, and a lady who laughed at all of it.

HE WAS OLD fashioned. They were blockading Cervera

when Quorn left public school. His silent lips framed words—

"There'll be a hot time, in the old town—"

He left the verse unfinished. An electric torch directed at Blake's face bathed him, head and shoulders, in a sphere of light. He looked like a sleeping spirit borne on the waves of a pale astral sea. His dark hair, straying on the pillow, moved in the draught from the open window.

"Drowning," Quorn muttered. "He's a likely enough lad, but she'll drown him—drown him. In her river of gold she'll drown him."

Then he wondered why he thought that, and why the thought seemed clear and sane, even though the words were nonsense.

Presently Blake opened his eyes with the steady, intelligent stare of a man who is devoid of fears and hates.

"Who is it?" he asked, puzzled but not frightened. "What do you want?" He saw along the shaft of light at last.

"Good galloping hallelujah! What in the name of drink and rioting does this mean? Madam—"

He sat up, staring. The torch wavered; it showed other faces—vaguely. Blake smiled, suddenly sure of himself, a gentleman aware that there was nothing in the world he could not face on even terms, instinctively feeling his pajama jacket to make sure it was buttoned.

"Madam, will you let me light the lantern?"

He was answered by a voice that thrilled with inner laughter and was mellow, tolerant, feminine, but vibrant with daring.

"If you are nervous, certainly. Otherwise—you see, I am incognito—I don't wish to be recognized."

"Uh-huh. Am I also incognito? Is this to be a strictly confidential chat?" Blake asked her. "I agree, of course. But why the witnesses?"

"I did not know you. Now I will send my ladies away if you wish. But if I trust you, you must trust me."

Blake was thoroughly used to being trusted; not so used to trusting others blindly—and particularly not strange ladies in the dark. Men trained in the secret service learn, usually lesson No. 1, the deadly, subtle danger of confiding women.

"Do you wish me not to know your name?" he asked her.

She laughed—low, with a sort of challenge in it.

"You will know that soon enough. But I have heard of unofficial conversations between the representatives of powers—nothing written—nothing even murmured afterwards. You understand me?"

"Whom do you represent?" Blake asked her. "Do you wish me not to know that either?"

"You shall know all I came to tell you when I have your promise. I don't mean your official promise. I mean your own word—you to me."

"Very well," said Blake, "you have it. But hadn't we better make sure there are no eavesdroppers? Lend me that torch a moment."

Quorn chose not to be caught. Self assertion was better.

"It's all right, sir. There's only me here—Ben Quorn. I saw 'em enter, and I guess they saw me."

"Tell him who I am, Ben Quorn."

"You mean it, miss? I'd never have told, I guess you know that. Mr. Blake, sir, this is her—the princess—I beg pardon, her Highness the ranee of Narada. Them four ladies with her, I don't know their names."

"Is this usual?" Blake asked her, draping the sheet around him and then swinging his feet to the floor.

"I mean, do you conduct all your diplomacy this way? Where are your manners, Quorn? Bring up some chairs, man."

QUORN DRAGGED UP a cane seated lounge, threw a mattress on it from the bed that stood against the far wall, then pillows, and retired to his own corner. Blake stood, bashfully draped in the sheet, until the ladies had arranged themselves, five in a row.

"I'll get out of here and get dressed if you'll wait five minutes," he said awkwardly.

"No, I would rather not wait. I must be miles away before daylight. Queens, you know, are not supposed to visit people in their bedrooms. I have come to find out whether you are friend or enemy."

"I am the friend of every lovely woman and the enemy of all your enemies," said Blake.

"I will hate you if you talk like that," she answered. "I have risked everything—literally everything, to steal this talk with you alone and to get to know you. I don't want silly compliments. Hasn't Ben Quorn told you what I am? Perhaps he was afraid to. Let me tell you. No. Judge rather for yourself. I am seventeen years old and I have won my throne. I have a kingdom and no money. Half my subjects are against me. Nearly every priest in Narada is my deadly enemy. You have been sent by the British government to save me from myself— Oh, I know the formula. You are to listen to all sides. You are even to lend ear to my father's lies against me, even though you British know he abdicated to save himself from being bundled off the throne. Tactfully, patiently, firmly, you are to reduce me to a figurehead. I want to know whether or not you intend to try to do that?"

"Aren't you rather ahead of the clock?" Blake asked her, trying to sound reserved and stilted. But his voice would not behave itself.

"I've a letter, of course, that covers my instructions, to be presented to you at a proper audience. Officially—"

"This is unofficial," she retorted. "What I want to know is, unofficially, will you play on my side and against my enemies?"

"But my dear young lady—"

"Don't dare to call me that. I won't endure it. When you English call people dear young ladies, it means you have made up your minds, and the dear young ladies may just as well take a back seat. But I refuse to take a back seat. I am the ranee of Narada. I intend to govern. What I want from you is help, not sermons."

"For instance, what sort of help?" Blake asked her.

"The sort of help you would like if you were in my shoes and I in yours. I want a fair field. I don't want the British, as well as all my other enemies down on me. I want a friend to whom I can turn for advice at any time."

"My instructions are, in part, to give you advice whenever you ask for it," said Blake.

"Oh, yes. And when I don't ask for it—then especially. And between times. Nice, dry, official advice, all full of warnings and talk about precedents, typewritten out in advance and a copy sent to Delhi for the files. Like Colonel Max. I thank you. My secretary shall invariably acknowledge the advice in writing, and he shall hunt through all the official records to find the most flowery official compliments."

"Well, your meaning is plain enough," said Blake. "But I'm blowed if I know whether you really want my personal advice behind the scenes, or whether you're trying to jockey me into a false position. Do you realize what it would mean if I were even suspected of aiding and abetting—er—anything outside the rules of the game?"

"You don't have to," she answered. "I only want yes or no. Are you my friend or enemy? Which is it?"

"I could give you good advice this minute," Blake retorted. "However, I haven't presented my credentials yet, so I don't have to advise you. I will answer you instead. I am no woman's enemy—certainly no young woman's—assuredly not yours, at any time. I will be your firm friend as long as you play the game according to what I believe are the right rules. Prove to me that I may trust you, and you may trust me to the limit. Men's limitations vary, you must remember, but I will do my best."

"Oh, well, I suppose you are just another Englishman," she answered. "Are they all alike, the English? Are you all Colonel Max and Henry the Eighth and Lloyd George?"

"No," Blake answered. "Some of us are almost human—I've been accused of being that. For instance, I'm curious. How did you get here? How do you propose to get home again? Are you protected? It's a dangerous hour of the night, you know. And what is this river of gold of yours, of which Quorn has been telling me?"

The ranee appeared to hesitate; in the dark it was hard to

tell what she was doing. Suddenly she stood up—she and her ladies, so of course, Blake also had to stand.

"You will soon know the answer to all those questions. May I thank you for your courtesy in suffering this invasion, and apologize for my own discourtesy in waking you?" **BLAKE WAS NOT** allowed time to answer. She and her ladies vanished, less like ghosts than like shadows of ghosts. Blake listened, but there was no sound of horses or any escort, and his manners were too old fashioned to permit him to follow and try to discover how she managed her escape from the scene. At last he struck a match and lighted the lantern.

"Quorn," he said, "you appear to be in her confidence. If she gives you a chance you may say that I said born leaders, and people of genius, fail less often through their own mistakes than because they lack followers, who have faith and vision. Those women she had with her are dummies— mute, stupid, scared out of their wits. Has she five women and five men that she can really count on—ten incorruptibles?"

"No, sir."

But Quorn's reply seemed a magic formula that evoked unsuspected life from the black without. A shot rang through the night that sent him hurrying out to take care of Asoka, who was like a fussy, panicky old bachelor when things happened suddenly in darkness without his express permission. It needed Quorn to make him confident that he, Asoka, had so ordered things and all was therefore as it should be. There was something like panic, too, among the horses; somebody was heaping fuel on the watch fire and the grooms were shouting. Blake unloaded his revolver on general principles; he was sure of himself but aware that his servant Abdul had a way of forcing short cuts to an issue. He summoned Abdul and ordered him to lock up the revolver in a suitcase.

"By the beard of the Prophet, now I know we are in danger," Abdul grumbled. "When my sahib puts away his weapon which he knows very well how to use, and relies on his intelligence which is a doubtful quantity, then we are at the mercy of Allah who is often much more just than convenient."

Another shot rang out. Blake went out on the veranda where he could see the glare of torches—crimson between a mystery of phantom trees. There was shouting—excited, sporadic, full of purpose; and there was purpose in the intermittent motion of the torches. Suddenly the spreading crimson streamed out through the jungle into the clearing, and now men were visible, ten, twelve of them, hunting something.

A tiger, one hind log dragging, broken by a bullet, was trying to escape, and they were heading him back with the torches, taking great risks, standing when he charged and making a hedge of whirling fire. But for what purpose?

That swiftly became evident. There came a thundering of hoofs—a phantom horseman charging full tilt past the bungalow—a thing of sound and no dimensions until it burst into the ring of torchlight—a lithe, lean Rajput riding a bay Arab mare, and whirling a long lance as they whirl it when they ride at tent pegs, or at the wild boar. The tiger sprang, but the lance took him full in the throat. In the confusion of flare and shadow, he seemed to turn completely over backward in the air, and fell dead, lance upward. The mare was now unmanageable. She burst through the ring of torchlights and vanished into darkness with her rider.

Blake strode over to where Quorn was managing Asoka, giving him idiotic things to do to keep his mind off idiocy of his own. He was making him lift a heavy log and set it down—lift it—set it down again.

"Who is that sportsman with the lance?" Blake asked him.

"Prince Rana Raj Singh, damn his eyes! Look out, sir, this animal's skeered. He's like to cut loose any minute. Hey, you. Kneel. You hear me? Get down on your knees or I'll knock your block off. So, that's better.

"Nobody but Rana Raj Singh could ha' done that stunt. Nobody else'd be crazy loon enough to think o' doing it. He's all guts and nice manners—and no more sense o' civilized behavior than a ten ounce trout. He thinks death's a joke. You'll have to excuse me, sir. I dassen't put an extra chain on this animal or he'll think I don't trust him, and there won't be any peace for three days.

"Better get out o' the way of him, sir, he's dangerous in this mood. Hey, you. Come on now—swing your smeller this way—pick me up and put me on your neck where I belong."

BLAKE STROLLED BACK to the veranda. He would have liked to meet the men who faced that tiger with their torches, but he had an intuition that Rana Raj Singh would look for him in his proper place. And so it happened.

The prince came riding out of tar black darkness into the circle of lantern light, swung out of the saddle, threw the reins over a post and smiled. He was the handsomest

Rajput Blake had ever seen—too full of inborn dignity, to waste a gesture on pride or self assertion. He was one of those rare men who knew his own worth and was always quietly looking for equal worth in others. Tolerant, too, when he did not find it. Aware of eternity—plenty of time for every one to learn what manhood is. Death a gay vacation, probably, and life an interesting school.

"Mr. Blake? I expect apologies wouldn't interest you. I have heard that you appreciate that other people have their problems. That tiger had to be put out of the way—man eater—killed two women last week. Too bad, though, that he had to choose your bedroom, as it were, for the last act of his drama. I am Rana Raj Singh."

"Come in and be comfortable," Blake suggested.

"Sorry. I'm acting escort at the moment. Comfort and responsibility don't always go in double harness."

Blake did not care to mention his recent visitors, but it was rather a load off his mind to learn that they had protection on their way home.

"All right," he said. "Glad to have met you. Don't keep anybody waiting. Drop in and see me in Narada. I'll look forward to it."

Rana Raj Singh laughed.

"I am your escort," he said, as if that were the most natural thing in the world, and he was rather surprised at Blake's not knowing it.

"Mine? Damned good of you, of course. But what in hell do I want an escort for?"

"For instance, tigers," the prince answered.

But it was plain that he did not mean that. He had a way of brushing his beard upward and then stroking his mustache, that showed a smile as full of information as it was devoid of malice. His eyes, too, were the eyes of a man aware of enemies, although not afraid of them. He appeared to be listening while he talked. Coolies had appeared from somewhere; they had trussed the tiger's carcass to a pole and carried it away. Rana Raj Singh's men had beaten out their torches; left them smoking in a heap, and vanished.

"I never ask such a man as you to tell me what he doesn't care to tell," said Blake. "But it seems I'm in some way involved in a mystery. Don't say anything in confidence, because that might handicap me. I prefer to be free to make use of information. But tell me anything you don't mind telling."

"If you should be killed on the way to Narada, who would be blamed for it?" asked Rana Raj Singh.

"Her Highness, the ranee's government, undoubtedly," Blake answered.

He said that stiffly. As official resident, his person was sacred. One did not speak lightly about such essentials as that. If representatives of governments were not inviolable, civilization would cease.

"Her enemies," said the prince, "would have cause to congratulate themselves. And her arch enemy—if he should be sufficiently indignant—"

"I get you. I get you perfectly," Blake interrupted.

From what he had been told about the rajah who had abdicated, it seemed likely he was capable of killing any one for any reason. Also it was common knowledge that he wished himself back on the throne.

"What is needed," said Rana Raj Singh, "is a golden

river on which her Highness, the present ranee, may float her boat to—"

"Float it to what?" Blake asked him. But Rana Raj Singh did not choose to answer that. Instead, he asked—

"Would you—would you in principle object to helping her to discover and own that golden river?"

"Hell's bells! This is like a law court," Blake retorted. "Too many hypothetical questions. I'm neither a professional witness nor a lawyer. You—and some one else, too, who came to sound me out tonight, must use your own judgment. Treat me as friend or enemy, and take the consequences, either way."

THE HORSE SHIED suddenly and then stood trembling. Asoka loomed out of the night, a mass of elephantine dignity, aware of having done that most difficult of all things. He had overcome panic. He was consequently superbly pleased with himself. He curved up his trunk, caught Quorn in it, and set him on his feet in front of Blake, then pushed Quorn's turban down over his eyes as a mark of special affection.

"Hey! Where are you sticking that beak, you old fathead. Watch out or I'll telescope it plumb inside you." Quorn took hold of the trunk to keep it out of mischief. "If I might horn in, sir—"

"You appear to be in. Speak your mind," Blake interrupted.

Quorn turned to face Prince Rana Raj Singh, but he jerked his head in Blake's direction.

"Him," he said, "he's special extra, No. 1, O.K. I doped him out. You'll trust him if you take my tip."

Then he turned to Blake and jerked his head toward the prince.

"What I don't know, sir, 'd fill lots o' libraries. But I'm good at elephants, and judging character seems to go along wi' that without making me any kind of a Solomon some other ways. I'm giving you the lowdown when I tell you the prince is the real goods. He ain't one o' these here politicians, and he don't play with marked cards or deal from the middle. He comes mighty close to being my idee o' the elephant's front end, sir, if you asked me."

HE MOVED OFF into the darkness, leading Asoka by the trunk. Words were exchanged that he did not hear—short, swift speech of two men seeking for each other's confidence. It was the prince who called him back.

"You tell him. Tell him all you know," he ordered.

He swung into the saddle and cantered away into the velvet blackness of the night.

"Sir," said Quorn, "there are things that no sensible man would believe, that are facts notwithstanding. And there are things that all the wise ones fall for, that are as false as company promoters' ads. So, take it or leave it, you won't offend me any. Once on a time there was so much gold hereabouts that they still talk of that time as the age of the golden river. The stuff came out o' the mountains, nobody knows exactly where. There was so much of it that there didn't have to be no taxes. And human nature was about the same then, I reckon, as it is now, so the kings and ministers of less fortunate states cooked up a manifesto about how their honor had been insulted and nothing but bloody warfare could set that to rights.

"They explained how they weren't jealous. They was

simply brimming full o' righteous indignation. So they set out to invade Narada, and there was fighting, right here in the pass near where we are tonight. Narada didn't have a dog's chance, but her rajah was dog in a manger minded, and the folks back o' the fighting line felt the same way about it. They found some way of hiding the mouth of the mine, and it has stayed hid ever since—although they do say that the priests of a certain temple know the secret. Now if our young ranee can find that so called golden river—"

"Reminds me," Blake remarked, "of the people who play roulette in the hope of winning enough to buy contentment for the unemployed."

"Sounds like a pipe dream, don't it, sir? The trouble is, her father—the rajah, that is, that, abdicated, knows she's looking for it. And 'tis said that the priests who know the secret o' the mine are playing his game. If she finds it, they'll either doublecross her somehow, or else kill her, or else deed the mine to *him* in such a way that *she* can't get it. Outmatch her they may, but scare her off they know they can't. They know that if she gets the mine, she'll run Narada to her own taste, which is a long way from being their taste. She will answer their sermons with certified checks, which are an antidote for hokum that works as snappy as vaccination against smallpox. As I understand it, sir, the point is, are you for the ranee or ag'in' her?"

"Does she think she knows where the mine is?" Blake asked.

But Quorn seemed suddenly to lose his fluency of thought and speech—or else his confidence in Blake.

"I couldn't say, sir."

"Dammit!" Blake remarked. "Do you see my difficulty? No matter how much I might like the princess, I'm obliged by the terms of my commission to keep a watchful eye on her, to report her doings and to stop any unlawful, or even any unusual conduct of affairs until the Indian government has time to pass on it. Where do you suppose the ranee is?"

"I couldn't say, sir."

"Where is Rana Raj Singh?"

"Anywhere near by, sir—difficult to find, impossible to get away from. You see, sir, the troops can't be trusted; they might easy be bought by the ex-rajah. And besides, troops is too official; anything done by a soldier means the government is guilty. Any one who has one soldier to the other fellow's two, is guilty, no matter what happens. So the army is doing sentry duty where it can't get into mischief—much, and Prince Rana Raj Singh, who ain't nobody's hired man, nor no man's fool, and whose followers can't be bought—they'd fry with him in hell for half a smile—is jes' hanging around, so to speak, strictly unofficial, to make sure no murder gets done."

Blake thought seriously for a moment about his job, then sentimentally, as all true sportsmen must, it being sentiment that sharpens chivalry to cut the humorless thongs of logic.

"I haven't presented my credentials yet," he said at last. "There's nothing necessarily official about me until that happens. If the princess knew where the mine is—if she knew now, and if you know where she is—I could act unofficially, and I might be useful."

"Shall I call your servant, sir, or do you dress without his help? Me and this here elephant are ready soon as you are,"

Quorn suggested. "I've a heathen as can come with us and fry an egg or two at day-break."

ASOKA WAS SADDLED and waiting when Blake came striding through the darkness. Like many solitary men, Quorn sometimes thought aloud; at other times he talked to any dumb brute that was near him. Blake overheard him talking to Asoka and then, for the first time, he was absolutely sure that there was only one side which a sportsman should take in this hotbed of intrigue into which he had been plunged. Quorn's actual words, though, had little to do with the mystery.

"Hold up your foot, you old bum, while I feel for thorns. Pity you can't talk, you fossil; me and you agree fine. It'd sound good to hear some one tell me I ain't crazy. Did you get what I did? That man Blake's a bird. He trusts us absolute—no joker up his sleeve. If he had even thought o' bringing his own servant, I'd ha' took him anywhere 'cept where we're going. It'd ha' been too bad how we missed the ranee, but we'd ha' missed her sure as me an' you is buddies. Him being what he is, we'll treat him handsome— No, there ain't no thorns—so mind your durbar manners and give him a good, comfortable ride, you big bum. And speaking o' durbars, I'm thinking that nex' time me an' you lead the circus parade, there'll be no more o' that radiator bronze. We'll have you sugared up wi' pure gold leaf."

BLAKE SAT AND smoked, and swayed through the night. Asoka seemed to have forgotten tigers and hysteria; he was all elephant again—owner, that is, of all eternity and distance, of night and jungle—part of it—heart of it— gray with experience—all tolerant because he knew that nothing matters much and men pay for obedience in corn and sugar cane. So night and the leagues were one, and when the dawn drew near, the trail was nearly as spent as the darkness.

Two or three times there were hoof beats; now and then a shod hoof rang on rock. And once, Blake caught the clank of stirrups touching, as if more than one horseman followed. But when morning came, there was no escort anywhere in sight.

Dawn broke over the little lake that men call the Mirror of Parvati. There was no sound, except where water splashed and tumbled down the spillway by the high dam at the lower end.

Blake called a halt beside the dam. He found it interesting. It was high and narrow, wedged between the spurs of flanking hills. It seemed to have been built by herculean masons before history was written, and then added to perhaps a thousand years ago. The upper half was of limestone, squared and dressed, yellow and gray and green beneath time's brush; the lower portion—granite—was of undressed rocks so huge that only giants could have hurled them into place; hurled them and, it may be, squeezed them until they fitted.

Standing on the dam, Blake saw the sunlight sweep along the lake until it touched a promontory at the upper end. It was a tree hidden mass of rocks that might have fallen from a hillside centuries ago, and on its edge, reflected in the lake, stood a temple hardly large enough to deserve the name, but so exquisitely beautiful—in that setting— as to make the beholder almost gasp for breath. A flight of perfectly proportioned steps descended from it to the water. Midway down the steps, the ranee stood, alone and motionless. She might have been the goddess of the place.

When she saw Blake at last, she called to him—a sound that burst syllabic boundaries and spread along the water like a bell note, and a thousand birds took flight, unterrified, yet awakened by the magic.

Blake hastened, and as he left the dam, a dozen horsemen rode out from the trees behind him, on the far side of the spillway. They had four pack horses in their midst, burdened with small wooden barrels. Blake, who had an eye for color and composition, was too interested in the ranee on the temple steps to turn and look behind him. But Quorn saw. He saw the horsemen ride below the dam, and he concluded they had business there, but he was an expert at observation without comment.

It was perhaps ten minutes before Blake had reached the grass grown road and settled down into the swaying howdah, with Asoka putting best foot foremost because he craved a plunge into the lake and knew he could not have it before the journey's end was reached. They had gone perhaps fifty paces when a blow like the ring of sledge on anvil came from somewhere behind. Blake turned to see what caused it, but by that time, the dam was like a curtain cutting off the view.

"Possibly I dislodged one of those loose stones at the top," he remarked.

"Maybe, sir." Quorn was not disposed to argue.

"Strange, though, that it should have waited so long before falling."

"Yes, sir. Falling stars is strange, too. I counted thirteen of 'em before daylight. Somebody's out o' luck."

"Do you believe in luck?"

"Me?" Quorn was a long time pondering his answer. "Why—yes, sir. I was lucky to git born, I reckon. I feel lucky every time the sun gets up o' mornings. I'm like this old bum we're riding; the smell o' breakfast makes him kid himself he's lucky. Lucky when he starts out for some exercise. Lucky when he gets home for a rest. We're all lucky we don't get what's coming to us. There's a mint o' mercy somewhere."

"All right. But in your philosophy, who can be out of luck?"

"Easy, sir, that's easy. The sucker who ain't satisfied 'cause things ain't worse than what they are—he don't know what luck is, that sucker don't. And if he don't know what it is, he can't recognize it when it swings his way. And if he can't recognize it, what's the use? He's like a bird asking its ma what air is. Or he'd be like me and you, sir, if we was to ask each other what's an interesting job. Believe in luck, sir? Yes, I've had some."

FOR A MOMENT, as they approached the temple, Blake suspected Quorn. He had spoken of a heathen who might come with them to fry an egg or two. There had been no sign of any servant all night long, and now there was no sign of the young ranee though he had clearly seen her standing on the temple steps. But there was a fragrant smell of breakfast and he presently beheld a tent with a table in it, and a civilized meal all ready on clean linen and expensive plates. Not far away, spread ready on a board, was a heap of hill rice for Asoka, with a pile of hay beside it. Yet not a servant was in sight, nor any sound of one.

Blake said nothing, but he wondered whether he would

have been tempted to make that side trip had he known in advance that everything was planned for his reception. He would have liked to ask pointed questions, but decided not to, and he was relieved, too, when he saw that Quorn's breakfast had been set beside Asoka's pile of hay. It would have been difficult to sit at the same table with him and be silent without appearing surly.

As he ate his breakfast, he reviewed Quorn's conversation of the previous day and night. He was suspicious. Nevertheless, the more he pondered it, the more inclined he found himself to give Quorn credit for honest opportunism and loyalty to his employer.

"But the ranee? I'd better watch—"

That thought was interrupted. There arrived a perfect cavalcade of horsemen. Rajputs to a man. All Rajputs have the right to carry arms, and it is a point of pride with them to exercise the privilege, so there was nothing to arouse comment in the fact that every one of the twenty-five had either sword or lance. But there was a truculence that stirred Blake's sense of well being—a rather more than vague suggestion in their attitude that they had caught him where he had no right to be.

As a matter of fact, he had a perfect right to be there unless the ranee should object. But perhaps she did object. Why else had she disappeared? Was all this mystery a complicated trap set for the purpose of tempting him into indiscretion, to be used against him for political purposes later on?

That line of thinking set him thoroughly on guard, so when the leader of the party dismounted, gave his reins to an attendant and approached, Blake was feeling none of that after breakfast geniality that was normal with him. Even his cigar was rather tasteless. He acted the part of an iceberg, and the more his visitor assumed an air of confident self-assurance, the colder and more distant Blake became. He even looked away to watch Asoka, rice all finished and hay neglected, plunge into the emerald green where limestone shelved into the lake. He bit the cigar clean through when the visitor introduced himself as the recently abdicated rajah.

"SIT DOWN, WON'T you?" Blake's voice was as inhospitable as a banker's when the interest is overdue. "Do you always travel around with a young army at your back?"

The ranee's father stared at him, but accepted the proffered seat, refusing Blake's cigar and rather deliberately lighting one of his own cigarets. He was a rather splendid man to look at, not so worn as some princes that self-indulgence has demoted. His enormous private wealth had saved him from the usual self-pity that crowns failure with contempt, and horsemanship had kept him in good physical condition. A yellow turban made him look much younger than he was. Well fitting silk shirt and breeches suggested iron muscles. He was dark, and rather more arrogant in manner than a man should be who knows the justice of his own cause, but he in no way resembled the fly blown looking criminal that Blake had pictured him.

"I have to take care of myself," he said at last, when he had thrown away one cigaret for no apparent reason and had lighted another. "My life is constantly in danger."

"So?" said Blake, a trifle tartly. It was meant to irritate.

"Yes. Your government would doubtless punish somebody if I were killed. They would quite likely punish the wrong person. Incredible though it may seem, I prefer to live. So I ride protected. Am I right in supposing you are the new resident?"

"You are," said Blake.

"Well, it is, of course, none of my business why you are in this place instead of on your way to Narada. If I should ask, doubtless you wouldn't tell me. I must get that information from your government in Delhi. I keep a permanent agent in Delhi; he can ask, even if he gets no answer."

"It may save you trouble if I consider myself insulted to begin with," Blake suggested. "Let's call that settled and now get to business—if there is any."

"Business?" The ex-rajah snorted. "What business have you here, helping to desecrate ancient monuments and to make light of religion?"

"I have had a most excellent breakfast and have greatly enjoyed the view," Blake assured him. "There is a species of wild goose here that I have never seen before."

The ex-rajah's thin lips hesitated between a smile and a sneer.

"Wild goose?" he said. "Yes, indeed—a true word spoken in jest. This *is* a wild goose chase. I hope to make you realize it. Will you listen?"

"Speak your mind," said Blake, lighting a fresh cigar. "But please understand that I don't wish to hear anything from you in confidence. Whatever information you may choose to give me, I shall use as I see fit. Now go ahead."

THE INDIAN BIT his thumb nail. Habit made it hard for him not to answer venomously. However, some good comes of almost everything; ill temper made him short and to the point.

"I abdicated, but I was tricked into doing it. My daughter, to whom I have been never less than an indulgent parent, tricked me. Therefore, I saw fit to refuse her any portion of the private wealth that has always enabled my family to rule without taxing the people for our support. Consequently she is in straits for money. Therefore she is ready to commit sacrilege or any other crime.

"She wishes to marry a penniless adventurer, who looks to her for the money with which to make himself her husband. Even as she tricked me into abdicating, she has tricked you into visiting this place so that she may be assumed to have official British sanction for the desecration she intends. You know, I suppose, that this is a sacred lake—forbidden to all except certain priests and the members of a certain cult?"

"The cult of loveliness, I hope," said Blake. "That possibly excuses both of us for being here. However, don't let me interrupt you."

"Somewhere near here," the ex-rajah went on, "was the ancient source of our family's wealth. It was known as the Golden River. In plain words, it was a gold mine. It was closed up during an invasion. The country was conquered and for more than three hundred years my family lived in exile. The secret of the mine was so well kept that it was utterly forgotten by all except certain priests who became its traditional keepers, and who have invented the superstition that the Golden River will never be found again until the gods see need for it. I have offered them a liberal share, but they have always refused to tell me where the entrance is."

"Deuced consistent of you. You propose now to help the

priests to keep the secret and to prevent the sacrilege, the perpetration of which, you formerly tried to promote," said Blake. "Continue, do—I'm interested."

"I would have used the wealth for my people, Mr. Blake. That reckless child who is now ranee would squander it, not only on the penniless adventurer whom she hopes to marry, but on the gods only know what other mischief. How she discovered the secret no one knows, but the priests feel sure she has discovered it—perhaps some old document hidden away in the palace—there is no guessing.

"The priests have appealed to me to use my influence. I was on my way to meet you when information reached me of your having turned off in this direction. So I rode all night to have this interview. I am not here to ask favors. I am here to warn you, the representative of the British government, that sacrilege is about to be committed and that its inevitable consequences will be rebellion, blood-shed, anarchy."

"Your horses look remarkably fresh after an all night ride," Blake suggested, but the ex-rajah ignored that, strok-ing his mustache to hide the corners of his mouth.

"I warn you," he said, looking straight at Blake, "that if any attempt is made to enter that small temple or to raise the floor stones, I shall resist it with all the violence at my command, in the name of the people's religion and respect for sacred monuments."

"Very praiseworthy. I'm sure, but rather premature, I think," Blake commented. "Time enough, surely, to talk like that when somebody invades the temple. Did you fall off your horse on your way? I see dirt stains on your elbows. Hope you weren't hurt."

"Damn you!" said the ex-rajah. "Well, I've warned you."

He stood up, no longer making any attempt to hide the mud stains on his white silk shirt.

"Good morning."

"Let me warn you in turn before you go," Blake answered. "I don't see any objection to your protecting that little temple if you see fit. If there are any priests in there you may as well protect them too. Why not? The temple is superbly beautiful and the priests seem not to have neglected it, so they are morally as well as legally entitled to respect. But—now please listen carefully—I doubt your word and mistrust your motive. If you interfere with any one who is not attempting to violate that temple, it will be my more or less unpleasant duty to bring you to book for it. May I lend you a clean shirt? There is one in my bag in the howdah. No? Well—happy to have met you. Lovely weather, isn't it? Beautiful view. Good morning."

QUORN CAME, AFTER tossing pebbles at Asoka who was floating nine-tenths submerged, and in no mood to come out and be valeted.

"Elephants, sir," he said, "are most remarkable like small boys at a swimming hole. The way they stay in, hour after hour, you'd think some one had stole their pants, or a cop was waiting for 'em on the bank."

He noticed that Blake was not listening, followed the direction of Blake's gaze, watched for a few moments the ex-rajah and his twenty-five armed riders standing at their ease about fifty feet away from the temple, shifted his chew of tobacco and spat—with dignity and courtesy, down wind.

"Some folks don't know when they're well off," he remarked. "Some folks are always hunting trouble."

"Has he been hunting for anything else?" Blake hazarded.

"Him? Let's see—ten—eleven—thirteen days now he's been camped within a mile of here. He ain't hunting—he ain't fishing. He ain't got no social engagements in the shape o' women hereabouts. I seen a wagon load o' picks and shovels unpacked in Narada and repacked on the back of elephants. And I know they was his private elephants. And I seen 'em return to Narada without no loads whatever. Yes, sir, I'd say he's looking for something, if it's only trouble."

"Well," said Blake. "I can't say I believe the story about the Golden River mine. It sounds too fabulous. I've seen too many similar fables vanish into thin air. But if the tale should be true, and the ex-rajah should be the first to rediscover the entrance, he might possibly be able to claim—"

"Sir," Quorn interrupted, "he'd claim *anything*. He'd claim the blue sky to prevent our young ranee from seeing the sun by day or the moon by night. He'd claim sole right to the use of castor oil if she had tummy ache. He'd claim sole right to die if he thought she'd half a chance to get to heaven. He's had at least ten tries to poison her. He blamed her for the weevils in the cotton, for the horse bott, for the high rate of exchange and for the short monsoon. He'd rather see her fail as ranee of Narada than see the Golden Age return. He'd rather die than let her live. He'd rather have earache than see her happy. We've a word in the United States—"

"Yes, I've heard that word," Blake interrupted. "Quiet, man. See who's coming." Blake, like many another sportsman of his type, was old fashioned in his choice of language before women.

"Did you enjoy your breakfast? Plenty of dead animals to eat? I haven't yet learned how to feed an Englishman—I had to take the servants' word for it, and I didn't let them stay to wait on you for fear you might not like to swear in front of them. I didn't want to spoil your appetite."

The ranee's voice was gorgeous. Blake stood, bowed, smiled, stared at her mannish costume that was, nevertheless, as feminine as Indian skill could make it, wondered at the laughter in her eyes, at her courage, and at the skill with which she, so recently a *purdah-nashin,* had acquired that easy, graceful manner in the presence of men.

"That was hardly breakfast," he said, "it was a feast in paradise. And now—an angel," he added gallantly.

"No," she said, "just now I'm the mere fussy owner of a rather fine elephant on whose back I once rode to a throne. I'm very fond of him. Mr. Quorn, will you please call Asoka up out of the lake."

"He won't come, miss. He's plumb cussed. He figures he's done a full night's work and allows he'll take a full day off. I've called him and I've hove rocks at him. He's—"

"Will you do my bidding, Mr. Quorn?"

It was neither a whip lash nor was it petulant. It was royal recognition of ability, and a command to do what could be done. Quorn recognized it.

"Yes, miss."

BLAKE MISSED THAT interlude because the ranee chose to keep him standing facing her, so he did not see Quorn plunge into the water and go swimming out to where Asoka wallowed and loafed, squirting up water in jets like an amateur whale, and then swimming away in slowly widening circles, thoroughly enjoying Quorn's blasphemous indignation.

The lake was nowhere wide; the elephant was nearly in the middle before he let Quorn overtake him, and then raised a knee so that Quorn might scramble on to his head. Beyond the ranee, hardly a quarter of a mile away, Blake could see the ex-rajah and his followers in a group beside the temple.

He was questioning the ranee, and she parrying his questions—watching the ex-rajah and wondering what the man intended to do next, thinking of half a dozen things at once and chiefly conscious of the sheer impossibility of seeming wise and dignified when you feel unwise and a bit ridiculous—when a sudden, terrific explosion scattered the ex-rajah's horses and seemed to shake the lake's foundation.

A mushroom column of black powder smoke appeared above the dam. There was a noise as of mountains falling. Perceptibly, inch by inch, the surface of the lake began to fall. And the ranee cried aloud. She did not scream; Blake noticed that. It was a moan of pity, sorrow and excitement—anything but weakness.

The dam was down—at least the upper half of it. The lake was pouring down the ancient river bed. There was a current in midstream that swept Asoka onward toward the broken dam, turning him tail first. Quorn seemed to be trying to get him headed downstream, so that he might escape diagonally toward one bank or the other.

About half of the ex-rajah's men were running in pursuit of stampeded horses; the remainder had mounted and looked to their weapons. Toward them, along the side of the lake on which Blake and the ranee stood, there were fourteen Rajputs galloping hell bent for leather, led by a man—Prince Rana Raj Singh.

"Your Highness," said Blake, "let me caution you. If those are your men coming it is your duty to control them. It will be my duty to report whether or not you used your influence to prevent bloodshed."

She glanced at him once, very swiftly, and then away to where Asoka battled with the torrent.

"Yes," she said, "isn't it dreadful how duty and inclination clash. You would love to see them fight. I also. Look. There go a faithful friend and a beast that I would not have traded willingly for all the Golden River. Krishna! No, no, no—he's winning. Quorn has—Quorn has saved him. Mr. Blake—"

Be hugged by a young ranee and then say what Blake's sensations were. Diplomacy is all impersonal. A diplomat in the embrace of Eastern loveliness, age seventeen, is personal beyond the limits of imagination of the men who write blue books and codify rule and precedent. She did not kiss him—otherwise Blake might have utterly lost his standing as a diplomat—might also have found himself the target of the lance of Rana Raj Singh. What she did was to give way to one of those rare, honest outbursts of emotion, that make friends of kings and queens and commoners. Thenceforward Blake might have to caution her, but—

"Is the Golden River mine?" she asked him.

"If you can find it, count on my friendship," he answered.

"Find it?" she retorted. "Look!"

The level of the lake was down five feet already. To one side of the temple steps, and yet only a few inches above the water, there appeared what plainly was the summit of an arch, supported by columns, all carved out of the solid rock wall which underlay the jumbled debris on which the temple stood. It resembled the end of a modern railway tunnel.

"I'll bet a thousand it leads upward," Blake remarked. "If that's the entrance to a mine, I'll bet it's dry. I'll bet it drains into the lake. I'll bet the mine is up there in the mountain."

WHERE THERE SHELVED into the lake that limestone ledge from which Asoka had gone plunging to his bath, appeared the smooth beginning of a rock road, rutted with the wear of wheels, that led around the curving corner of the lake and dipped by easy gradations toward the tunnel entrance. And the mine dump now grew visible; a ridge like a monster's backbone, principally broken quartz, began to creep, as it were, above water. It appeared that nearly half the lake was filled with débris from the mine, to what depth none might guess, but there was dump enough in sight to prove that the ancient workings were enormous.

The ex-rajah appeared to be in a quandary whether to stay where he was and defend the temple, which yet might turn out to be the real entrance, or perhaps might hide the chamber where the ancients kept their refined gold, or to lead his men down to the rock road and defend the mouth of the tunnel against all comers.

He decided too late. Rana Raj Singh, galloping like the wind, led his dozen thundering across the limestone, headlong down the curving rock road, and drew rein at the tunnel mouth, knee deep in water.

"Heeyah!" he laughed. His men roared, and they shook their lances toward the ranee.

"Goal! Our goal!" cried Rana Raj Singh, and the ranee kissed her hand to him.

"Your goal it is," said Blake. "As referee—"

No sooner thought than done, he took the ranee's hand and led her down the rock road.

"Possession," he said, "is nine points of the law. I saw Asoka reach dry land some minutes ago. If Quorn should bring him this way, and if the beast isn't too exhausted, we'll have him clear away enough of that loose masonry to let us into the tunnel. I would like to be able to swear your Highness stood within the mine and claimed it as your own in my presence."

Sheer nonsense? Probably. The biggest nonsense in the world is thought of by the diplomats endeavoring to forestall rival claimants. Nine-tenths of the acreage of the world is held by titles based on logic weaker than that. Nothing was more certain—more instantly certain than that the ex-rajah was prepared to dispute that, or any other claim whatever.

His men had caught their horses; he had twenty-five now to the ranee's lover's twelve, so he deserted the temple at last and at a walking pace descended the rock road behind the ranee, almost overtaking her and Blake, perhaps refraining only because Blake was at pains to hold the middle of the road and might not easily be passed without offense. Even an ex-rajah, with no throne to lose, may hesitate before he thrusts to the wall the agent of the British-Indian government.

And last along the rock road came Asoka, glistening wet, with Quorn on his head, ill tempered because of the scare he had had, and the drenching. But the elephant was happy, being pleased with his own prowess. He kept curving his trunk backward over his head as though to whisper in his own left ear, which is a sign among all elephants that nothing whatever is wrong with the world, or anything, or anybody.

"You great big bum. Maybe you'll listen to your poppa nex' time when he tells you to come out. You big stiff. Kid yourself you're smart, eh? See what you done to that lake, you fathead. Busted it. You get the fire hose after this— fifteen minutes, neither more nor less, until you get into your durned old thick head that when your poppa says it's time to quit, that's exac'ly when you come out and behave."

But Asoka kept on whispering into his own left ear, and any circus man can tell you that when elephants do that the luck runs even better than when three white horses and a brown one drawing hay are met coming toward you at daybreak.

"Durn you and your optimism," Quorn objected. "If you had to sit like me in wet pants on the fat head of an idjit, you'd think different."

By now, the water level was a foot below the tunnel entrance, laying bare the pediments of the two high columns, and about an acre of platform made of quartz and débris from the dump, laboriously smoothed and leveled. It was so firm and free from hollows as to be dry almost as soon as the lake receded; the only remaining water lay in the ruts made by ancient wheels.

THE EX-RAJAH TOOK a gold flask from a holster and drank deeply when he drew rein on that level platform. There was no room for him to draw near the mouth of the tunnel. That was guarded by Rana Raj Singh's men. Also it appeared he chose to keep his distance from Blake and his daughter, whom he had never recognized as the ranee, whom he had never treated with even distant courtesy since she displaced him on the throne. He affected not to see her. But he kept his eyes on Rana Raj Singh—eyed him with such malice that his own horse felt the vibrance of it and grew restless.

"Bring up that elephant," cried Rana Raj Singh, after a short whispered conference with Blake. "Clear the tunnel entrance."

So Asoka swayed along between the rival groups of horsemen and began to drag away the rocks that blocked the tunnel mouth, choosing key rocks with an elephant's uncanny skill. The pile tumbled of its own weight. An hour passed. Asoka was growing sulky—he being a durbar elephant and no mere work animal—when at last an opening appeared through which it was possible to pass one man at a time.

The ex-rajah finished the drink in his flask. He watched Blake and Rana Raj Singh debating whether it was safe to let the ranee lead the way into the tunnel. As they reached a decision he shouted, halting them. He rode about twenty paces forward and, behind him, his men quietly closed ranks.

"I forbid any one to enter that tunnel," he announced. "This is the Golden River, of which I am the rightful owner by inheritance. It is not and it never has been crown property. It is personal property, as the priests of the temple will testify. I am here to take possession."

"Damned deuced awkward," Blake remarked. "The fellow may be right at that. However, my dear, you are ranee. It is up to you to make the next move. I'm supposed to be neutral. Dammit, is there something in my eye?"

He covered both his eyes and rubbed them. If he made a gesture with his elbow toward the tunnel opening, no unprejudiced observer could have sworn that he intended that. If, when he had rubbed his eyes, he looked first at Rana Raj Singh, and then at the ex-rajah, that was natural enough. They were there. He had a right to look at them. And Rana Raj Singh had a right to put his own interpretation on the glance. So had the ex-rajah.

And by that time the ranee was within the tunnel entrance, her sandals slipping on wet rock and her voice sounding like bubbling underground springs as she talked excitedly. She thrust her head back through the opening.

"Has nobody a torch? An electric torch?"

One of Rana Raj Singh's men dismounted, took a torch out of a holster and followed her in through the gap. Rana Raj Singh drew up the rest of his men, knee to knee, before the tunnel mouth.

"Make ready," he commanded, and each man looked to his saber, but as yet no one drew.

Then he leaned out of the saddle and spoke to Blake.

"There will possibly be an incident. Would you care to take cover behind my men? Perhaps the tunnel mouth?"

"No," said Blake. "I wouldn't be able to see much from the tunnel mouth."

He strode out to the middle of the open space, about half way between the groups of horsemen, and stood there, thoughtfully selecting a cigar and lighting it. Then he put one hand behind his back, and it seemed to Quorn, who was up on Asoka's neck, that the movements of that hand had some significance.

He moved Asoka forward, close enough to Blake to be able to hear anything that might be said above a whisper. Asoka's great bulk blocked the way effectively; in order to attack Rana Raj Singh at the tunnel entrance, the ex-rajah would have to divide his force, or else shift ground and approach from another angle.

The ex-rajah chose the latter alternative. He moved his men toward the throat of the curving rock road, thus taking slightly higher ground and cutting off Bana Raj Singh's only possible line of retreat. The curve of the road was such that the lake lay behind them with the road on their left flank, and by that time there was a sheer drop of about five feet from the platform down to water level. Blake's hand moved again. Quorn moved Asoka forward in a semicircle so that again he faced the ex-rajah's men.

"SIR," SAID QUORN, "I get you. Sir, I get you. Me and you is neutral. This here elephant has prejudices. He don't know no better."

Pugnacity can be aroused in every living creature if you know the trick. Quorn whispered and Asoka began mumbling to himself. The ex-rajah found a second flask in his holster and drank from it. Rana Raj Singh spoke in low tones to his men.

Then the ranee came forth, glowing with excitement. She spoke rapidly to Rana Raj Singh, laughing as she showed the stains on her clothing. He nodded gravely. His men all uttered exclamations and the horses became restless, sensing the excitement, which increased as the man who had followed the ranee into the tunnel came out, mounted, and began to talk in low tones. Suddenly, before Rana Raj Singh could prevent her, the ranee slipped past the horses and ran to Blake's side, laughing and almost breathless.

"The tunnel leads upward—up into the mountain. It looks wide enough to take a four horse team, but there's no air up there. To the left of the entrance there's a passage leading to a chamber that must be underneath that little temple. There was a wooden door. It was rotten. We broke it down. We broke straight into the treasury. They not only hid the mouth of the mine by raising the lake level when the country was invaded, but they hid their treasure in there too—gold bars, numberless, and a bag of jewels. The bag was rotten—rubies, emeralds, sapphires all spilled— look!"

She showed him half a dozen great stones in the hollow of her hand.

"Better get up on that elephant," said Blake. "There may be trouble. There's no saddle on him. Can you sit on his head?"

"I will stand with you," she answered, and there was no time after that for Blake to argue with her.

Brandy in the brain of the ex-rajah had decided to precipitate an issue. He began by abusing Blake in order to tempt him into indiscretion.

"I suppose you expect to grow rich and retire out of the proceeds of this outrage," he shouted. "People of your rank, you know, are supposed to try to be honest. Bribes and commissions—"

"We agreed I am already insulted thoroughly," said Blake. "Why labor the point?"

He was imperturbable and vastly more exasperating than if he had hurled hot insults in return. Exasperating, and yet chilling. He increased the ex-rajah's wish that some one else would start the fight. Rana Raj Singh was the man who should start it—a Rajput prince, a man of high standards of personal honor, easy enough, surely, to incite.

The ex-rajah began heaping insults on his daughter, using words that made her stiffen as she stood beside Blake. As a woman who had cast away the laws of *purdah,* and had turned her back on every convention that could not justify itself in common sense, she was a rather easy target for the vile tongue of a rogue half drunk with brandy. He used lacerating speech. He stripped away the rags of his own self-respect in order to destroy hers. But he drew no answer. He was face to face with dignity that would not stoop to recognize his vileness.

So he turned on Rana Raj Singh, calling him a kept man, pawn of a strumpet, one who hoped to be a ranee's puppet husband and be given pocket money for his pains. But Rana Raj Singh utterly ignored him. It was Quorn who hurled the hot retort back.

"Poisoner! I've seen the poison that you tried to kill her with. I've seen the written confession of the servants you bribed to take it to her. I ain't dignified. Me, I'm nobody— I'll fight you. Get down off that horse and take your licking!"

A SILLY SHOT at Serajevo plunged all Europe into war. Quorn's challenge, shouted from Asoka's neck, snapped the last shred of the ex-rajah's self-control. He gestured to his men and sent them charging headlong toward the tunnel mouth—reserving himself, perhaps, for future outrage.

He counted, though, without Quorn and Asoka, and the vibrant scream with which an elephant can scare the wits out of a horse. An elephant's speed for fifty yards is swifter than the swiftest cavalry. A charging elephant is five tons of horrible frenzy. Not a horse stood up to it. They wheeled and fled, Asoka screaming at their rear, and to a horse they plunged into the lake, ridiculous, indignant, with every last ounce of their enthusiasm gone. It was impossible to climb out of the lake without swimming several hundred yards to shallow water.

"Now would you care to act sensibly?" asked Blake, advancing.

It occurred to him that in conversation out of earshot of the others, he might be able to persuade the man to go home. But the ex-rajah either mistook Blake's motive, or was too maddened by the brandy and the ridiculous plight of his men, to use what reason he had left. He drew an automatic pistol, aimed it at Blake, changed his mind, and fired deliberately past him at the ranee.

He missed her, and he also missed his last chance of escape from retribution. Rana Raj Singh shouted—twice he shouted—once to Quorn to get out of the way with Asoka, once to his own men, halting them as they spurred to avenge the pistol shot.

"Behind me," he commanded. "Halt and wait there."

They obeyed. He took a long lance from the nearest man.

For a few paces he rode forward at a walk, giving the ex-rajah time to realize that he was face to face at last with an antagonist who would not give or ask any quarter. Then he broke into a trot, the lance held carelessly, point upward.

It was then that the ex-rajah fired—than that the lance

came swiftly into rest. The spurs went home and the horse shot forward, snorting like hell's own messenger.

Shot after shot came singing from the automatic, each one nearer to the target then the last, but the steady lance point, never swerving, was hypnotic. The ex-rajah could not take his eyes off it. He spurred his horse and tried to wheel out of the way, then fired his last shot wildly as the long lance took him in the throat, unhorsed him and pinned him, dying, to the earth.

The ranee ran to her father's side. He could not speak, but he could recognize her. It appeared that he could hear her.

"Don't die angry. Laugh! You're getting less than you deserve. You're dying at a Rajput's hands—that's no disgrace. Bear no grudges now. I bear none. Smile at me."

Perhaps he was too far gone and could not. He died with his eyes averted from her, staring at the entrance of the Golden River mine.

"Some folks," said Quorn sententiously, from his seat on Asoka's neck, "don't know when they're lucky. Come on, you old bum. The ex-rajah's men'll be all wet and wanting a job. They'll be anxious to show us what well behaved boys they are. We'll put 'em to work to lift your howdah on. Our young miss is the Golden River ranee now. We'll give her a joy ride home."

A TUCKET OF DRUMS

*A Novelette of Ben Quorn and the Red
Headed Bandit of the Indian Hills*

THE PALACE GROUNDS were a half square mile of wooded darkness and lamplit marble within a high wall, against which the wind and rain drove in furious gusts. Except for the sound of the rain against it, the wall had to be guessed; but where the lamplight shone above the guardhouse there was a glimpse of water streaming from the overhanging eaves, and of a dim, irregular segment of wall upon either hand. A puddle beneath the lamp shone like a pool of liquid fire.

It was Indian night. No sound except that swish of rain against the wall and the sighing of wind swept trees. There was nothing to make the guardhouse gate seem real, or to make the sounds seem other than the formless, melancholy welter of chaos, until a tucket of drums sobbed from the point where the long wall dissolved into the darkness. Then the splash of shod feet. Then, in a lull between the blasts of wind, the clink of it might be rifle swivels, or spurs, or both. But no lantern to show who was coming. Only the splash now and then of shod feet in step, and the sodden thump of three wet sheepskin drums. But that brought a world into being. It suggested purpose. It redeemed the dismal night.

Three drummers, then an elephant with two men on his back, who looked like something from another world, with overcoat collars up over their ears and bare legs wet and

glistening; then an officer, spurred and sabered, splashing
gamely through the mud and struggling to hold a cheap
umbrella against the wind; behind him an almost naked
servant helping him to hold the umbrella; then eight
sepoys, overcoated and trying to keep the rain out of their
ancient rifle locks; and last of all, a small cart drawn by

one humped bullock, driven by a nearly naked man who
twisted the bullock's tail and kicked at the animal cease-
lessly with his bare toes, passed in under the guard room
archway. There were doors that faced each other under the
arch. Two sentries, smothered in shawls and overcoats,
awoke out of the doorway shadows, presented arms at each
other because the procession had already passed them,
retired again into the shadows and resumed their sleep.

On one side of the arch was the room in which distinguished visitors wrote their names in an ancient parchment

book, in proof that they had called at the palace to parade their courtesy. Light through a hole in the blind sent a streak of mellow gold across the paving stones under the arch—a streak of warmth  that made the gloom beyond look more impenetrable.

Within the room, with a cigar in his mouth and his feet on the table, sat Brazenose Blake. On the table were a whisky bottle, a siphon, a box of cigars and three tall glasses. Facing him sat Parbit Singh, the palace chamberlain, dressed in a blue serge European cut suit and dark blue turban, that emphasized the darkness of his eyes. He was a very handsome man, as perfectly at ease with Blake as with Quorn, the other member of the party. Quorn, who made no claim to anything other than his position as superintendent of the ranee's elephants, wore a crimson turban, and a pepper and salt suit.

"WHY A 'TUCKET' of drums?" asked Blake. "The word is obsolete and it means a flourish of trumpets."

"Well, there were no trumpets," said Parbit Singh. "They only had three drums but a tucket was ordered, so they did their best. They marched around the wall sounding a tucket about every fifty yards. The bandit heard them and took to his heels, believing a large force was coming. That was more than a hundred years ago, when we had an English mercenary officer commanding the state troops. He gave all his orders in English because he was too drunken and lazy to do anything else, but he saved the palace from the bandits by giving that order. And tucket is an easy word to remember. So tucket it is. And ever since that night the march around the walls has been repeated. I don't think you should try to upset such harmless ancient customs as our tucket."

Blake laughed.

"I would as soon think of changing the custom of guarding Buckingham Palace. But here is the point, Parbit Singh. There is a bandit at large, and from all accounts he has a considerable following. If your young ranee is to continue to rule, she must subdue that bandit—capture him—bring him to justice and protect her subjects from anything like armed banditry in future. This tucket of drums may have served its purpose a hundred years ago, but isn't it rather ridiculous now, as a means of—"

"No," said Parbit Singh. He shook his head. "Not at all. You don't understand. We have only fifty soldiers, not counting officers. Those bandits realize our position and respect our difficulties. If we should discontinue that tucket they would say we were not showing them the proper respect. But as long as we continue it, as a sort of gesture of courtesy, they take no serious steps against a government which they recognize as necessary for the good of all concerned. Without orderly government, Mr. Blake, even banditry would cease to be profitable. They understand that. We also understand it. So we arrive at a working compromise."

"Unfortunately," said Blake, "your ranee's enemies have sent complaints to our state department. They say a man's life isn't safe outside the city."

Quorn interrupted:

"That's them rascally priests, sir. Them priests'd take the side of Satan himself against the ranee. Give them bandits justice and we'd pay 'em a bounty for killing off Brahmin priests."

Blake blew his nose behind a big silk handkerchief.

"But the roads should be safe, Quorn."

"Sir, they're safer than if there was a cop at every crossroads. Them bandits don't stand for competition. If you and me was to hold up somebody we'd have 'em down on us in fifteen minutes. The bandits cost much less than the priests. It's cheaper and easier to pay 'em a small fee for protection than it would be to bribe police. It only costs me ten rupees a month to protect all my grass cutters."

"—who cut grass for her Highness the ranee's elephants," said Blake. "That won't do, Quorn. You know it won't. This is not the Middle Ages."

"Well, sir, her Highness has fifty sepoys. Dope it out to suit yourself—only take a look first at the sepoys. Me and my mahouts could beat 'em easy with some pop-guns and a brass band."

Parbit Singh appeared more relieved than annoyed by that summary of the situation. As palace chamberlain he would hardly have cared to speak so plainly.

"Well," said Blake after a moment's silence, "the night is young and it's raining too hard to go home. We have this room to ourselves. Let's try to solve the riddle. What is the bandit leader's name?"

"Nobody knows his real name. He is known as Bagh— and Bagh means tiger," said Parbit Singh. "He came to Narada many years ago from nobody knows where and he has lived in our mountains ever since. He limps a little, but has enormously strong shoulders and arms. He is said to be able to leap into a tree out of the saddle and to escape through the forest like a monkey. But that may be exaggeration."

"Are his men afraid of him, or do they like him?" Blake asked.

"Both."

"That's bad," said Blake. "Fear and affection is the Napoleonic combination. Where does he bank his money? There must be some one in the city who transacts business for him."

"Nobody knows," said Parbit Singh.

"Nonsense," Blake retorted. "A bandit without influential friends is an impossibility. He couldn't last ten days. He couldn't cash his loot to pay his men. He couldn't get warning of ambush. He couldn't keep himself informed as to the political situation. He couldn't issue his own propaganda. He would be at the mercy of the first policeman with a pair of handcuffs and a club. Name me his agent in the city and I will show you how to catch your bandit without much trouble."

"But we have no proof," said Parbit Singh—so lamely that Blake stared.

"Well," he answered after a moment, "I don't want to have to ask for British troops."

THE RAIN SWISHED and splashed torrentially. A cloud of smoke blew out into the room and everybody coughed.

Blake was about to speak again when a door creaked beside the fireplace. For a moment he thought the storm caused it, but he glanced at the door and saw a hand was holding it open. He had supposed the door concealed a closet, but a strong draught swirled through, suggesting a passage leading into the palace grounds.

"Eavesdroppers," he remarked unpleasantly. "Come in, whoever you are."

There were several men in the passage, for he heard feet shuffling. However, only one man came in and he closed the door behind him. Parbit Singh muttered an exclamation and Quorn grinned. Blake sat bolt upright, bringing his feet to the floor with a crash, nearly upsetting the whisky as he jerked his chair around to face the stranger, whose manner was a blend of careless self-confidence and half mocking deference.

"Good evening," he said in English.

Vaguely, with his shock of beeswax colored hair, he resembled an orang-outang. He had enormous shoulders and a pair of arms that nearly reached his knees. His pug nose had been flattened at some time, and unskillfully restored. His face was framed by tangled red whiskers and tanned by the weather, his teeth were clean and extremely regular, and his mouth was sensitively humorous. Altogether, he was not displeasing. He wore no head covering. From the waist down he was dressed native style in dripping wet cotton pantaloons, with naked feet. He had evidently left his sandals outside the door. From the waist up he had made some attempt at European costume. He wore a coat and vest of brown velvet with brass buttons over a bright green silk shirt. At his hip was a pistol holster and he wore a belt full of ammunition.

"Good evening," he said again, since no one answered. "I am Bagh. You have heard of me?" He looked at Blake, and humor shone in his greenish gray eyes. "No," he went on, "there is no use trying to summon the guard. My men have locked the guardhouse door. See—I have the key here."

He tapped the monstrous iron thing on the table.

"Shall I sit down? *Krishna!* But I would try to show better manners if you were visiting me in my village."

"Oh, so you have a village? Yes," said Blake, "sit down by all means. Give him a chair, Quorn, won't you?"

But the stranger had already taken one and was holding his legs to the fire to draw the rain steaming from his pantaloons.

"It was reported to me," he said, looking at Blake over his shoulder, "that you told the ranee that you meant to have some unofficial conversations with a view to solving the bandit problem for her. I'm the bandit. Let's talk. Where did I learn English? In England, since you wish to know. I was born in Surrey. I tried clerking in a bank, then prize fighting, because I had heard that Corbett did that, but my punch was not so good as my nerve. I tried the army, but they wouldn't have me because my chest is out of all proportion to my waist—or some such nonsense. So I came to India as a fireman on a Belgian tramp, deserted, led the holy life for two or three years begging by the wayside, tried after that to get a job as railway guard, but was kicked on the hip by a Eurasian for getting in his way. He died a trifle suddenly. I took to the holy man life again until I reached this place, where the bandit business looked too good to pass up. It was. I like it. It's more respectable than banking and less exhausting than being punched by experts. There's no big money in it and I miss seeing the newspapers, but it's a fairly lazy life and I get all the comforts I need. Now tell me who you are."

"The man who is going to put you out of business," Blake
assured him.

"Yes, I left you a pretty wide opening there, didn't I.
However, now that the referee has counted me out and
you have had all the applause, suppose you tell me who
you really are. Are you one of the Blakes of Blakewood?
Oh. Not Marmaduke Brazenose Blake, by any chance—
captain of the Surrey eleven twenty years ago? Oh, well.
My uncle strung and pegged your cricket bats. Remember
that time when you fought the cattle drover in Kingston
Marketplace—the man who beat his dog to death? I saw
that. I was one of three who swore to the police that your
name was Jones and that you lived at Elm Road Surbiton.
You owe me a lie in return."

"I am told that you caught a man recently and skinned
him alive," said Blake disgustedly.

"That will do for the lie. The account stands even. You
referred, I suppose, to the money lender. He should have
been skinned, but he wasn't. I let him buy his choice of
all the ways of dying. He could have been skinned alive
for ten rupees. The easy ways, of course, are the expensive
ones. He chose to die a natural death—he has the dropsy
anyhow—and that's costing him more per month than I
though he had per annum. The climate appears to suit him
up there in the mountains and I rather think he likes the
separation from his wife."

"Well," said Blake, "your banditry has got to cease."

"That's what I came to discuss. May I have some whisky?"

Blake nodded. Quorn poured him a stiff drink. Blake
pushed the box of cigars toward him.

"Excellent, I dare say, but I'm not a judge of whisky," said

Bagh. "For too many years I have had to drink and smoke what I could get. You know what that means. No sense of taste or smell left. However, I hear perfectly. Before I came in at your invitation, I heard you say something about British troops. I suppose you mean a regiment of Sikhs or some other blackguards who will rape the whole countryside and force me to carry out reprisals. I hope you won't think of it. It wouldn't be like a Blake of Blakestone to try to solve a riddle that way. Any cad could do that."

Blake scowled. Nearly all Englishmen do when they are struggling against their naturally friendly instincts.

"But somebody was skinned alive," he insisted.

"Oh, yes. One of my men was. We caught him stealing from the money lender—which was the same thing as robbing us, of course."

"So you skinned him alive, eh?"

"Not unless you're talking in terms of occult philosophy. We didn't even hang him. We drove him away to try to live with honest men. Cruel, I admit, but life is that way. He was caught by the police, who shot him. I suppose he knew too much about them. After that they skinned him in order to make out a case against me. The body was no longer recognizable, so they said it was the money lender's. According to Karma, I suppose I skinned that fellow. But as one man to another, you might say I have an alibi."

"If you're telling the truth."

"I always do. It's so safe. It gets you a reputation for sagacity and cunning that is worth a thousand men, and gives you much less trouble than the men would. Let me tell you some more truth."

"Fill your glass first," Blake suggested.

"No, thanks. If that whisky's as strong as I suspect, I might get altogether too gentlemanly. I don't think you would take advantage of me, but I suspect the palace chamberlain. I have done him so many favors that he might welcome the chance to turn against me."

PARBIT SINGH LOOKED scandalized. He had far too perfect manners to defend himself. He appeared pained, yet cognizant of the fact that life is full of slander and false evidence. Quorn nodded unconsciously; it appeared he also had his views. But the bandit sensed the situation and proceeded at once to complicate it by explaining:

"You see, he owes his job to me. I keep the ranee on the throne. The priests are against her because she defies tradition and most of the laws of caste. The priests are great talkers, and some people are good listeners. The less prosperous ones can listen with three ears. Consequently there are at least ten thousand people in Narada who would like to start a revolution and bring in the British. The ranee's fifty soldiers can't prevent them. But I can.

"I inform them that at the first sign of a revolt against the ranee, I will loot the temples, the shops and the banks; furthermore, that I will fight the British troops and spread havoc all over the countryside. I point out to them that I cost much less than a standing army, and almost infinitely less than an invasion by the British troops."

"Nevertheless," said Blake, "this banditry has got to cease. This is an unofficial conversation. I would appreciate your suggestions as to how the problem can be solved. You understand, don't you? At a word from me our government would send sufficient troops to wipe you and your followers off the slate."

"It would take a hundred thousand men, or else several years," Bagh answered. "Even with poison gas and airplanes. Have you any idea how difficult this country is to penetrate with troops? How easy it is for me to hide? How much damage I could do? How easy it is for me to get what few supplies I need? How thoroughly I would enjoy the sport of playing even a losing game against the whole bally British Empire? And besides, there's politics to think of. You see, I'm educated, although I admit I don't see the newspapers very often. I think I know enough to stir the patriotic stink in the noses of sensitive men and women. I think I could set about a fifth of India, say, two fifths of the House of Commons, all Europe and half the United States howling about imperialism and capitalistic greed. If you don't believe it, try me. Maybe I'm wrong. I'm no Lenin—no Trotsky—no Mussolini. I'm new to that wholesale heads-I-win-and-tails-you-lose stuff. It rather scares me. Too many scruples, I suppose. But I will stake my scruples against yours. Summon the troops and I'll cut loose. On the other hand, play on-side and I'll obey the rules too. I think now I'll change my mind and have just one more whisky—not too much soda, Mr. Quorn. When! That's perfect, thank you."

"What do you think of it?" Blake asked suddenly, staring at Parbit Singh.

"I think he has put the situation in a nutshell. On the one hand, he keeps excellent order on the countryside and the roads are safe to any one who pays a little tribute. They are safe to the poor at all times. On the other, it is not compatible with dignity or economically sound, according to the text books, to allow a bandit to do the police work.

Others might take example from him. There might soon be no government if this were allowed to continue."

"I agree with that," said Blake. "Now what about it?"

He stared at the bandit truculently. Bagh ran his fingers through his beeswax colored hair and grinned.

"Play fair," he said. "It's your turn. I've talked enough. I suspect, if I had one more whisky, I would tell you my right name."

"I shall have to inform myself," said Blake, "as to how many men you have and just how strong your position really is."

"Good. I like that. Almost any other diplomat would have tried to disguise the fact that my strength or weakness makes all the difference."

"It makes some difference," said Blake. "I prefer to know how many troops to ask for."

"I would have liked you even better," said the bandit, "if you had admitted that your government particularly does not want to send troops. There's nothing like telling the truth. Oh, yes, I know they *could* send them. But I happen to know that your instructions are to keep peace if possible."

"I'd like to know where you had that misinformation," Blake retorted. He glared at Parbit Singh, who looked like a man who knows the world is full of false accusers, but that innocence will justify itself in God's good time.

The bandit grinned again.

"Well," he said, "I grant you full protection and free passage for yourself and a few servants to visit me at my headquarters. You see anything you want to see, only don't bring any soldiers or policemen. I will provide the bodyguards. It's beastly weather. You will find horses can't manage the mud. Better come on an elephant. If you'd care to shoot a tiger bring your rifle. I can't offer you any decent whisky or cigars, so bring your own. And by the way, have you any old newspapers? I got a copy of the *Times* three months ago. I almost know the advertisements by heart."

"I'll bring a pile of them," Blake answered.

"Thanks," said Bagh. He stood up. "Care to shake hands?"

"No, not yet," Blake answered. "I hope to be glad to shake hands with you before we've finished."

"Well—if I give you the key of the guard room, will you promise not to let those soldiers out until ten minutes after I've gone? Now and then they shoot straight by accident. They mean all right. It's a pity to have to *strafe* them."

"Very well," said Blake, "I promise. Ten minutes by my watch."

THE BANDIT WENT out by the same door through which he had come, closing it silently behind him. There was only a glimpse of armed men in the passage. Thereafter, though Blake listened intently, there was not a sound. He was sure that they did not go out through the guard room arch.

"It's pretty obvious they've friends in the palace grounds," he said, and stared again at Parbit Singh, who said nothing. It was Quorn who spoke:

"Sir, they've friends everywhere since that man captained 'em. I doubt if you could find in all Narada fifty men who'd take the field against 'em. Some wouldn't dare. Some wouldn't care to. And every living man and woman would be tipping the bandits off to every move you made. The fifty that you might raise by paying 'em handsome would be tipping off hardest of all, for two reasons: first, the longer the campaign lasted the more money they'd get; and second, they wouldn't want to risk their skins. Barring all that the job might be easy."

Blake allowed fifteen minutes to elapse instead of ten, then he unlocked the guard room door. It was none of his business, but he suspected that if Parbit Singh had done it there might have been some sort of official hocus-pocus afterwards. There was no sense in making scapegoats of a few cold, sleepy sepoys. Blake was a trouble hunter, not a maker, and he liked to go deep into the hearts of things before he set surfaces ruffling.

He wished Parbit Singh a good night and, turning his overcoat over his ears, went splashing through the mud toward the great lonely bungalow where he had to live in state, representing the most perplexed, determined and inconsistent—because alive, alert and constantly evolving—government in all the world. He had been chosen to go to Narada because he was daring and unconventional; but he would be chosen for the limbo of retirement on half pay if he should dare too much, or interfere too little.

"Abdul," he said, as his servant came struggling out of the night toward him holding an umbrella and a lantern, "no man can hold his pants up and succeed at anything. Take off your pants and carry them. Give me the lantern. Then you can do one job half decently. Yes, you may hold the umbrella yourself. I would rather be wet."

QUORN FOUND HIS way to the elephant lines, where the great brutes were chained so that they could stand in the rain, or take shelter beneath brick arches as they wished. Most of them stood in the downpour, glistening like wet rocks when the flickering firelight overcame the smoke where the mahouts, who had run out of opium and could not sleep, were trying to warm themselves. Lately, Quorn had put a cot in the shed where the corn and medicines were kept, to cut down pilfering. That was the chief reason why the mahouts could buy no more opium until next pay day. One of them, splashing through the puddles, followed Quorn toward the shed door, where he watched him light the lamp and tuck the mosquito netting carefully under the mattress before turning in.

"Protector of the poor," he whined, when Quorn noticed him at last.

"Strut your stuff," Quorn answered, and then changed into the local dialect. "You know better than to ask favors unless you've earned 'em. Yes, I know, two opium pills would make me your father and your mother and the shadow of God upon earth. I've heard that several times. Yes, and you'll tell me something I ought to know. I've heard that—frequent. Whenever I pay you fellers in advance I get nothing but lies, so give me your news first. And mind you, I can kick like fifteen mules if that's my judgment, so save your breath if you've been cooking up a yarn over the fire there to get me to open the medicine chest. Also make it short and snappy, since it's long past bedtime."

"Heaven Born, there came a robber from the hills—a follower of that one whom they call Bagh, the Redhead. He besought corn for his horse, which your servant gave him, being chief mahout and knowing well your honor's generosity. No, sahib, it is true there was no key to the corn-bin, but there is a little loose plank where a rat gnawed and an arm can reach in—"

"Lord, but I'll get the better o' you heathen yet! So that's where all the corn's been going."

"Heaven Born, that robber may have been a liar, but your servant tells the truth. He said your honor will be asked to take two or three elephants into the hills, conveying Beelaik sahib and his servants; and that you must not be frightened because Bagh, the Redhead, has not forgotten how you let him hide in your house—"

"The man's a damned liar," said Quorn. "I never knew he was in the house or I'd have opened a bottle. I never knew he'd been there until I missed a couple o' newspapers. And I wouldn't ha' known then, only I started to whack my servant, so he came out with the truth. But go on with your story."

"That was all, sahib. You should not be frightened and you should follow the trail to the place where a tiger slew three charcoal burners."

"And you want opium pills for that? If it weren't such a raw wet night I'd take an ankus to you. Here you are—how many of you shivering by the fire there? Well, here's two each, and no holding out on the others—two for each of you, you thankless bums."

He put a lump of the stuff into his pocket and faced the rain again, splashing his way with a lantern to where the monster, Asoka stood, half under his arch and half out of it, catching the drip from the eaves on his back. It was one of Quorn's obsessions that prolonged rain was as depressing to the elephant as to himself, and the beast was clever enough not to dissuade him.

"Here you are, you big stiff. This'll warm your insides."

He made the great beast get back under the arch, and

swore because the mahouts had not provided enough gravel to prevent the dirt from being churned into a slough. Then, under the arch, he went through the regular routine of saying good night. There was a box on which he sat. There was a box of matches in a dark hole where a brick had been displaced. He lighted his pipe.

"You big bum. Ain't you 'shamed of all the trouble you got me into along o' being your friend? Just because I takes a fancy to you and tames one o' your tantrums, I has to assume responsibilities that'd drive a bishop crazy. And the more I spoils you the more you wish on me in the way o' circuses. It stands to reason, luck like me and you've been having can't last forever."

WHEN MORNING CAME, he was sure that prophecy was right. The blankets were damp and so was his tobacco. There were beads of water all over the walls of the shed he slept in. He could hear rain drumming on the roof; and the feet of the man who awakened him came splashing through a slippery lake of mud that would have depressed any one except worms and elephants. He opened the shed door and glared at a man with a gunny sack over his head. He listened in scandalized silence. He spat sarcastically.

"Sure," he answered, "my middle name is Noah. I'm the guy what swam Niagara Falls. I'm web footed. I've a twin six submarine sedan for just such social visits of a nice bright morning. Breakfast? No, sir, I don't eat it. Coffee? I'm like my elephants, I never heard of it. I'm one o' these here frogs that get fat on water. But say, you cut along home and tell her Highness Ben Quorn's coming, but he ain't going to wear no top hat nor no gilt plush suit. I'm coming in a gee string and umbrella, and if I manage to swim that distance and actually get there, she'll have to talk to me down the periscope."

What he actually did was to ride an elephant, so that he reached the palace a long way ahead of the messenger. And though his tweed suit was drenched and his turban was a wet red rag that dripped cheap dye all over his face, he was, as usual, so pleased to be received inside the palace, and so delighted by the prospect of intrigue, that his ill humor vanished. He was not kept waiting. The ranee and two of her ladies entered almost before he had had time to look into one of the mirrors and wipe the dye off his face with his handkerchief.

THE YOUNG RANEE appeared weatherproof. She was as radiantly lovely and as mischievously merry as he had ever seen her. She wore no jewels whatever, but was just a charmingly dressed young girl, with flowers in her hair, obviously pleased to see a friend upon whom she knew she could rely for anything, in or out of reason. He refused to be seated for fear his wet clothes would spoil the furniture, but she sent for a cane chair and refused to reveal her business until he was comfortable, one leg crossed over the other, and the servant had left the room.

"Are you ready for an expedition, Mr. Quorn?" she asked then.

"Yes, miss. And you may as well tell me the worst first. I was telling Asoka last night, him and me's due for grief o' some sort."

"Last night? Where were you last night? Weren't you in the visitors' room at the gate house?"

"Yes, miss."

"And you met Bagh—the Redhead?"

"Yes, miss."

"Tell me in ten words what you thought of him?"

"One's enough, miss. He's scared."

She nodded.

"Was any one else scared?"

"Yes, miss. Parbit Singh was. Him and Bagh has been cahooting and maybe there's been some money changing hands. Parbit Singh kept a straight face, but he was scared stiff thinking the Redhead might give him away. And Bagh, he talked a sight too promiscuous about fighting the whole British Empire for him to kid me he wasn't bluffing. And if you was to ask me, I don't think he bluffed Mr. Blake worth ten cents."

The ranee frowned a moment, pondering. Possibly she was trying to scowl, but she could not keep her mouth from looking mischievous, or her eyes from shining happily.

"Well, Mr. Quorn, I am only a girl on a throne, and my throne seems to me to be dreadfully insecure. If it is left to the statesmen to prop it up, it will fall, undoubtedly. Can you think of a way to help me?"

"No, miss."

"Oh, I'm so relieved! I believe I could get along nicely if it weren't for being helped so often. Were you ever a bandit?"

"No, miss."

"Isn't that splendid. You would really believe them, wouldn't you, if they threatened most terrible things."

"Not me, miss. I've drove bandits in a taxicab. They was the scaredest guys I've ever seen. I was afraid the guy that held a gun against my ribs would loose it off because his teeth was chattering."

"Ah! I *knew* I could depend on you. You know, don't you, that nobody is really dangerous until he is afraid."

"Man or beast, miss."

"Even Mr. Brazenose Blake."

"Yes, miss. But he ain't so easy to frighten."

"I don't want him frightened. But I don't want him to frighten the bandits. Do you think you could bear that in mind if you should take Mr. Blake to see Bagh? Oh yes, I know all about that. He sent a man last night to tell me he invited Mr. Blake to come and see him. Bagh was afraid I might forbid it on the grounds of danger. He has brains. He wants to get the situation straightened out before the rains are over and it might be convenient for the British to send troops."

"It'll be awful mean traveling through the jungle, miss, this weather. Skeeters and malaria—"

"Quinine," she answered. "Use lots of oil of eucalyptus, and I'll give you a new mosquito net to use at night. You won't enjoy it much, but when you come back I will buy you a new Ford car to drive around in, and you shall have a uniformed attendant to take care of it."

"Miss, I'd rather have the corn bin rebuilt. Them mahouts—"

"Very well, you shall have that done too. And I'll let you fire all the mahouts and hire new ones if you like."

"No, miss, thank you kindly. Them I have is bad enough. When do we start on this here expedition."

"Today, if possible. Not later than tomorrow. I learned that Mr. Blake was up before daybreak giving orders to his secretary and his servants. I expect a visit from him as soon as he thinks it's decent to come—he is the most considerate, informal man I ever knew. He is probably itching to go, but afraid to get me up too early in the morning.

"If he only knew how I am itching to see him started! But then, he wouldn't go at all, because he's a diplomat. The way to make him take the worst risks is to persuade him I am anxious about his safety. Do you think you could do that?"

"I could try, miss. He ain't credulous. He likes to let on he believes you. Being a decent feller, he'll go on pretending, so long as no harm comes of it. But he's awful wise under that easy going, gentlemanly manner. My way with him is to tell him just the plain plumb truth and not too much of it at any one time. Then let him throttle his own twin two. He's good at it."

"It would be terrible," she answered, "it would be disastrous if an accident should happen to Mr. Blake. That is why I wish you, and nobody but you, to take him. Do you understand me? I am really anxious about Mr. Blake's safety."

Quorn scratched his head. He thought he understood but he was not quite sure. Perhaps she did not wish him to understand.

"I'll keep him out o' danger," he said looking at her slyly with his goatish, agate colored eyes. He resented half confidences.

"You will mind your own business!" she retorted angrily. She looked contemptuous, as if Quorn were untrustworthy after all.

"Don't you know that danger is the only element in which he thrives? He is one of those men who are no good, can't use their wits unless they are in danger. Danger arouses all his faculties; he becomes wise and does unexpected things. I don't want him frightened. And the only thing that can really frighten him is the thought that he is making a fool of himself. Whereas it is only when he is making a fool of himself that he is really any good. So he mustn't be frightened on any account. He must think he is in deadly danger, and that I am afraid for his safety. Then he will proceed to show me what a Duke of Wellington and Solomon he is by playing beautifully into my hands, and thinking it was he who saved my throne, when, as a matter of fact, I intend to get him promoted for being so stupid that even the statesmen think him wonderful."

"I get you, miss," said Quorn. "I get you. I'll manage my elephant perfect. Barring that, I don't know nothing excep' that quinine is good for skeeter bites, and tuck the net in good under the mattress afore you turn in. And now I'll go and get Asoka's back rubbed good and dry afore we put the howdah on him. I'll be ready to start, miss, whenever you give the word."

THE START WAS made that afternoon in a drumming rain. Two elephants, loaded with tents, supplies and servants, splashed behind Asoka, who was in holiday mood because the rain amused him. He was like a dog who delights to roll in unspeakable things. He wanted to stop and smear himself with mud; he wished to fill his trunk with water from the pools and squirt it at his passenger. He chose the slippery places where he could act like a skidding motor car and slide with all four feet together. At times he hurried for no reason, and then Quorn and Blake were drenched by the shower from overhanging branches. At other times he preferred to dawdle, breaking off branches which he

alternately chewed and flourished. He pretended to smell
tigers in the undergrowth—as if any self-respecting tiger
would be out in such abominable weather—and simulated
fear. And through it all, Quorn humored him with the
patience of understanding.

"He's betwixt and between two memories, sir. What he
was, and what he is. And he don't know jes' exactly what
he'd like to be. There ain't no harm in him—and tomorrow
he'll act like an old gent smoking a cigar."

That first night they camped in a clearing where there
was a huge shed without sides, under which piles of firewood had been stacked. But the roof leaked, there were
snakes in the wood, and the mosquitos were there in myriads, so that the storm outside was almost preferable.

Blake invited Quorn to sup with him and they sat
together under the tent awning, where Quorn could watch
the elephants eating their enormous rations of freshly
cooked flat cakes.

"You appear to know where Bagh keeps himself," Blake
hazarded.

"No, sir."

"Good Lord! Do you propose to wander about in the
jungle until we stumble on him?"

"No, sir. I reckon it's up to him to find us. He knows
we've started. I saw one of his men go running naked away
ahead of us, soon as we pulled our freight away from your
front door. Them heathen can run like rattlesnakes. I'll bet
you it was Bagh who had that there firewood stacked ready
for us. He's prob'ly got relays of runners, and they'll signal
to each other from tops o' trees and what not."

"Too bad a man with all his brains and energy should be

an outlaw," said Blake. "I've been wondering what I would do in his place. He might kidnap me, and while the troops were looking for me he might make his own escape—possibly even to Europe. Even so, I don't see how he'd get away with any booty."

"Booty, sir? He has to split with grafters. Power, he has. But money? Not much."

"How do you know?"

"I don't know," Quorn retorted.

But Blake doubted that. He studied Quorn's face a long time in the flickering firelight before he threw away the stump of his cigar and turned in.

QUORN SET HIS cot beside the elephants, just out of reach of their trunks, so that they could not damage his mosquito net. After he had smoked his customary pipe beside Asoka, he slept like a man who has no troubles upon his mind. Let Blake and Bagh worry. All three elephants had full bellies and sound feet, and there were no sore backs. If the bridges were down and the fords in flood, then the going would be even worse tomorrow, but the difference would not be worth swearing about.

It was drum beats that aroused Quorn finally. An elephant, that to his experienced eye looked in far too good condition to have come any distance, loomed into the zone of firelight with four men upon his back, three of whom thumped at sodden drums while the fourth, who guided the elephant, sat silent under an umbrella.

Blake poked his head out of the tent but they took no notice of him. He went back to bed. Quorn fell asleep again.

There was no more disturbance all that night. The

servants awoke finally and there was the usual shouting and excitement as they slew snakes that had invaded the woodpile while the camp slept. Then Blake came out in his pajamas, and the four who had come in the night watched him narrowly until he sat down in the camp chair. Then they came before him, making suitable obeisance.

"We are headmen," they said, "of three villages that lie near together about one day's march away. This fourth man is the cousin of a money lender whom the bandit called Bagh, has imprisoned in the hills until he can extort all his money. We have come to have speech with your honor concerning that."

"Why all the noise in the night?" Blake asked them.

"We were afraid of tigers. We were also afraid of Bagh, who is terrible."

"You supposed that that drumming would drive him away?"

"No, sahib. It was to let him know that we were not hiding from him. Therefore he knew that we would pay the *takkus* on demand—for each of us one anna, the elephant as well—five annas altogether."

"And if you didn't pay it?"

"Our bellies slitted, our elephant stolen, our homes robbed during our absence. It is very cheap."

"Then what have you come to complain about?"

"This, sahib. We have heard that your honor intends to abolish Bagh, the Red Head, and that in his place there will come constabeels and sepoys who will inflict on us more *takkus* and less peace."

"What says the money lender's cousin?"

"Sahib, it has been said that your honor means to procure

the release of that money lender, which, if true, is a calamity. He will set himself to worse extortion than before to recompense himself for all the money Bagh took from him. Though I am his father's brother's son, he sold my heritage; nevertheless, I am still in debt to him. But we pay no interest while he is Bagh's guest. And it may be that Bagh will persuade him to relinquish all those documents by means of which he keeps us impoverished and himself rich."

"How many men has Bagh?"

"No one knows, sahib, except Bagh himself."

"Where is he now?"

"Who are we that we should know that?"

Blake summoned Quorn.

"Do you know where we go from here?"

"Not me, sir. But there's only one trail as you might say navigable."

Blake ate breakfast leisurely, hoping the rain would cease, then spent half an hour in conversation with the village headmen. Good humoredly, he allayed suspicion of himself and won the admission that each of the men knew Bagh intimately. But he could not learn where Bagh's headquarters were, nor where he kept his army.

"Are you sure he has a thousand men?"

"Perhaps more," said the money lender's cousin.

Finally Blake decided to ride forward.

The headmen led the way until Asoka, who was used to lead all processions, bunted their elephant out of the road and set such a pace that he was presently out of their sight. He and his passengers were in another wet universe all by themselves. He left not even a track to follow; the jungle floor was inches deep in water, and there were plenty of places where even the general direction he had taken might be in doubt.

"We'll be lucky if they overtake us with the beds and grub by nightfall," Blake grumbled.

Quorn remembered the ranee and her rather vague instructions.

"We'll be lucky if we keep our scalps on," he retorted. "I've lost the way. For that matter I never knew the way. This ain't a way; it don't seem to me to lead nowhere."

But it did, and Quorn knew it. Where a great rock heaved itself above the jungle, and a flooded stream on the right hand left only a six foot passage, they emerged through a volley of driving rain into a charcoal burners' clearing, where the clumsy kilns stood like damaged beehives and abandoned, grass roofed huts were falling into ruin.

A woman with only a cotton cloth around her waist, her bare breasts glistening in the rain and a naked child on the ground beside her, stood waving her arms and wailing. Blake shouted to her in a dialect that he thought she might understand. Quorn stopped the elephant. He shouted too, but the woman went on wailing. Then they became aware of ghostlike figures closing in upon them from the surrounding trees.

There were spearmen and bow and arrow men among them, although the greater part had only sticks and long knives. They were stealthy, and closed in rapidly. The woman gathered up her child and slipped away between them, laughing. Then a man raised his spear and spoke to Quorn in a voice that suggested no doubt of obedience.

"He says we're prisoners, sir. I might charge Asoka through them, but they might get you with an arrow."

"No," said Blake. "Let's let them entertain us. I haven't been a prisoner since Cronje caught me in the Boer War. Ask them what they propose to do with us."

"We're to go with them to Bagh, sir."

"Are they part of his army?"

"They say not, sir. They say it's none of your business who they are."

"That's the way to talk! We're to ride, I suppose?"

"They say yes, sir—if we act discreet."

"Excellent. Cronje took my boots and made me walk twenty miles. Do they know I've a rifle up here and an automatic pistol? No? Well, you needn't tell them. Say I'm ready to start when they are."

THE RAIN SWISHED down more dismally than ever, but Blake's spirits rose until he started whistling. He checked himself abruptly for fear of seeming too indifferent to danger. Many a latent danger gathers itself and bursts for lack of flattery.

"It pays to let the masters of a situation feel important," he remarked to Quorn in an expansive moment. He even tried to look dejected and drew down the corners of his mouth, but happiness exuded from him like smell from an onion. He was the least dejected looking prisoner who ever rode an elephant through a driving rain while captors trudged the mud before, behind, and upon either side of him.

They were a gentle looking mob of cutthroats, dressed in cotton clothing that clung wetly to their bodies like loosened skin. They carried their weapons in the manner of a Robin Hood chorus—that is, more for the sake of completing the picture than producing spinal chills. It was fair to doubt whether any one of them had ever drawn a drop of blood in anger in his life.

"But such men," said Blake to Quorn, "can be more terrible than seasoned soldiers if aroused, although the fury does not often last long." Quorn said nothing.

As they plunged into the jungle, Blake began to try to make his captors feel that they had a most important prisoner, who never for a moment doubted their humane intention. As an amateur actor he shone. He deceived himself at any rate—it stands written in his diary, which he only shows to beautiful women and intimate friends, that he acted the part perfectly. What he actually looked like was a well bred Englishman having a glorious time.

Ben Quorn had no complaint to make except that he was wet and getting hungry. He had long since learned that his eyes, and his resemblance to the legendary Gunga Sahib were a passport that rendered him safe from end to end of Narada. There was not a bandit in the country who would hurt a hair of his head. His only dread was lest he should spoil the young ranee's game, whatever that might be; and even that dread was vague—he was so sure of her ability to conjure triumph out of any mess of circumstances.

There was no food when they paused at noon. Asoka was allowed to break off branches, which he chewed contentedly; but Blake and Quorn had nothing except tobacco so dampened that it was difficult to light, and even harder to keep burning. Their captors closed around them and Blake tried, with Quorn as interpreter, to glean a little information. But either Quorn was none too skilful with the dialect, or the captors were determined to keep up a screen of mystery, for it availed Blake little.

"They say, sir, Bagh's army don't never show itself in daytime—and never all at a time in one place unless there's serious fighting to be done."

"How often is there serious fighting?"

"They say not often, sir."

"How long ago was the last?"

"They don't rightly remember, sir. They say, who wants to fight Bagh anyhow?"

"What happens if they don't pay his tax?"

"They say they don't know, sir. Everybody pays it."

"Why have they taken me prisoner instead of letting his army do it?"

"They say they don't want his army quartered on them, sir. Too many men to feed and too much trouble."

"What sort of weapons has his army?"

"They say terrible weapons, sir. Rifles, revolvers, swords, machine guns."

"Funny," remarked Blake. "Where did they get them, I wonder. Have they ammunition?"

"Quantities, sir."

Blake began to whistle to himself again. He scented serious intrigue, perhaps involving agents of a foreign power. Treaties are agreements as to what should not be done, behind the screen of which each party undermines the other; it is awfully embarrassing to a friendly power to discover its secret, so to speak, minor treacheries, and there is no better fun in the world.

"Tell them to get a move on," Blake suggested.

THEY RESUMED THE journey, splashing through rain

until night-fall, when the crimson glow of village fires came twinkling through a stake fence and the smell of smoke along the wind was sweeter than balm in Gilead. All the village turned out to receive them. It was a place of several hundred huts surrounded partly by a mud and stone wall, partly by a stake fence and, for about one third of its circumference, by the sheer flank of a somber looking flat topped mountain—an outlying spur of the range that isolates Narada from the humdrum world.

Near a huge tree in the midst there was a big hut where the village elders gathered. There they fed Blake and provided him with a cot to sleep on. Quorn was given quarters in another, smaller hut, beside which Asoka gorged himself on rice and warm cakes at his hosts' expense. There was a great deal of quiet curiosity—eyes peering in at Blake, and whispering—eyes peering at Quorn comparing him to the legendary Gunga Sahib—but there was no whispering for fear he might work a miracle. Thrilling though it is to hear of miracles, no sane man wants to see one.

Blake inquired why he had been made a prisoner.

"I would have accepted an invitation," he said blandly.

"Who should know that? Bagh said we are to bring you to him." The village elders were diffident, firm—but evidently nervous. "We didn't want Bagh's army down on us."

"Don't you realize that British troops might be sent to look for me."

"That would be bad, but Bagh, Redhead, would defeat them. He is terrible. Nevertheless, he will do no harm to you unless you disobey him. Obedience—good always comes of that."

Blake went out to see the night sky, hoping that tomorrow's clouds might let the sun through for a while. He saw a row of smoky crimson watchfires spaced along the flat rim of the mountain.

"Redhead's men," they told him. "They will be gone by morning. They protect us."

"From what?"

"God knows. There are terrible things that never happen as long as Bagh guards us and we pay the *takkus*."

"What does he do with all that money?"

"It is not much. Indeed it is very little. It is hard to say how he pays his army and has something for himself. Nevertheless when need arises, Bagh is always generous. It was he who paid the Sikh *apoti-kari* to come and live among us and cure the eye sickness."

"Where is Bagh?"

"No one knows. We will send you forth. Other men will show which way to take. We hope your honor will find no fault with us when your honor speaks with Bagh. We are poor men but we have done our best for you."

Blake turned in, but for a long time he did not sleep because of the sound of sodden drum beats. Drummers appeared to be marching around outside the village wall—two-thirds of the circumference and back again. He awoke the man who had been stationed near the door to watch him and demanded what the noise meant.

"It is the custom. It is the tucket. Redhead says if we do that nightly there shall never be sahibs sent to trouble us. There came a sahib once—in the night—but he heard the tucket and it frightened him away. Redhead said so. So we always sound the tucket, taking turns, no matter what else happens."

Meantime Quorn held conversation by a fireside with some men who were not village elders and whose statements of fact were therefore less conservative.

"Me, I'm thinking loving thoughts, you pockmarked sons of baboons. But that man Blake is another matter. He's important. Making him prisoner is twice as dangerous as setting fire to the whole doggone country."

"Bagh will deal with him. Bagh will show him his army, so he will doubtless tell the British they should keep away. Bagh would never let the British reach our village. Bagh kept the Germans out of Narada. He told us so. He told them he would fight them with his army if they came, so they didn't come."

"Were there bandits before Bagh came?"

"Innumerable bandits, sahib. There was fighting until Bagh conquered them. Since then there has been no bad trouble of any kind. Only we pay the *takkus*. But that is not much. It is cheaper than being plundered."

"Well, you guys have brought yourselves trouble this time. You've taken prisoner the lord high pussy footin' snooper of the British raj—which he's a decent feller, but he's on his dignity because that's what he's paid a salary to do. There ain't nothing left for him to do but act nasty."

They laughed, at his efforts to translate slang into their dialect.

"The sahib is pleased to jest with us, and we are merry men, so why not? But we know you are the Gunga Sahib, reborn after a thousand years according to the prophecy. And yonder is your great elephant Asoka. Therefore we know no harm will come to us, because we know that if the Beelaik sahib should seek to injure us you would prevent that."

"Me?" Quorn muttered. "Once I drove a taxicab! Well," he continued aloud, "you suckers, I've seen strange things happen, and I know a young ranee what knows her onions. I've seen that old fat head Asoka there, in one of his tantrums, step careful sideways so's to miss hurtin' a child. And I've seen the blooming British army, guns and all, go back to barracks because some one in a top hat said so. But I'm a nigger if I can see any clear way out o' this mess. You'd better catch Bagh and hand him over."

"Sahib! Eh? Eh? It is not wise thus to speak of Bagh. He has long ears and a long arm."

"Where are them other two elephants what's bringing our loads and the servants?"

"No one knows, sahib."

"Meaning nobody won't tell. Them are the ranee's elephants. Can't you guys see that if you treat her disrespectful there won't be no government?"

"There is the Redhead Bagh."

"Well—don't say afterwards I didn't warn you. That man Blake is picked for pulling just such plugs as this one. He's the unravelingest guy as ever took the kinks out of a snarl. He'll outwit Bagh and bring you all to your senses jes' as sure as this is monsoon weather."

Quorn meant kindly. He also meant to obey the ranee's orders and play into Blake's hands, by impressing the natives with Blake's importance and imbuing them with a sense of Blake's skill, so that they would treat Blake respectfully and make him pleased with himself. But the best intentions have a curiously devious way, sometimes, of straying from their object.

There was nothing more said. Quorn smoked his bedtime pipe beside Asoka and then turned in. But when morning came he was aware of another feeling in the village—nothing overt, nothing even tangible, and nothing in the least unfriendly to himself. He saw suspicious, lowering glances aimed at Blake when Blake was not looking. But if Blake detected any of them in the mirror while he shaved in the watery light outside the hut he made no comment.

THERE WAS A delay about starting, for no satisfactory reason—all sorts of excuses. Somebody was gaining time for something. Then the start was sudden; Blake was rather bruskly ordered to mount the elephant and follow a dozen guides, who demanded his rifle and pistol, saying they would return them to him if Bagh said so. Blake refused to give them up.

"You needn't worry," he assured them. "I won't shoot you or Bagh. That is not my business."

They waived the point because it seemed that at last they were in a hurry. They led the way at the mail runners' swift jog that presently left Asoka two or three hundred yards behind them, because Quorn was sparing him, not knowing how long the march might be. The track led before long between steep flanked hills; it became a river bed along whose ragged banks Asoka scrambled, grumbling, until they reached a gorge through which a flood poured that almost swept Asoka off his feet. He turned and refused to face it. Quorn looked for a way around but there was none. It was a cleft between two granite mountains, shaped like a wedge, as if earth had shrunk and split as skin does on a calloused hand.

"I'm afraid you'll have to use that ankus more severely," Blake suggested. "Animals are like people, Mr. Quorn; they need spurring at times. There's nothing there that he can't scramble through if he tries."

"No, sir. But I know the old skate. He ain't loafing. He's talking back. He knows what I want him to do and he ain't obstinate—not now he ain't. There's something wrong."

He urged the elephant again, forcing him up to within ten feet of the gap, rushing him at it. But again Asoka planted, raising his trunk and swinging to the right toward the ankus, which was a mad way to behave. As he turned, a dozen boulders tumbled from a ledge a hundred feet above and crashed into the gap exactly where Asoka would have been had he obeyed orders.

"There are men up there. They pushed those over," Blake remarked. But Quorn was busy reestablishing relations with Asoka.

"You big bum. For a jinx you're a fair to middling fist o' loaded craps. Now cut out the hysterics or I'll bean you with the butt end. Come on now, snap out of it. Poppa listened to you that time. Now you listen to poppa. Fallen rocks can't pick 'emselves up and repeat, so in you go—you hear me? Do you want me to knock your block off? So, that's more like it."

Asoka went through like a tank going over the top, not thoughtful of the comfort of his passengers. On the far side there was a space of level ground ten feet above the water and there they waited for Bagh's promised guides who were to meet them. Meanwhile the twelve villagers kept their distance, squatting in the rain in two groups, and no amount of shouting could induce them to come near enough for conversation.

"Wait. Wait here for Bagh's men," was the only answer.

And at last only one man came, but he so sure of himself and strode with such easy dignity along a goat track that he looked like the lord of all that countryside. The villagers vanished at sight of him. Blake dubbed him Robinson Crusoe because he wore a goatskin hat and jacket and carried a big, cheap cotton umbrella which turned inside out in the wind whenever he tried to use it. He grinned genially, appeared to know no language that Blake or Quorn could speak, and treated Asoka with utmost reverence, saluting him—perhaps as the biggest elephant he had ever seen. He was armed with a two edged sword and a dagger, both stuck into a girdle that looked as if it might have come from some one's gay silk dressing gown. When he turned to lead the way he gestured like a bandmaster with his loosely closed umbrella, turning now and then to grin with seductive familiarity. He led all day long over difficult mountain trails that made Asoka grumble like an earthquake.

Toward nightfall it occurred to Blake that they had moved in a wide semicircle.

"Quorn," he said, "in my judgment we are not much farther from Narada than we were last night."

However, they were in a maze of tumbled mountains and it might be that there was no other way of reaching their destination. The weariless guide trudged on until he brought them at last within sight of a slope that was scattered with glacial débris behind which a considerable army could have taken cover. Smoke was rising from behind one group of stones. Not far away from it a sodden, soiled flag of some kind drooped from a roughly trimmed pole. One man was visible for a moment standing upon a boulder, from which he gazed, shading his eyes with his hand. He dropped out of sight suddenly and a blast of bugle music came down wind. Then the guide, with a grin and a final wave of his umbrella, turned aside, motioning Quorn forward; and when Asoka had passed him he turned back along the path by which they came; striding as if the long day's march had only whetted his desire for exercise.

Asoka needed no directing; he could smell the sharp smoke and the aroma of flour cakes cooking. He made great haste along a well worn narrow path that wound among rocks, and came to a stand in the mouth of a cave that had been lined with timber and hung with gray grass matting. There was cordwood heaped up at the entrance. Inside there were evidently three caves that shared one opening, and from the center one, which seemed to be the largest, smoke was finding its way out through a hole between the boulders overhead. One man was filling a great basket with the cordwood, a spearman beside him. In another moment Bagh himself stood in the opening with his legs apart, hands on his hips, a jovial grin on his face. He wore a bathrobe of yellow toweling over his green shirt, and his feet were encased in beautifully polished riding boots.

"Junction!" he shouted. "All change! Restaurant is on the platform and the hard boiled eggs are guaranteed!"

He motioned to Quorn to make Asoka kneel, and extended a hand to help Blake out of the howdah.

"Welcome to Tunnel Inn—three rooms, all heated.

There's a room to himself for the elephant—first on the right and mind the low bridge as you enter—plenty of hay in there and lots of fresh cakes. Supper is ready as soon as you've washed your hands—eight courses and—and did you bring me any newspapers?"

BLAKE FOLLOWED HIM into the cavern, noticing the hollow rumbling of two voices in the smaller cavern on the left. The only people in the larger cave were the spearman and four servants who were exceedingly busy with pots and pans in a smoke cloud at the far end. There were some blankets hung to make the wooden walls look cheerful. From the overhead beams hung several sorts of oil lanterns and lamps that confused light, smoke and shadow into one dim golden haze. There were some camp chairs, a few stools, several comfortable looking heaps of rugs and blankets, and a teak table that might have belonged to a king; but there was no extravagant luxury and there was nothing that even remotely suggested the headquarters of a dangerous bandit. There were not even any weapons on display.

"Did you see anything of your escort?" Bagh asked when a deaf and dumb man with a split lip had removed Blake's raincoat and had wiped his boots.

Blake lighted a cigar and sat down in a canvas chair. He decided to seize that opening.

"No," he answered, "unless it was your men who tried to drop boulders on me. I caught a glimpse of those blackguards. I was taken prisoner—"

"Harmed or insulted?"

"No, except that of course it was a very serious insult to the raj to subject its representative to that indignity."

The redheaded Bagh drew up a chair and sat down facing him.

"I hope you brought plenty of smokes," he said. "Yes, thanks, I believe I will have one. My own are pretty bad. How do you keep yours so dry in monsoon weather? You must show me that trick. The whisky you brought is here at the back of the cave."

"Where are those pack elephants?" Blake demanded.

"Gone home. Would you like a drink now? So would I. Let's take a snifter and feel good tempered."

The service could hardly have been improved. A man set a table between them with a tray and long glasses. There was soda water, wind cooled in a chattie. And the whisky of course, being Blake's, was excellent.

"Wonderful," said Bagh. He drank like a man who might drink gluttonously if he should let himself go. "The worst of a bandit's life in this part of the world is the poor quality of the only liquor and cigars obtainable—that and the lack of newspapers. But there are flaws in everything—even in banditry."

"You promised me protection," Blake resumed, "yet your men tumbled rocks on my head."

"Yes—there are even flaws in popularity. I heard all the details of that incident two hours ago and I have already sent to inflict punishment. The perpetrators shall be beaten. Their own villagers shall beat them—thoroughly, I assure you. The alternative would be a visitation by my army; nobody wants that to happen."

Quorn came in, having seen to Asoka's needs in the other cavern. Bagh ordered a drink for him. Blake gestured to him to be seated, but Quorn refused.

"Soak me," he sneered, "if you want to. I'm a human and I can take my dose of dirty, underhanded foul play standing up. But dropping rocks on a decent elephant—I won't drink with you. You're no sport."

"It was your fault," Bagh answered. "Sit down and be sensible."

"My fault? You're a liar! If you're a man you'll come outside and put your hands up. Suppose you'd broke Asoka's back. Come on—come outside and fight!"

"Yes," said Bagh, "your fault, Mr. Quorn; but it's the world, so somebody else is getting punished. Sit down, I say, and be sensible. Do you want to be made to sit down? I have only to—"

Blake gestured, and Quorn took the proffered chair, but he eyed the untouched drink with baleful contempt.

"Entirely your fault," said Bagh. "In addition to my army I have two very efficient means of controlling this area— propaganda and intelligence. I am thoroughly and almost instantly informed of anything unusual that takes place within my bailiwick. And you are quite unusual, you know. You told several villagers who were seated with you around a fire that Mr. Blake is wise and powerful enough to wipe me off the slate. You even advised them to seize me and hand me over."

"Very foolish of you, Quorn," Blake commented.

"And so," said Bagh, "since they prefer me to any other form of government, they decided to kill Mr. Blake. They are stupid people, or of course they wouldn't prefer my tyranny to the sweet seductiveness of constables and soldiers. But there you are. They were also afraid they had incurred my wrath already. You see, I ordered them to meet you and bring you safely to me. To make doubly sure they made you prisoners. In other words, they exceeded their instructions. They supposed that a fatal accident might serve to cover up that indiscretion."

"You're plausible, aren't you," said Quorn, half mollified.

"I have to be," said Bagh.

"Do you keep your promises?" Blake wondered. "I was told I should see your army."

Bagh smiled. For the moment he seemed unable to suppress the vanity he felt.

"Yes," he said, "you shall review my army—in the morning."

"How many men did you say you have?"

"I didn't say," he answered. "You might not believe if I told you. But tomorrow, if you care to take the time to count them—"

A man summoned them to dinner at the carved teak table. It was excellently cooked and well served on imported chinaware, but few of the plates were of the same pattern.

"My servants are clumsy and break things," Bagh commented. "It would surprise you how rarely we rob any one who has china to match my dinner set. I have one of your plates here. Do you recognize it? It was a present from your *hamal*, whom I recommended to your butler. You dismissed the *hamal* afterwards or I wouldn't have mentioned it. This other plate is from the ranee's palace—too ornate—rather bad taste, don't you think? But isn't she a delightful little woman?"

THAT GAVE BLAKE another opening. He stepped into it blithely, as a rather too confident pugilist steps forward into his opponent's trap. And the trap was so well laid that

Blake grew more and more sure of himself and blundered through sheer obtuseness into a solution of his problem. So that Quorn, who had no notion as yet what the answer to the problem might be, sat still and neglected his meal, marveling at the young ranees' unerring judgment of the man.

"She is more than delightful," said Blake. "She is a young woman of rare character and ability. But she is in a very difficult situation. She is limited by treaty to an army of only fifty men, and yet the Indian government expects her to stamp out banditry if she is to be allowed to carry on. The alternative, of course, would be some form of advisory commission that would take the reins out of her hands, leaving her a mere figurehead; and the advisory commission would undoubtedly call for British troops—at the expense of this state—to handle the bandit situation. If you admire her, as you say you do, I imagine you might care to save her—and incidentally yourself from what, in my opinion, would be something of a catastrophe."

"Have some more whisky," suggested Bagh. "Finished eating. Let's take our glasses over by the fire."

The servants had built a fire on the rock threshold of the cave and had placed the chairs there, so that they might sit and be free from mosquitos in the not unpleasant veil of thin, dry hardwood smoke.

"You are asking me," said Bagh, when they had settled themselves, "to disband a loyal army, to leave all this district at the mercy of any ruthless rascals who care to set up in the bandit business, and to retire myself into oblivion. In exchange for what?"

"I am not sure, of course—this is entirely unofficial—

but I believe I can assure you of a pardon and your liberty," said Blake.

"Very good," said Bagh, "let's be unofficial for the moment. How do you suggest that the ranee should rule this countryside? What steps is she to take to keep other bandits from taking over if I resign? What is to prevent my disbanded army from raising a reign of terror? Won't that mean British troops anyhow, sooner or later?"

"I had thought of that," Blake answered.

"So had I," said Bagh. "And between you and me, I would rather stay and fight the British troops, and get the fun of that, and get killed finally. In the long run it would mean less hardship for the villagers—less hardship, I mean, than the anarchy that would follow if I should retire."

Blake was always a man to man diplomat. He believed in straightforward appeals to people's better nature.

"Why fight?" he asked. "You're not an ordinary brigand. You're a man of good sense and public spirit—something of a genius, I daresay. Why not give me time to get a sufficient number of troops quietly into the country—just a handful, you understand—enough to keep the country quiet until the ranee can develop stable government. Then you retire—"

"With a ticket of leave, I suppose, to be indorsed by the police of every town I visit? No, sir! I have established a nuisance value, if nothing else," said Bagh. "Have you another of those cigars? You shall judge for yourself in the morning whether my army can fight or not."

"Well, what do you want?" Blake asked him.

"What do you offer?"

They sat in silence, staring at each other across the glowing embers. From the distance came the sudden thumping of drums, as it might be of men on the march. The whole dark world outside seemed full of a mystery ready to spring. There were no stars visible, although the rain had ceased.

"Would you like a post under the ranee's government?" Blake asked him suddenly.

Quorn sat so still that the other two almost forgot his presence, but he had hard work not to chuckle. Bagh studied Blake's face in the firelight for a long time before he answered.

"Are you a man of your word? Or are you offering something you can't perform, in order to get me in your power?"

"I can't pledge my government," Blake answered, "but I assure you my recommendations carry weight, particularly if there should be no incidents such as might get into the newspapers."

"Do you mean by that," said Bagh, "that your government would prefer to solve this amicably? Yes? Then why not say so? I'm not the one asking favors. By your own showing, I could put the ranee practically out of business and put your government to a lot of expense and loss of life besides. You've been pretty personal, so why shouldn't I be? I can imagine your future career depending to some extent on how you handle this situation. Am I right?"

Blake squirmed a little, not so visibly as worms do, yet not so secretly that Quorn did not notice it. He was watching with owl-like solemnity, but he was finding it hard to do that. He got up, muttering an excuse about Asoka in the next cave. There in the dark he could let himself go without risk of throwing any light on the proceedings.

"IF ME AND you, you big bum, was as innocent as our

young ranee—and as wise as Blake and the Redhead—
Lordy, Lordy, Lordy! Hold me before I die o' laughing!"
He buried his face against Asoka's trunk. "She's talked with
the Redhead, and she's talked with Blake, and she's talked
with me—if I didn't know better I'd swear she talked the
monsoon into making all this rain! And she'll leave 'em
both thinking they did it 'emselves! But how's she going
to handle Bagh's army? Durn 'em, they'll mutiny, soon as
they learn he's quit the bandit business. You be still now
while I go back and hear the rest of it."

He left the great brute swaying in the dark, stood in the
cavern entrance for a moment listening to a far off drum
beat and then returned to his chair between Blake and
Bagh.

"Elephant's restless," he explained. "Strange quarters."
But they had not missed him. They took no notice.

"Officially, our government has no actual knowledge of
banditry in this area," said Blake. "It would be quite simple
to deny the rumors if the banditry should actually cease. I
think I can persuade her Highness, the ranee, to appoint
you minister of forests, on salary of course—"

Quorn spluttered, but blew his nose by way of alibi.
Blake shot an impatient glance at him but remembered
he was only an elephant superintendent who could not
be expected to have perfect manners. Quorn spat into the
embers and was still.

"If the budget could stand the strain of paying them, do
you think your army would consent to build roads?" Blake
suggested. "They could be turned into road builders, with
possibly some sort of vague police power for the protection

of the roads, so as to make them feel important—save their faces for them, so to speak. Do you think they would do it?"

"They might," said Bagh. "Do you think the ranee could employ so many?"

"I would urge her to reduce other expenditure. The roads would be a good investment. How much a month would it call for?"

"We will estimate that in the morning," Bagh answered. "Do you wish to make terms with me tonight? Very well, I'll agree to five hundred rupees a month for me as minister of roads and forests, plus magisterial authority to protect the roads. For my men—five rupees a day for officers, who are to become foremen; a rupee and a half a day for the rank and file, who are to become laborers. My commission to be for a minimum of ten years, with a pension of half pay on retirement."

"Reasonable enough," said Blake. "I believe I can put that through. I am willing to recommend it."

"The trouble with me," said Bagh, "is that I'm a man of my word. If I agree to a thing, I do it. If I threaten, I perform. You see, I have to be that way; I make a virtue of necessity. If I should agree with you tonight, definitely, you could count on my keeping the terms. On the other hand, if we don't agree you can bet your boots I'll use my army for another purpose. Wait till you've seen my army. It's the most efficient and best disciplined body of men you ever set eyes on. It would follow me till hell's bells clang for all of us."

"Well, I'll agree with you," Blake answered. "I'm glad to do it. I would hate to see a man of your genius and good sense hunted by troopers and shot like a dog in the end.

But if I accept your word, you must accept mine. All that I can promise is to put this arrangement through if possible. I will return to Narada, interview the ranee, wire the central government for its approval, and send you notice as soon as I receive confirmation."

"Very well," said Bagh. "Is it time to shake hands now? And shall we have another drink? Now I'll be frank with you. My real reason for yielding is newspapers. I find life almost unendurable without them; I'll be able to get them once a week from now on. When you see my army in the morning you'll realize that newspapers mean as much to me as dope does to some other people. We all have our weak spots—dammit!"

Blake was well pleased. He saw a knighthood in the offing. Few men have the opportunity, by sheer diplomacy, without expenditure of one man's life or one cartridge, entirely to abolish banditry in a native state. When he turned in at last on a pile of rugs he lay awake, listening to the drum beats of Bagh's approaching army, which seemed to be coming from three directions. There was drumming and then silence, all night long. He would have liked to go out there in the dark and watch group after group arrive. He wondered at the silence after they had come. He marveled at the discipline, admiring Bagh as any good sportsman admires the good points of his adversary. He was proud of himself for having solved the problem so adroitly. And he was rather annoyed with Quorn for making such atrocious noises in his sleep.

STRANGELY ENOUGH, BLAKE slept toward daybreak, and when he awoke, with sunlight pouring into the cavern, Asoka's great bulk blocked so much of the entrance that he could not see outside. Thereafter there was dignity to be observed, so he permitted Bagh's servants to bring breakfast to his bedside before he displayed any curiosity. But he was thrilled and made restless by the thunder of the drums outside—not many drums but big ones, beaten in staccato quick time—the most exciting sound on earth.

Then the redheaded Bagh came, gentle and grinning, disguising vanity, Blake thought, beneath an air of casualness. He still wore the dressing gown over his green shirt— no hat—no weapons.

"If you'll mount the elephant," he said, "I'll march them past you. Afterward we'll line them up and you may count them if you choose."

So Blake climbed up into the howdah and took post outside the cavern mouth. For a moment he felt rather disagreeably surprised because he saw no army. He could not even see the drummers. But Bagh stood on a rock beside him, looking proud, and he supposed it was part of Bagh's vanity to want to show how suddenly his army could appear from hiding behind the glacial boulders. The drumming had ceased. Bagh blew a whistle and it commenced again. From behind a great rock, line abreast, twelve drummers marched and thumped their bullhide instruments until a thunder pulsed from hill to hill and down along the valley, echoing among the great forest trees. Behind the drummers marched exactly twelve men. They were armed with swords and muzzle loading guns.

"We agreed," said Bagh, "didn't we?" He appeared excited—almost nervous, Blake thought. "You and I pledged our words of honor?"

"Yes," Blake answered. "Where's your army?"

"That's it."

Blake was able to control himself because Quorn provided distraction. Seated on Asoka's head he doubled himself up forward, spluttering with laughter that almost shook him to the ground. Blake felt furious with him. He called it damned bad manners. He regretted having given Quorn a drink or two the night before. He stared at Quorn's back as if eyesight could wither him, scorch him, burn him up. He exploded at last—

"Dammit, fellow, are you forgetting yourself?"

The army, having marched past, changed direction and deployed itself until it faced Blake at a distance of fifty paces. There it halted and there was silence until Bagh once more blew his whistle. Then a tucket of drums beat out a salute.

"That's what I've terrorized the country with," said Bagh. "Any fool could do it with a thousand men. My limit has been twenty-five—plus propaganda and information. They're all officers—they're to get five rupees a day each. Don't forget that."

"Damn 'em, they must have worked last night—to stage all that drumming," Blake remarked.

"They did. And for two rupees a day. Think how well they'll work for five!"

ALL THE WAY home Quorn was very careful not to resent Blake's irritability. He who has trained elephants understands better than most men that irritability must find an outlet—a target that cannot be hurt, if possible. He endured all things, including a lack of Havana cigars, without a murmur even though Blake himself smoked incessantly and the aroma tantalized Quorn's nostrils. And because Blake was a good sportsman, it eventually dawned upon him that Quorn had saved an awkward moment. So he made amends before they reached Narada, and characteristically he made them handsomely:

"I intend to recommend you for a raise of pay," he said. "I don't see why the budget can't be stretched a bit to manage that."

But there was some one else to whom no thought was necessary, because, as Quorn had said, she knew her onions. She knew Quorn, at any rate. She met him in the doorway of the palace reception room, when he came from delivering Blake at his house.

"Did all go well?" she demanded.

"Yes, miss."

"Did Mr. Blake see the Redhead's army?"

"No, miss."

"Did he see the four and twenty that I advised Bagh to show him?"

"Yes, miss."

"And was Mr. Blake satisfied?"

"Yes, miss."

"Excellent! Then I can have my Redhead to help me govern, and we'll build roads, and there'll still be a hundred first class bandits under his orders to keep the villagers in hand at no expense to me! I will make a great state of Narada, Mr. Quorn, before I have finished."

"Yes, miss."

"I will show you a government."

"Yes, miss. About that corn bin—could I have the palace blacksmiths put a metal lining in it? Them mahouts is thieves; they'd steal the shadow off a wall."

He rode Asoka home in pitch black darkness, laughing, talking aloud to the elephant, as his habit was when there was no one else to hear.

"You big bum, you're a better diplomat than Blake," he said. "You talk less. How much would you give, for all that money lender's mortgages by the time Bagh turns him loose? He'll have to cancel 'em. And I'll bet you the borrowers get back what they're overpaid him. Bandits? Hell! We couldn't live without 'em!"

As they reached the elephant lines they heard the thunder of three sodden drums. The tucket was being sounded around the palace wall, protecting all Narada against outlaws.

IN OLD NARADA FORT

A Novelette of Modern India

THE RANEE QUOTED high authority of very ancient vintage.

"A man's ears," she said, "were never meant for closing. His mouth was."

Ben Quorn sat respectfully in front of her on the edge of a chair, in a room that smelt vaguely of sandalwood and rose leaves. Ben Quorn smelt of the elephant lines, although he did not know it, but the ranee, who had much more tact than most young women of her age, never so much as wrinkled her beautiful nose; she knew that no amount of soft soap will remove the smell of elephants. And though so royal that the line of her ancestry fades into a mystery of fabulous mixed marriages of gods and men, she always made Quorn be seated in her presence.

Her servants, who were rather shocked by it, tried to excuse it on the ground that Ben Quorn was really a reincarnation of the legendary Gunga sahib, whose face, carved on the marketplace wall resembled his. But the truth was that the ranee, in spite of her youth—or perhaps because of it—had sane ideas regarding the treatment of faithful friends in her employ.

But that did not prevent Ben Quorn from fidgeting with his helmet; it is a long way from driving a taxicab in Philadelphia to being seated in an ancient Indian palace and

being consulted by the unmarried and very lovely young ruler of a native state. He was always nervous in her presence, although his agate eyes met hers fearlessly, and with the thrill that comes of mutual understanding.

"Yes, miss," he said solemnly.

She liked him to call her miss because it sounded modern and democratic.

"Mr. Quorn, I have too many advisers and too many servants, but not enough friends."

"God save you from too many friends, miss. They're worse than the others. They get sore at you if you don't do what they say; and they blame you for it if you do. A friend is an enemy still in the egg, if you'll pardon my saying so."

The truth was, Quorn was homesick, though he had never had a home worth mentioning. He yearned for the roar and fog of Philadelphia. He was tired of talking in an alien tongue to aliens who treated him with superstitious

awe, but who viewed life so differently. He was devoted to the young ranee, and to her elephants; particularly to the biggest of them all, Asoka, an intelligent but touchy monster who, in his frequent tantrums, was unmanageable by any one but Quorn himself. But he would have liked some pepper-pot and scrapple, some bootleg beer and a Sunday paper. He did not want to drive a taxicab again, but he craved to lead his elephants in procession through Philadelphia and be looked up to by old acquaintances. Childish, of course, but human. Fortunately the ranee realized that he was homesick.

"I will give you a vacation on full pay, Mr. Quorn, as soon as I can spare you. Meanwhile you must look for some one whom you can trust to take care of the elephants in your absence. And just now there are some other matters."

"Yes, miss. I suspected trouble from the way you had me sit on this here fancy chair in place of a cheap one. Maybe you'd better tell the worst first. All the rest looks easy when the worst is over."

"Mr. Quorn, it is highly irregular for me to talk to you like this. If you should repeat what I say to any one—to any one—you understand me?"

"Yes, miss."

"Mr. Brazenose Blake, for instance. He is the nicest man, I think, who ever was sent by a viceroy and council to prevent a little ranee of a lonely little native state from having her own way in important matters. I like him and he appears to like me. He is such a gentleman that he yields in unimportant matters without even pretending that the destiny of a universe depends on them. When I ask him for good advice he gives it, from his own viewpoint, of course, but utterly honestly. He even shows me, sometimes, how to evade the strictures of the central government. But he represents the central government. So he mustn't even know I have talked with you—except, of course, about the elephants, which are your proper business."

"Yes, miss."

"A rebellion is brewing."

"I'VE A .45, miss, and a blackjack. I'm for you. But I weren't never trained for fighting. Me and Asoka between us might do quite a piece o' damage. But—"

"I wish to avoid fighting. I intend to win, not to be rescued by the British and be reduced to a sort of political doll. It will be difficult to win, but I intend to do it."

"Yes, miss."

"Since I rediscovered the Golden River mine everything has gone wrong instead of better, as should have been. In the first place, the mine needs enormous amounts of money to put it in working order. I haven't the money and Mr. Blake won't let me negotiate with foreign capital. The central Indian government would like to have a finger in the pie. There are financiers in London. They are not Englishmen; they are of the international type and they have enormous influence. They have heard of the mine through Bamjee, my purchasing agent, who is a treacherous little reptile. Bamjee smuggled their expert investigators into the mine—"

"I could kill Bamjee, easy," Quorn assured her.

"Anybody could," she answered. "But I need him in order to trap all the others. There has arrived in Narada a Mr. Ginsberg."

"Yes, miss. I seen him. He claims he's here to shoot tigers. He's staying at the abandoned mission and my servant Moses counted six rifles he has, but I'll bet he never fired one. He don't know which end is which. And he ain't in no hurry either. He claims he can't get guides to suit him. I could guide him, miss, and dump him in the river along with all them alligators. How would that be? Or maybe the German government—"

"He isn't German," said the ranee, "and he isn't a Jew, and his name isn't really Ginsberg, although he has a passport and ail the proper credentials. In one sense he is a trap set for me. If harm should happen to him there would be a hue and cry raised instantly from all sorts of directions; hundreds of newspapers would print nonsense about a state of lawlessness in Narada; fifty reasons would be found for taking the mine away from me—and perhaps for removing me from the throne. You see, I have information."

"Yes, miss."

"Mr. Blake is a gentleman."

"Yes, miss."

"Meanwhile, this Mr. Ginsberg, with the help of Bamjee, who pretends to be hunting for suitable guides for him, is spreading stories about how rich the mine is and how foolish my subjects are to let me keep it closed up. Ginsberg tells them that perhaps I am working it secretly and that my ignorant agents will damage the mine so that it will take years to get proper production from it. He knows that is naked nonsense but he keeps on saying it. He says I am preventing the mine from being developed by people who would employ thousands of men at high wages. He says I have set my face against prosperity because I wish to keep people in subjection. Have you heard any of that talk?"

"Yes, miss."

"Why didn't you tell me?"

"Miss, my job is elephants."

"You are likely to lose your job unless I can checkmate Mr. Ginsberg and his friends. The priests have taken sides with him, although they don't know who he is. You know how the priests hate me because I repudiate caste and encourage people to ignore their insolent pretensions. The high priest of the temple of Siva has set up a claim that the mine really belongs to the temple. It is a false claim and he knows it is false, but he asserts it openly in order to stir up the people against me. He would like to stir rebellion because that would mean my deposition. He will succeed unless I find some means of making him ridiculous."

"Miss, if that guy ain't ridiculous I'm the Prince o' Wales. Have you seen his automobile? Bamjee sent for me to fix its carburetor." Quorn shook his head.

"Yes," she answered, "but he must be made to *feel* ridiculous, and others, who think he is wonderful, must be made to *know* he is very ridiculous. But there must be no bloodshed, because bloodshed would be taken as proof that I can't rule. And I have only fifty soldiers."

"Yes, miss. I know them soldiers."

The ranee ignored that comment. After all, they were her soldiers and she was loyal to them.

"Rebellion is brewing," she repeated. "The conspirators' headquarters is in the Old Fort, where the high priest goes at internals to conduct a service in the sacred cave that is somewhere under the main building. There was no need for him to revive that service; he only did it as an excuse for encouraging the conspirators. I have nobody but you on whom I can depend to defeat the high priest."

"Me, miss?"

"Yes, you. The people believe you are the reincarnation of Gunga sahib, and that Asoka is a reincarnation of the Gunga sahib's elephant. The Gunga sahib was a hero and his elephant was as sacred as himself. Nobody would harm you; not even the high priest would dare to put you even to indignity. The high priest realizes that. My information is that Bamjee has been told to try to win you over. That is why I told you the proverb about a man's mouth."

"Yes, miss."

"And I don't know what will happen—not exactly what will happen; but I want you to walk into Bamjee's trap. The man whom I will some day marry—Prince Rana Raj Singh—will come to your assistance; perhaps at the last minute. Mr. Brazenose Blake is as friendly as he dares. I believe I can trap Mr. Ginsberg. You must depend on me to do my utmost not to leave you in the lurch. Can I count on you? Do you promise?"

"Yes, miss."

Quorn rolled his eyes. " 'Deed you can, miss."

THERE WAS NO other possible answer that Quorn could have given. He was as putty in the ranee's hands, he loved her so. To him she was the fairy princess he had dreamed of as a child when his mother told him stories to put him to sleep. To be invited to the palace and talked with in confidence was bliss; it was almost ecstasy. But Quorn was homesick, all the same, and there were two trends running in his mind. On his way through the gorgeous palace garden toward the elephant lines, he was perfectly frank with himself about his predicament.

"Ben Quorn, you're crazy. She's a pippin. She's as pretty as light on dancing water, or one o' them buds with dew on it. There ain't a scrap o' meanness in her and she sticks to her friends like road oil to new paint. But they've got her number, them priests have, and she's slated for the ash can just as sure as my name ain't Napoleon. I'm a damned fool not to pull my freight for Philadelphia before I get mine too. I'll get it worse than she will. Mine 'll be poison, or else a bullet. But you can't cure damn' fools. No, sir, you can't cure 'em. And if I choose to be a dad blamed idiot, that's my affair. Great jumping Jupiter, what does it matter what happens to *me?*"

But that line of philosophy made him no less irritable. When he reached the elephant lines, where four and thirty great brutes swayed and tossed up dust with their trunks until the air was a shimmering haze through which the surrounding green foliage looked like a painted back drop—the stage where Quorn himself was emperor and high priest, doctor, teacher, disciplinarian and man of mystery in one, he loosed the dogs of anger at the first victim in sight. There was a monkey—a sacred, untouchable, privileged, impudent, flea bitten, scrofulous thief from a neighboring temple helping himself to the grain from the feeding board of a young elephant, whose sore back had spoiled his appetite. He had grown incautious from long immunity. Quorn caught him unawares, his one regret being that he was wearing light shoes instead of hob nailed English boots.

"Goal!" he remarked as the monkey sailed in a parabola across the compound wall and landed backward in a tree. "Now, who's next?"

He chose the chief mahout, who happened to be nearest. He scandalized him, making him take the hose in his own important hands and wash from the young elephant's sore back every trace of the thrice sacred priestly remedies that had been applied with proper incantations by the full light of last night's moon. From his medicine shed he then brought an enormous bag of epsom salts, which he laid on thick, with water, and covered with dozens of gunny sacks to keep it moist, delivering meanwhile, by way of incantation, a profane, even blasphemous, but expert homily on how to load young elephants.

"And then you call 'em treacherous—dumb brutes that must put up with your damn' lazy cruelty!"

He threatened the chief mahout with mayhem and then went to cool off, sitting on one of Asoka's feet while he examined him for corns, which are the bane of all big elephants.

"You big bum," he complained affectionately. "You're more trouble to fix than flat tires are. And if corn and hay was to cost the same as oil and gas, your tusks'd be decorating some one's mantelpiece. Eating like a orphanage, looking like a long nosed bishop, and raising hell is all you're good for. Shove that other foot this way."

Asoka was in one of his playful moods. He pushed Quorn's new red turban down over his eyes and then did the new trick that Quorn had taught him—rifled the handkerchief out of his pocket and wiped Quorn's nose with it.

"You sucker! Do you kid yourself you're Dempsey? You've bloodied my nose, you doggone lunatic! Here, give me that handkerchief."

Quorn stanched the nosebleed and, because he was Asoka's guide, philosopher and friend, he refrained from retaliation. But of all the discomforts that could make him fighting angry, a blow on the nose was worst. He craved a victim. He looked for one, and the mahouts, aware that somebody was going to catch it, became studiously busy cleaning up the lines. It was then, on the crest of that climax, that Bamjee sauntered up, oozing innocence like benignant honey.

"What a lovely day," he murmured.

Quorn, seated on Asoka's forefoot, bit off a piece of tobacco and stared. Bamjee was a harmony in cream and chocolate; the only accents were his watch chain, cuff links, gold rimmed spectacles and the silver handle of his silk umbrella. Cream colored pants and vest, chocolate colored socks and turban, tan shoes and brown alpaca jacket blended with his old ivory skin. He was a little man with wrinkles at the corners of his eyes and a walk that suggested affluence.

"A lovely day," he repeated, a trifle louder.

"Sure, you could fry tripe on a chair seat. Are you looking for trouble? Try me! Start something."

AS PURCHASING AGENT, Bamjee had the right to make exasperating trouble if he chose, but he had never found it profitable to annoy Quorn. Just now he was almost over acting suavity.

"You and I, Mr. Quorn, have been very useful to each other many times. We have trusted each other. I would like you to trust me again. I wish to speak to you in confidence."

"I'd sooner trust a scorpion," Quorn answered, busily scraping the bowl of his pipe.

"That is not polite. That is not courteous."

"The hell you say!"

"Mr. Quorn, it is plain that your nose has been hurt. But it was not I who hit your nose. It would do you no good to hit mine."

"Wouldn't it?"

"Why are you rude to me?"

"Forty-eight rupees, eight annas," Quorn retorted. "That's half, as per bargain, of the price you charged the high priest o' Siva's temple for fixing his automobile. I did the work and it's a shame to take the money, but you took it, so divvy up."

"Mr. Quorn, I came to do that."

"What's preventing you? There ain't no such thing as a lovely day when a man o' your—o' your piety owes me money. Cough up."

Bamjee counted forty-eight rupees, eight annas. Quorn stuffed them into his pocket.

"As a matter of fact," said Bamjee, "the high priest's treasurer has not yet paid me, but never mind, I have always treated you fairly. We are good friends, aren't we, Mr. Quorn? You like your little jokes at my expense—your little crudities. Perhaps that is one reason why we are friends. I wish to speak to you in friendship for your own good—privately, where none can overhear us."

"See a chance to line your pocket, eh?"

"Possibly. But yours also, Mr. Quorn. It is a secret. Will you walk with me to the Old Fort? Or I can send for my carriage and we will drive together."

Quorn leisurely filled his pipe, then looked up at Bamjee with a pair of agate colored eyes that betrayed no trace of anything but faint curiosity.

"Tell you what," he said. "This elephant's getting over his corns nicely. He needs exercise. I'll take you riding."

So presently they dawdled through the crowded streets, Quorn on Asoka's neck, ankus in hand, face inscrutable. Bamjee was in the howdah so that he had to talk at Quorn's back—a condition that forces direct speech. Quorn, on the other hand, was not obliged to answer with more than grunts; he had all the excuse he wanted to be taciturn and dignified.

He was more than a circus parade, and he knew it. He was history, high on the neck of the tallest elephant in India, parading through the streets of time. He might know himself for an ex-taxi driver and Bamjee might think him a possible dupe; but the great elephant acknowledged him as master, and all Narada knew him as the reincarnation of the Gunga sahib. Quorn was not nearly so home-sick just then, nor so irritable.

"Mr. Quorn," said Bamjee, "it is necessary to use great frankness with you. Our beloved ranee is in such grave danger that you and I must find a way to preserve her life, even though her throne can no longer be saved."

"I thought something o' that sort was coming," said Quorn.

He shifted his quid of tobacco and glanced backward.

"I was sure you'd be on her side. Shoot the works."

"Then you know rebellion is coming to a head?"

"Not me."

"You have spoken with the ranee?"

"Not me. Only about elephants."

"Oh well, I suppose every one is talking of it. Of course, rebellion is silly. The people don't realize how swiftly the central government will send troops to enforce order. Nevertheless, I am in favor of rebellion because it will lead to early exploitation of the gold mine and that will be highly profitable for us all. It is thought, Mr. Quorn, that if you—in your capacity of Gunga sahib on Asoka—should identify yourself with the rebellion, doubters would be much more readily convinced and there would be far less bloodshed; perhaps none at all. And as the Gunga sahib you insure that the ranee shall be well treated and not molested in person. You would not need to say anything, or even to do anything except to be seen in certain places on your elephant. The priests, and certain others, would do all the talking."

Quorn turned his head suddenly.

"What do I get out of it?" he demanded.

He knew that Bamjee would expect that, and he guessed that Bamjee would never really trust him unless there was a money stipulation to explain the apparent willingness to join the conspirators. He also guessed that, Bamjee having confessed his own treachery so frankly, he himself would be poisoned or stabbed before midnight unless he should satisfy the agent that he was really willing to betray the ranee.

"How much and when?"

"You must leave that to the generosity of those whose business that is," said Bamjee.

QUORN CHEWED ON that reflectively. Finally he spat.

"I was a sucker once," he said. "I weren't never exactly sweet, but I was innocent. I was ashamed of circus bill-boards because I thought they understated facts to a point where they was plumb untruthful. I believed the pictures in the seedmen's catalogues. I believed what the minister said about going to hell. I used to give my nickel to the missionaries reg'lar. I believed the world was made in six days and I wondered whether the Lord worked union hours and, if so, what was happening sixteen hours out o' twenty-four. I believed you had only to be trusting and simple and truthful. And then I took to driving taxicabs. How much, and when do I get it?"

"You must make your bargain with the committee. There is much bargaining going on and you are in a good position to get favorable terms because the high priest of Siva's temple, who is a very influential Brahmin, is also a shrewd bargainer. He has stipulated that the Committee of Reform and Progress, as it has been named, must be able to guarantee your not being on the ranee's side; otherwise he will observe neutrality, which would be disastrous to the cause because so many thousands watch for his example and behave accordingly. You see, although he regards you as an ignorant person and, for that matter, as an impostor, he knows that the people regard you as Gunga sahib. They are almost as superstitious about you as they are about him, so it would be bad policy to take sides openly against you—especially since he had to admit publicly that you are the Gunga sahib. They could easily kill you, of course. I think he would prefer that. He is very tired of seeing you so honored and respected. But *they* see the advantage of letting you live, for a while at least, if they can show you to the public as being on their side.

"So your only possible course is to make your bargain, take your profit and then escape to the United States. Otherwise they will make a scapegoat of you when the British send troops to subdue the rebellion. They will say it was you who caused it all. On the other hand, of course, they can kill you now and say the ranee's agents did it by her orders. Then they can say it was your murder that caused the rebellion by arousing popular indignation.

"The high priest would like that best because it would give him also an excuse to be indignant; but of course, he will not openly advocate murder, or even secretly advise it in so many words. He merely says it is a pity you are such a nuisance."

"And to think I fixed his automobile for forty-eight rupees, eight annas!" Quorn reflected. "And I'm to walk into the trap, I am. Ben Quorn acting mouse bait like a maggoty lump o' cheese. I'm on the hook already." He began to whistle to himself.

Asoka mistook the whistling for impatience. As the rightful leader of all royal processions, he resented anything ahead of him, so he began to hurry. The dreamy city flowed past like a panorama, green gold sunlight streaming by temple roofs through splendid *neem* trees, on to coppery skins and multicolored turbans that moved in and out of shadows against sunlit walls. The ox carts dawdled and Asoka began rumbling ominously.

"Hey there! Behave yourself, you big stiff!" Quorn commanded for the dozenth time. "Act reasonable. This here is a stroll along Fifth Avenue, you sucker, not a fire call."

But Asoka, just as a thoroughbred horse will, had sensed Quorn's mood, and it is the mood of the trainer that governs his animal's response to circumstances and conditions. The vibrations of Quorn's discontent had passed like coded messages along every fiber of him until, by way of his knees tucked under Asoka's ears, they reached Asoka's brain. Emotionally, then, the two were one.

Down a cross-street came a vehicle that stirred Quorn's sense of the proprieties, as well as his sense of ridicule. It struck the match of anger. It aroused hatred. And it blocked Asoka's way. The fulminate of passion, ever ready in Asoka's blood, exploded and awoke a tantrum in which all the anger of all the elephants of time had outlet.

THAT WHICH SWUNG into the street and filled it nearly from wall to wall was the high priest's automobile. It was gilded and much more enormous than any circus wagon. Its high wheels, looking far too fragile for the weight imposed upon them, supported a boxlike compartment that had only one small window set in a narrow door on the left side.

Over that, towering above the eaves of houses, teetered and trembled a great pagoda, upon which a pantheon of gilded gods with many arms were represented posturing in attitudes symbolical of alternating life and death, evolving each out of the other.

It was a car weighing several tons. The high priest and his assistants were concealed inside it, doubtless in a torment of unventilated heat. On the outside were more than a dozen attendants, some of whom beat gongs, others cymbals, bells and drums. For centuries past that car had been drawn through the streets of Narada by eighteen elephants. As such it served its purpose as a symbol of the absolute eternity of moments and the unreality of time.

But the modern movement has had strange vagaries in the byways of the world. Even in Hindu temples, even in Narada, restlessness has given birth to change, and change to incongruity. Some younger priests had mocked at the team of eighteen elephants. A treasurer had grumbled at expense. And like a Puritan grandmother in an era of skirts above the knees, the high priest had compromised; he had kept the car but changed the method of propulsion. Also, he had been roundly cheated by a salesman of second hand engines, who had tricked him with a petrol hoisting engine, geared to the wheels by a system of chains and belts. The speed was less than the vibration and the noise resembled target practise on the range with muzzle loading rifles.

There was no muffler on the exhaust; flame and foul smoke belched astern and stung the sensitive membrane of Asoka's trunk, and Asoka decided to slay the damnable, abominable thing. He rushed it.

"Why the hell didn't God make elephants with four wheel brakes?" said Quorn, as he tried to stop the monster.

But the rapping of the ankus on Asoka's angry skull was simply irritation applied to prehistoric, cataclysmic wrath. The great head crashed against the rear end of the gilded mystery on wheels; the sacerdotal engine backfired with a noise like an anti-aircraft gun. It scorched Asoka and he screamed. He lost awareness of Quorn's voice. He tried to drive his tusks into the horror—to crack it, crush it, smash it, trample on it—to destroy it and then escape from its very memory. A chain snapped, and suddenly, like a gilded galleon before a dreadnought's guns, the thing lay at Asoka's mercy.

He behaved like a petulant five ton baby. He wrenched his tusk free, filling the echoing street with frightful trumpetings, arching his back to hurl himself in spasms at the thing he hated.

There was panic. Owners of booths and shop fronts rushed to get their awnings down and shutters up. Crowds poured into the street from doors and alleys. The high priest, torn between fear and dignity, tried to peer through the only window; six priests, less obsessed by dignity, struggled and wrenched at the one narrow door; but the door had become jammed by Asoka's efforts. Volleys of tiles were coming from the housetops now and every blow that struck Asoka spurred him to fresh effort.

Quorn began bleeding from cuts on the head and Bamjee, in the howdah, yelled with pain and fear as he tried to dodge the missiles. A new tumult added itself as owners of the houses fought with sticks and blasphemy to save their roofs from being stripped. And in the midst of it all, Asoka changed his mind.

He decided he could not destroy that horror. He must get away from it and run. He would run away from it forever to dimly remembered mountain ranges that he used to roam some half a century ago. He might have turned, but an angry elephant goes through and not around things. He saw daylight between the side of the abomination and a shop front that was heaped with crockery and cheap glass lanterns, so he jammed his shoulders in between the carriage and the wall. Quorn saved his legs from being crushed by raising them and clinging to the howdah, but he stuck to his post on the elephant's neck because in such moments a man shows the stuff of which he is made. There was no thought about it, he just stuck there.

"Who'll go your bail, you big fool?" he wondered. "Do you know you're playing hockey with a high priest?"

A wall beam splintered like a piece of kindling. Half a roof came crashing through the floor above the shop as the wall collapsed inward; and Asoka's rump swung around amid smashing glass and crockery until he had the priestly vehicle in flank, and faced the door through which the priests were trying to escape. They scrambled over one another in panic, trying to climb into the pagoda, hoping to find a weak place where they could break through and reach the roof of the house on the other side of the street. They yelled as Asoka thrust his trunk in through the window. He tore the clothes off one of them before they all crouched, terrified, in a corner.

THEN HE BROKE the door and wrenched it off. He tried to climb in, being sure now that the priests inside the thing were the cause of all his anguish. And because the glass and crockery in the shop were breaking noisily, and the owner of the place was prodding him savagely under the tail with a broom stick, he drove his weight against the side of the car with all his might until at last the whole thing cracked like an eggshell and overturned, sending it thundering into the opposite wall. Being mainly of mud, the wall collapsed and crushed the gilded gods on the pagoda, bringing down the roof and the people on it who were hurtling missiles.

The upset wheels were spinning. One of them spun like an emery wheel against Asoka's tusk. He wrenched it off and hurled it through a shop front. Quorn yelled to the high priest's driver to shut off his switch and stop the engine, which was coughing and spraying gasoline; but the driver had departed thence, like a monkey in breech clouts, scampering down the street with visions of eternal wrath behind him.

Suddenly Asoka noticed that there was room to get by; he backed into the stricken shop for one last charge—heard Quorn's voice—wheeled in a havoc of dust and crockery and lit out down the street for sweet conservatism, liberty or death—no matter which. Behind him a thousand voices raised a cry of "Fire!" as the spark set alight the gasoline. The high priest's compromise with progress vanished in a ghastly veil of flame that set fire to the shops on either side of it.

Quorn tucked his knees again beneath the upraised ears and sat tight.

"Attaboy, bozo! Beat it! Get the hell out o' here to Roosia. You've made enemies."

There were booths and awnings all along the street—ox

carts to be overturned; groups of men and women to be scattered screaming down alleyways; horses and asses and mules to be stampeded. Asoka neglected nothing. There was an unwise, elderly and very sacred bull whose privilege it was to roam the streets and forage doles and steal from open shop fronts. Nobody had ever struck him and he doubted there was such a thing as haste; he stood and dared Asoka and—door posts, door and all—he vanished backward into the front room of a house where ladies lived whose modesty possessed a retail market price. Their screaming satisfied the bull that they and none other had done the indignity, so he wrecked the establishment and, being a sacred bull in a profane place, he wrecked it so thoroughly that people remarked afterward how the gods chastise by means of proper instruments.

Asoka carried on. There was plenty of scenery left that would come to pieces if properly tackled, and he had a reputation to live up to; a habit of doing more damage in one of his tantrums than all the other elephants, in all of theirs, could do in an elephant's lifetime, which is upward of a hundred years. But he was bruised and a trifle breathless, and he could hear Quorn's voice now, not exactly soothing but reminding him that there is always aftermath. He had had the better of every one who ever tried to manage him, always, excepting Quorn. Quorn had always been in at the finish; always even tempered and unflustered. Quorn had become as much a habit as the tantrums, and Quorn's voice, now that the rage was dying down and he could hear it, was a recognized overture to the return of reason.

"Cut it out now! Me and you'll catch hell enough for this

to last a lifetime. You've done plenty, you big lummox! Easy, do you hear me! If you haven't fried a high priest in his own fat with his own gasoline, you've scared him proper—and I guess that's worse. Them gentry don't like being made ridic'lous— Oh, holy mackerel! She said—she said he's got to be made ridic'lous! As my name's—"

He began to whistle. The familiar refrain began to penetrate Asoka's consciousness; he slowed down.

AT THE END of the street, two hundred yards ahead of him, the Old Fort stood in the midst of a public park all gay with lotus ponds and gorgeous flowers—gloom at the heart of gaiety. The very legends, clinging to the fort like the vines to its ancient walls, were enough to keep people away; but a grim portcullis gate, and drawbridge across the moat, were so forbidding that not even Quorn had ever entered there, although there were no guards in evidence and the portcullis was almost always raised, as it now was.

In theory the place was public property. In actual practise it was a common meeting ground of rival priests and other mysterious individuals, who were at pains to preserve the gruesome atmosphere for the sake of the privacy it afforded. Without being exactly superstitious about the place, Quorn would rather have forfeited a month's pay than cross the drawbridge. He tried to turn Asoka down a side street.

But Asoka had seen the lotus ponds. A bath appealed to him, and all Quorn's efforts with ankus, knee and voice were unavailing. Bamjee, behind in the howdah, by no means a physical coward, but a victim of nerves and imagination, screamed as the elephant cracked on speed and plunged with a five ton splash into a pond between him and the drawbridge.

Quorn was used to it but Bamjee, losing balance and forgetting to cling to the howdah rail, was catapulted head over heels into a slimy mess of ooze and lotus stalks, where he spluttered and struggled until Asoka noticed him.

Very few men understand the minds of elephants. Quorn did. Bamjee did not. Bamjee tried to work his way to Asoka in order to clamber back into the howdah and be carried to dry land. Quorn yelled to him to run for his life. Asoka, red eyed from his efforts, saw what he took to be the evil genius who had made him forget his dignity, resulting in all the misbehaviour. He gave chase. Terror lent Bamjee wings. He scrambled from the pond and fled toward the drawbridge, looking like a scrambled chocolate ice cream soda with his turban awry and his suit a wreck. Bamjee had held the record for the hundred meters at his university, but now he beat that easily, although out of training and impeded by a broken silk umbrella. Asoka lost several seconds because of his weight which made him sink into the mud at the edge of the pond.

Bamjee reached the draw, shouting to some one inside the fort to raise the bridge behind him, but Asoka came thundering over the span like a gun going into action. The nerves of Bamjee's spine were like guitar strings as he dodged to the right inside the gate, skidded on the flagstones and dived like a rat into a dark hole, ten or twelve inches ahead of the tip of Asoka's trunk.

The drawbridge rose behind Asoka's rump and down came the portcullis. Some one had done it who was ignorant of the mechanics of the thing; it came down much too fast and crashed on the stones, driving the elephant almost frantic. In front, about twenty feet away, was the mouth of a dark tunnel; he supposed that Bamjee had escaped into it. He rushed at it, screaming with anger, and Quorn had to cling to the masonry overhead to save himself from being crushed to death. His fingers found interstices in the carving, his knees slipped from under Asoka's ears, and he swung for a moment wondering whether his grip was strong enough to hold him. His first impulse was to drop to the flagstones below and to follow Asoka. He loved that elephant. Tantrum or not, he might be able to save him from making too big a fool of himself—possibly from danger, accident, death.

However, Quorn was not an acrobat; he dreaded falling. And it may be that the hand of destiny had hold of him. He saw that the ledge which his fingers gripped was fairly wide and that he could swing himself up on it. He accomplished that almost without reasoning about it and, once there, the drop to the flagstones looked too dangerous to attempt. He began to climb along the ledge in search of an easier way down, pausing at every other step to listen to the echoing thunder of Asoka's lone quest.

"The big lump! He's bad enough with me on his neck. What in hell he's doing down there without me to hinder him'd take two men and a boy to imagine!"

THERE WAS NO way down; the ledge ran straight into the wall at either end. But he found an embrasure—a sort of slot in the wall along whose face he was climbing, designed for the use of archers to protect the entrance if the drawbridge should be lowered. It was a narrow slot, but he was not very large. Excitement lent him strength and he forced his way through into a gallery that ran along three sides of a huge, ill lighted hall.

He could hear voices, but they rumbled and echoed so that it was impossible to tell from which direction they came. Once or twice he thought they were coming nearer, and as he did not want to be discovered until he knew first what had happened to Asoka, he hurried along the gallery until he found a door that opened into a long, high, narrow room.

The door was ajar when he came on it; the room had the intangible feeling of having been occupied only a few moments before. There was a smell of betelnut. There were about a dozen cushions on the floor. He felt one of them and it was warm.

"I'll bet they got to hell out of here when they heard us crash the gate. They'll have gone to find out what Asoka's doing. Good enough; they can see that as easy as I could. Maybe the old skate won't give 'em a scare!"

By the noise he could tell that Asoka was raising havoc somewhere. A sort of fatalism settled on him.

"What he'll do, he'll do. I can't alter it. Let's hope they haven't guns to shoot him with."

He began to imagine a world without his friend Asoka and it made him sad. Suddenly homesickness had him in its grip again and filled him with disgust for all things Oriental. In a fit of petulance he kicked one of the cushions across the room. There was a paper under it, smeared because it had been thrust under the cushion before the ink on it was dry. He picked it up. He was a duffer at reading native languages but he could make out that it was a list of signatures beneath some sort of contract or agreement.

Spitefully, rather than for any other reason, he thrust it inside his shirt.

"If it's important, maybe they'll worry. And if they worry, serve the suckers right," he muttered.

Then suddenly he felt ashamed—not of that sentiment, but because he had forgotten the ranee and her peril.

"Me, I was to walk into the trap," he muttered. "Hell, I'm in it! What next? Fine shape I'm in for bargaining, with two-tails busting up the landscape! I'll be just about as popular as a snake at a tea party. If the high priest wasn't roasted in his auto—and if he comes—oh, jiminy!"

He decided to hide. With luck he might be able to learn something about the conspirators and possibly even what they really intended doing. He did not believe much that Bamjee had told him—not now—in the cold light of loneliness.

Making as little noise as possible, he passed through a door at the end of the room into a smaller chamber. There was a trapdoor in the center with a great ring fixed to it. He raised the trap and found a stairway. It led downward in the general direction of Asoka.

When the door was shut it was not so dark as he expected. There was no need to strike matches. The stairway dropped downward between enormously thick walls, but the light grew stronger at every turn until he found himself in a doorless chamber somewhere about the level of the main floor. It was not damp. The room was well ventilated and he could see, through a barred window, in place of a courtyard a tank full of rankly smelling water. The bottom of the tank at one end sloped upward in the form of a ramp toward a platform and a row of columns; on the ramp lay a dozen alligators, some of them enormous. Quorn shuddered. He remembered the tales of how prisoners, held in the fort and tortured, were at last disposed of by feeding them to those reptiles.

"I wonder what the filthy devils get to eat nowadays?" he wondered. "What's their next meal? Me?"

He could no longer hear Asoka. He began to look for a way out of the room, but apparently there was none except the stairway by which he had descended. There were no chairs, no tables, but along the wall facing the window there were heavy teakwood chests from which the dust had recently been shaken; it stood on the floor in little ridges where it had fallen when the lids were raised. There was no particular reason why he should raise the covers and look inside; he was a man who normally respected other people's secrets and belongings almost to the point of monomania. He hated spying. But he had caught something of Asoka's terrible mood. His opening of those chests was possibly a faint vibration of Asoka's tantrum.

THEY CONTAINED NEW Brown Bess muskets, apparently unused, of the period somewhere between Clive's day and the Mutiny of '57. There was one whole chest of cartridges of the kind that had helped to cause the mutiny, with the grease on them caked and cracked. And there were two chests of cavalry sabers of about the same date. The muskets had been carefully oiled and the sabers, which had been recently cleaned, were tied in bundles. But the ammunition looked as promising as wooden money might on Wall Street.

"Hell!" said Quorn. "So that's their little game. I'll spike that."

He had no military knowledge, but he knew that the nearest British regiment was two or three hundred miles away. The ranee had only fifty soldiers, with weapons not calculably better than the muskets in those chests. For a teapot revolution in a city that contained no fighting men that arsenal was plenty—given secrecy, speed and determination.

"Here goes," he said, "if I get fed to them there alligators for it!"

He began to heave the muskets through the window, dreading the splash, pausing and listening, wondering how deep the water was; working feverishly to get it over with. Cartridges followed. Then the cutlasses. At last he closed the chests.

"What I need now," he remarked to himself, "is just the same thing that old Asoka needs, and that's a working alibi. They'd figure I was *some* sword swallower if they'd catch me in here. Me for the tall timber."

He climbed the stairs, gingerly raised the trapdoor, peered, listened, emerged and closed the trap behind him. But he had not remembered exactly how heavy it was; his fingers slipped and it closed with a thud that made him nearly jump out of his skin. Again he listened, and every inch of his skin began creeping. The worst of Asoka's tantrums had never frightened him half as much, and he caught himself wondering why. He heard a man cough. That was all—just one man coughing, but it made him feel he was in the presence of death. It made all the stories he had heard of the horrors of the Old Fort flash before his memory.

However, Quorn had courage. It took much more courage to go forward and investigate that cough than would have been needed for facing anything he could see. His heart was in his mouth as he tiptoed toward the door of the long room, cursing himself because he had left it barely ajar. He would have to move it before he could peer through the crack.

When he forced himself at last to press against it with the tips of his fingers, he went through physical contortions that expressed his state of mind. He expected to see at least one full sized, bullying conspirator, armed with a sword and perhaps a revolver. But when at last he had moved the door enough to be able to see through the crack he saw nobody but Bamjee. The little babu was still muddy and wet, but he was squatting on a cushion chewing betelnut as if he had no worries in the world.

It is mixtures that make explosions. Deep down in Quorn's emotional nature, thoroughly embedded in it, but crusted over by the scars of the world's unkindness, was a strong dramatic instinct. He could always admire the picture of himself making what the stage knows as a good entrance.

There was also a sense of relief; he was not afraid of Bamjee. Added to that was disgust with himself for having been afraid; contempt for Bamjee and indignation because Bamjee had set this trap and drawn him into it. So Quorn behaved otherwise than he might have done. He let dignity to the winds.

He combined one of Asoka's typhoon charges with the bouncing of an india-rubber devil and a tigerish snarl. He leaped upon Bamjee. He so terrified him that the little babu shrunk until his suit was like a loose wet shroud on him. He toppled him over backward and seized his throat. He shook him. He banged his head against the floor. He slapped his face. He punched him in the ribs. He did everything to him that he always had wanted to do to certain individuals, much as traffic cops for instance, who had done him an injustice for which he could not retaliate. And having won that glorious victory, Quorn sat down facing Bamjee, offered him a handkerchief to wipe his bloody nose and spoke to him friendlily.

"What about it?" he demanded. "That's out o' my system. I saw you dump those guns into the tank. What next?"

Bamjee gasped, spluttered, picked up his spectacles and put them on, spluttered again and stared at him.

"You have hurt me very seriously, Mr. Quorn. I am offended. But what do you mean? Those guns?"

"Yeah—guns in boxes down below there. I was watching and I saw you feed 'em to the alligators. Cartridges too, and cutlasses. I saw you. No use lying about it. I'm your friend. I've worked off every grudge I ever had. Now I'll save you from those conspirators if you'll tell me why you dumped the guns into the tank. Come clean now—shoot the works!"

"But, Mr. Quorn, I didn't!"

"I seen you. No use lying. Besides—" Quorn's fist looked more deadly than it was and Bamjee had imagination—"you said this morning it wouldn't do me no good to punch your nose. I've only hit it once yet. I'm curious to try what a second helping'd do to my—to my æsculapium or whatever it is where a man keeps his sense o' fitness. Better come clean, Bamjee. Use your judgment. Strut your stuff. Why did you dump those guns into the tank?"

BAMJEE STILL HESITATED. He was plainly in terror, and of something more than Quorn's clenched fist. He appeared to be trying to listen. He wiped his nose. He looked at Quorn. His eyes were wild with anguish. He appeared to be distracted between two, or it might be a dozen difficulties. He began to shiver. And then suddenly he yielded to the terror that was nearest because Quorn looked like resuming the state of warfare.

"You are too clever for me. I did not suppose that you are such a clever man. Mr. Quorn, I am sure that it was you who threw those weapons in the tank."

"I said I seen you do it," Quorn insisted.

"Unfortunately you would be believed. It was I who sold those guns to the conspirators. They will say it was I who threw them into the tank for fear that the sale might be traced. Oh, dear, it was very clever of you. Well—I am now for the ranee. I am her devoted servant."

"Why did you dump them guns into the tank?" Quorn demanded.

He had told the plain truth. Having pummeled Bamjee he now bore no grudge against him; he was even anxious to help Bamjee out of deadly danger. He proposed to make use of Bamjee's wits if he had any left.

"Of course, I did it in order to prevent the success of the conspiracy, Mr. Quorn."

"You had a change of heart?"

"Yes. Oh, why, yes—yes, certainly!"

"You lie! You were always for her, weren't you?"

"Yes, yes indeed. Of course, Mr. Quorn. You bewildered me with that blow on the nose or I would have answered that way the first time."

"Yeah. And what I did to you ain't nothing to what I will do if you change your mind again! You're for her, and you, always was for her—first, last and all the time. Get that into your system. Get it in good or I'll thump it into you. And what's the use o' your trying to kid me you sold them guns? You know you didn't. Are you crazy? Didn't some one steal them out o' your godown? Weren't they guns you'd bought to send to a second hand auction room in New York along o' my telling you there was a sucker market for just such trash as that? Lord, what a memory you've got!"

"Yes, Mr. Quorn. I remember. And I will remember your kindness always. But there is no need for them to find us here. Let me show you the way to escape."

"What? And leave Asoka for them hellions to drive into worse trouble than he's in already? You're a fine patriot, you are!"

"But Mr. Quorn, I know these people. We are in terrible danger. They will be desperate when they learn that you—I mean that I have destroyed their arsenal. Their one chance was to move swiftly. Without weapons they can do nothing. Even the ranee's fifty soldiers can control Narada if nobody else has weapons. What should they do now but murder us in order to prevent our telling tales about them?"

Quorn shuddered. The word murder always stirred his imagination more than the sight of bloodshed. He had a morbid dread of being murdered. However, he was Asoka's guardian—his friend.

"You're coming with me," he retorted. "You know your way about this fort. You'll show me or—"

"Yes, Mr. Quorn," said Bamjee. "I will show you."

Bamjee led in haste along the gallery and through the

passage at the farther end into a corridor, at the end of which an unglazed window overlooked a courtyard paved with granite cobblestones. There was the usual well in the center with a horizontal beam above it hung with ropes for drawing water. On the side of the courtyard, facing the window through which Quorn looked, was a row of stone columns supporting arches upon which the upper part of the building rested. It was dark underneath those arches—altogether too dark to make out any detail and, for a moment or two, Quorn supposed that the voices he heard came from beneath them. It was not until he leaned out of the window, trying to penetrate the gloom, that he realized the voices came from directly underneath him.

There were twenty men standing there upon either side and in front of an open door, and he could hear other men talking in the passage, or room, or whatever it was just inside the door. It was impossible to tell from above who the men were, but all except one wore turbans. The man without a turban wore a white sun helmet and European clothes. They were all staring toward the far right hand corner of the courtyard; they appeared to be excited and were all talking. It was impossible to distinguish words because of the hollow, rumbling echo.

"Come here."

Quorn took Bamjee by the neck and forced him to look downward through the window.

"Who's that—him in the helmet?"

Bamjee gave one glance, then struggled to withdraw his head.

"Mr. Ginsberg!" he gasped.

"No you don't! You stay here."

Bamjee tried to duck out of Quorn's grasp and run, but Quorn caught him by the coat collar. He pulled off Bamjee's turban, made a noose of its thirty yards of fine silk, slipped that around Bamjee's neck and tightened it to the point where he could breathe without very much discomfort.

"There's plenty left to tie your hands with," Quorn assured him. "And I could still gag you with the end of it."
HE AGAIN LOOKED out of the window, and presently discovered at what the men below were staring. He caught the glimpse of the end of an elephant's trunk that flicked out past a corner column and retired again into the shadow.

Instantly Quorn was a schoolboy again, imagining magnificent stage entrances; he wondered whether Asoka would come if he called him, and if so, whether he could drop on to his back from the window. Fortunately the height made him shudder and saved him from that indiscretion. He turned upon Bamjee.

"Show me how to get past them guys below there without them seeing. My elephant's in that far corner. Lead me to him."

"Impossible!" said Bamjee. "Yes, Mr. Quorn, impossible! From this side there is only that one door, and there they stand! How can we get past them without their seeing?"

"Dunno. That's for you to show me. Lead on, my bally-hoo-boy."

He tugged at the silken noose and Bamjee wilted.

They descended by a dim stone stairway into a corridor and slipped unseen behind the backs of fifty men into an empty room that had no door. There Bamjee nearly collapsed with terror. Quorn had to kick him to restore his self-control.

"You'll be all right when you've something to face," he whispered. His own nerves were on the ragged edge now. "It's your imagination scaring you. Nothing hurts until it happens. It don't take long happening. And it don't hurt afterwards—not if you're lucky. Come on."

He dragged Bamjee to the window, where they crouched so that only their eyes were above the sill. They could have reached out and touched the backs of several men. They had to look between them in order to see the far corner where Asoka was sulking in the darkness.

Bamjee clutched Quorn's arm as if superstition had him at last, and he, too, believed Quorn to be the Gunga sahib who could save situations by merely being present. And he who was supposed to be the Gunga sahib pressed his chin against the stone to keep his teeth from chattering.

"I'll take every last chance there is before I'll let 'em murder me!" he thought. And the thought was so vibrant that it almost had sound. It startled him.

"Shut up, you fool!" he muttered, actually using words with which to drown the thought. And because he used them Bamjee almost screamed.

Then Ginsberg began to show of what stuff he was made. As the only European in a group of Orientals, it behooved him, it appeared, to take the lead and to advise heroic methods. He had a rather thin voice. It suggested a sneer, though that, obviously, was not intended; it was the fault of his nose that looked mean, lean and inquisitive. There was nothing athletic about him, nor anything dramatic; he was casting himself for a part that were better played by a Booth in buskins. He stepped forward in the general direction of the danger—two full, fair paces—without contriving to seem heroic. His speech lacked stingo; there was none of the big gun note about it; it was too quick, too quarrelsome.

"Are you going to let that man Quorn spoil everything? It's true, we can't see him but he must be in there with the elephant. Otherwise the brute wouldn't stay in there. He's savage. He would be rushing out at us. But look, he doesn't attack me. What are you afraid of? Where are those weapons you spoke of? Bring your muskets out and shoot that elephant. If Quorn gets in the way of the bullets, that's his lookout. You have a good excuse for firing volleys at the brute, and the man made his own bed. Let him lie on it. Go on, somebody, and get the muskets. This will serve you for practise."

There was a movement toward the corridor, although Ginsberg remained in the doorway. About twenty or twenty-five men went up the stairs in search of weapons. The remainder clustered in the corridor, most of them laughing with the forced note of men under the strain of excitement. Ginsberg went on talking.

"It's all nonsense to say Quorn is necessary. I've maintained that from the first. It's just a ridiculous piece of superstition. Men like you, who call yourselves a committee of progress, ought to be ashamed of it. What is Quorn? He's a *gharri-wallah*—a man who drove cabs in the United States before he came here. Kill him, that's my advice, and you'll have an ignorant fool out of your way. Kill that elephant and you'll be rid of a public nuisance."

"Me and you, we'll have a bone to pick," Quorn muttered.

He turned suddenly upon Bamjee. He forced him to the floor. He set his teeth against Bamjee's ear and whispered:

"Get the hell out o' this. You go and find the ranee. You tell her you dumped them muskets in the tank. You tell her I said now's the time to make her spring. Tell her, make it snappy! And now listen here; if you don't find her quick, and if you don't give her that message, I'll blow the gaff on you to these bad boys. But if she gets the message quick she'll come quick—maybe in time to save me and Asoka. If she does, I'll swear away my soul that you honest to God did dump those muskets. That's all. Get a move on. Here— gimme that turban."

Bamjee removed his slippers.

"Mr. Quorn—" he whispered.

But Quorn scowled him into silence and the speech of gratitude was never uttered. Bamjee tiptoed to the door, paused, peered, saw his chance and vanished. Quorn raised his eyes to the window again. Ginsberg was talking.

"I THOUGHT IT stupid to write those names on paper. It commits you. It commits me. True, it makes it difficult for any one to back down or to betray the rest of us, because all the signatures are there on one sheet. But suppose, after this rebellion is over, that that paper should fall into the hands of the British troops when they come to restore order and take over the country? It's foolish. Why put yourselves into that kind of jeopardy? And why force me, of all people, to run that risk? Haven't I proved my friend- ship? And what sort of use could I be to you afterwards if that piece of paper were in the wrong hands, proving my connection with you? Who has the document? I wish one of you would go and get it. Let's burn the damned thing. I have matches."

Some one answered him in soft, liquid, almost womanly English—the voice of a special pleader:

"Surely we appreciate your friendship, Mr. Ginsberg, and we know you would not betray us or break your promises. But the high priest does not know you, so who shall blame him for insisting? It is he who will keep that paper in the secret temple archives. How can it get into the hands of the British?"

"I was a fool to sign it," Ginsberg answered. "I signed to encourage a few of you who did not wish to sign. Tell you what— I will pay five thousand rupees to whoever will bring me that paper. You shall see me burn it."

Quorn felt to make sure that the paper lay under his shirt. He grinned.

"You'd shoot my elephant!" he muttered.

It did not occur to him now that his own life was in danger. His imagination now excluded almost every thought except Ginsberg's threat against Asoka. No man loved a dog more loyally than Quorn loved that cranky elephant.

"Maybe it'll be our turn next— Shut up, you fool!" He had caught himself muttering almost aloud.

There was low talk in the corridor. Five thousand rupees was an offer that stirred the imagination, but apparently nobody knew who had the document that Ginsberg wanted.

"Better hurry," said Ginsberg. "They'll be down here with the muskets in a minute."

Then some one shouted, his voice echoing from the stairhead, and there was consternation. Ginsberg exploded.

"Nonsense! They can't be missing! I saw them an hour ago myself."

But the cries from the stairhead continued, and there began a concentrated rush to the chests where the muskets had been.

"Lord, what a chance!" Quorn muttered. "Could I shut the trap on' em? Could I catch 'em in there like a barrel o' rats?"

He could picture himself doing it, then sitting on the trap to listen to their buzzing underneath. But something saved him from attempting that forlorn hope; he heard Ginsberg talking to himself.

"A fine bunch of conspirators! Lost their muskets! God, what a crowd to have to deal with!"

Tiptoeing, Quorn crept into the corridor. Ginsberg stood there alone, facing the outside door that led into the courtyard. It was a heavy door with a strong bolt that, if once shut with a slam, could not be opened from the outside. Quorn loosened the noose in Bamjee's turban; he meant to treat Ginsberg none too handsomely. But Ginsberg turned and saw him.

Dynamite is not swifter than the hatred that flames when two men meet who recognize each other as born enemies. Ginsberg did not flatter himself; he believed he could read murder in Quorn's eyes and he stepped backward through the open door into the courtyard, where there would be room to run. He felt for his hip pocket where a pistol should have been, and his face turned white; somebody had stolen it.

"Good God!" he muttered.

"So you'd shoot my elephant?" said Quorn.

He, too, stepped out into the courtyard, slamming the door behind him. He was not nearly so heavy as Ginsberg, nor so tall, but Ginsberg did not deceive himself as to the outcome of a fight between them; he backed away. Quorn wished he had his ankus with him.

"What do you want?" demanded Ginsberg.

"You!"

"What d'you mean? What for? Keep back! Do you hear me? Keep back!"

"That way!"

Quorn began to drive him backward toward the corner where Asoka sulked in darkness.

"I'll teach you to murder a decent elephant!"

But Ginsberg was not to be forced so easily within the reach of Asoka's avenging tusks and knees. He sprang aside and Quorn made an effort to rope him with the end of Bamjee's turban. As a gesture it was foolish, ineffective, but it brought Quorn to his senses.

"Me?" he said. "I don't bear grudges—much. We'll let Asoka settle it."

It was Ginsberg who saw Asoka first. The great brute had heard Quorn's voice and had come forward a step or two to investigate with his far scenting trunk, and his short sighted eyes. Ginsberg shuddered and began to run, but there was nowhere to go; he tried the door that Quorn had slammed shut. Then he tried the enormous, foot thick wooden gate at the end of the courtyard, but that was held shut by an iron bolt high out of reach. There was nowhere to climb—except, perhaps, to the horizontal beam above the well, where he would still be within reach of Asoka's trunk. The best he could do was to keep the well between him and the elephant, hoping to dodge around it. He began to shout for help—about the worst possible course because it stirred the embers of Asoka's wrath.

QUORN WALKED TOWARD Asoka slowly, looking steadily at him. He was taking chances. Dozens of men had tried to manage the monster before Quorn came to Narada. He had had every kind of punishment inflicted upon him; and an elephant who has been cruelly punished falls into the habit of expecting punishment again, and terror causes him to kill his best friend.

"Kneel, you big bum!" Quorn commanded.

There was no response except an ominous rumble. Then Asoka began to sway his head and shift his feet in the sly, almost imperceptible motion of an elephant who means mischief. Suddenly Quorn thought of Bamjee's turban that he was still holding gathered in his right hand. He threw it away.

"You big idiot! What could I do to you with that thing? Don't you know your poppa never does you dirt, no matter how bad you've been? Come out o' that now. Come here. Put your knee up. Come on—put me up where I belong!"

Quorn's foot hardly touched the upraised knee. Asoka curved his trunk around him and hoisted him up to his place, where he drove his knees under the ears and settled himself for action.

"I've no *ankus,* you son of a gun! You made me drop it or I'd have killed a guy. There he is— D'ye see him? Like him? Like his smell? Take a look at him! Run him a piece!"

Urged by the pressure of Quorn's legs, Asoka swayed

slowly forward. Ginsberg made the courtyard echo with his shouting, then, utterly losing his head, he ran from the well. Asoka gave chase, uttering no sound, a little weary from the morning's tumult and not sure that he wished, or that Quorn wished him to overtake the fugitive. He followed almost as if it were a procession led by Ginsberg. And Quorn sat still, enjoying Ginsberg's terror.

"Shoot him, would you?" he shouted. "Shoot my elephant, would you? How about it?"

Twice around the courtyard Ginsberg fled, as if all hell followed him. Asoka gained little by little, unhurried, beginning to feel the laughter that was making Quorn's knees tremble. Ginsberg began gasping, hugging a stitch in his side.

"Step on her! Give her the gun or we'll catch you!" Quorn shouted.

Suddenly Ginsberg jerked like a pig that feels the spear, and darted toward the well. There was something about that that was reminiscent of the way Bamjee had escaped. It stirred Asoka's memory. He wheeled and gave chase— now in earnest. Ginsberg reached the well a yard ahead of him, his backbone creeping as he sensed, rather than saw, the outstretched trunk. He had meant to run around the well, but he could not make it. Maddened with fear he seized the upright and tried to swing himself to the overhead beam. Asoka only touched him, but the touch was plenty. He let go. He vanished. Quorn heard him plunge into the water. He leaned over but could see nothing. However, he could reach the rope that passed over the beam, and he made ready to pass that down.

"How about it down there?" he demanded. "Feel like shooting elephants?"

Hollow and spookish Ginsberg's voice came back to him—

"Lower the rope and I'll climb up after you take that brute away!"

"You ain't drowning?"

"No, I'm only chest deep."

"Too bad! You can see all right? Well, here's Asoka's compliments!"

He turned the elephant and made him raise his trunk over the well so that Ginsberg could see it plainly against the sky.

"Any message for your friends? Me and Asoka are off on a little hunting party. The rope's rotten—I wouldn't risk your precious life depending on it. See you along about supper time."

Quorn rode away, wondering how long it would be before Bamjee reached the ranee and delivered the message. He also wondered how far he could trust Asoka, who usually, but not always, became meek and slavishly obedient after his outbursts of passion.

"Them conspirators," he said, "is prob'ly still conspirating. There's only fifty sepoys and a colonel, Prince Rana Raj Singh and Mr. Brazenose Blake that she can count on. There ain't much Blake can do except give good advice; he has to keep his hands off. And Prince Rana Raj Singh has to be awful careful or the British might call him a—what is it they call 'em?—a disturbing element; they'd order him home to his empty hilltop castle somewhere away in Rajputana.

"No, she'll have to paddle her own canoe. But she can do it. And now what? What do me and two-tails do? It's a cinch we ain't going to stay here like a pair o' Ginsbergs in a booby trap."

He guided Asoka to the huge end gate, where he stood on the elephant's head and tried to reach the bolt that had been set high out of elephants' reach. He lacked three feet of reaching it, but he found an ancient ankus in a hole in the stonework, probably there for the purpose, and with that he hooked the bolt and slid it easily. Asoka pulled and the ponderous gate swung back. Quorn stared into the tunnel that passed underneath the whole breadth of the fort—the same dark tunnel into which Asoka had gone charging, from the other end, in search of Bamjee. He could see the bars of the portcullis and the raised drawbridge.

"I wonder how Bamjee got out? Maybe he didn't! Maybe he doublecrossed me." The tunnel was far lower than the gate, which had been built so as to fill a recess in the masonry; there were not two feet between a tall elephant's back and the top of the arch, so that in order to ride through the tunnel, it was necessary to lie prone. There was a rope with which to pull the gate shut. The bolt on the other side fell into place of its own weight. When he had shut the gate behind him, Quorn realized that he was now invisible; he could watch whatever should take place between him and the light and, so long as Asoka kept still, there was no reason why any one should even suspect his presence.

IT WAS EASY to keep Asoka quiet; by simply touching one side of his head, then the other, he got him swaying in the monotonous rhythm that probably expresses an elephant's consciousness of cosmic tides. The pitch black darkness, with the light in front of him, was the best possible condition to calm the great beast; that and the feel of Quorn's breast against his head restored him to his normal state of sentimental dignity.

And Asoka's increasing quietness was good for Quorn, calming his nerves and making it easier to think. But he could not conceive any way to raise the portcullis and lower the drawbridge without getting down from Asoka's back; and to get down would be like sawing off the branch he sat on. Asoka was speed, height, power and fearsomeness in one. Throw those away and he was simply Ben Quorn, stranger in a strange land, with cold chills up his spine.

The machinery for raising the portcullis and lowering the drawbridge was in plain sight. There were two cranks to be turned, either of which was manageable by one man; but one man could not manage both at the same time.

Some one came out of a door that opened into the tunnel and, after examining the machinery as if unfamiliar with it, slowly cranked up the portcullis, appearing annoyed by the noise of the ratchet that clattered over the cogs of the big iron wheel. Trying to lessen the noise by tinkering with the ratchet, he defeated his own purpose; the portcullis fell with a thunderous crash and Quorn almost laughed aloud.

"Lord, but I pity a guy what's more skeered than I am! What's his game, I wonder?"

The game soon was evident. Out of that same door in the tunnel all the conspirators came hurrying, treading upon one another's heels. Those in front called to the man at the crank to make haste and lower the drawbridge. The rats were deserting the sinking ship.

"The swine!" Quorn muttered. "Rob her of the chance to catch 'em, would they!"

That appeared to him so unreasonable, so utterly contrary to his dramatic sense of things that he entirely forgot the probability of pistols. He also forgot his own fear. He remembered that he and Asoka were the ranee's loyal servants, and that unless the ranee should score a decisive and undisputable victory, she might be reduced to a mere puppet. He grew furious at the thought of that. He urged Asoka forward.

"Wade in there and soak 'em!" he commanded. "Soak 'em proper!"

He had kept the ancient ankus with which he opened the courtyard gate. With the aid of that it was a simple trick to make Asoka thrust his trunk straight forward and utter hair raising screams as he rushed. A locomotive snorting and shrieking out of a tunnel mouth is a mild sight compared to an elephant with raised ears doing the same thing, because an elephant has no paralleled lines to limit his range of violence.

In less than thirty seconds there was not a man in sight except the one who had been cranking; he had climbed on the wheel and was swarming up the rope by which the portcullis was raised. The remainder had fled into the same dark hole used by Bamjee when Asoka first pursued him. It was a wide hole; there was room enough to follow, but it was no place for an elephant. There might be pitfalls, slippery stairs, anything. However, they could not escape unseen, and they could certainly see Asoka against the light so they were hardly likely to attempt it. He entirely forgot the risk of pistols; his one track mind was concentrated now upon means of escape across the drawbridge, perhaps to hold it from the far side.

He turned his attention to the man who was trying to climb the portcullis rope. He had done pretty well for a fat man—he was out of reach—but he could go no higher; he was trembling.

"If I was to lift that ratchet you'd go sky high kind o' quick," said Quorn. "Suppose you see sense and come down out o' that."

A GUN BARKED out of the dark hole like a mark of exclamation. The bullet missed Quorn by the thickness of a razor blade. Asoka screamed and backed away nervously. The man on the rope fell like a shot goose and Asoka tried to rush back into the tunnel, but Quorn got him under control. Plainly the man was not killed; when he had kicked a bit and felt himself he tried to crawl under the drum on which the portcullis rope was wound. The pistol shot, instead of frightening Quorn, had raised his spirits and quickened his intelligence; he noticed that it was quite easy to keep out of the way of any possible further bullets from that point.

"Hell," he remarked to the fat man, "this here elephant can pull you out o' that more'n twice as easy as you can crawl in. Spit on your hands and crank that drum some more afore I put you to an inconvenience."

The man obeyed him. Quorn sat on Asoka wondering what the conspirators would do next—particularly whether he could cross the drawbridge without being shot from behind.

"Maybe they ain't such good shots," he suggested to himself. "Gee, but I hope they don't pepper Asoka. The old loon might think I did it. He'd never forgive me."

The portcullis groaned up and at a nod from Quorn, the fat man turned his attention to the drawbridge crank, first staring at the blisters on his hands, then eying the elephant before he sighed and took hold of the handle.

"Hard work is hell for a fat man," said Quorn, "but the quicker you start the sooner it's over with. Hump yourself."

But nothing happened. Both of them saw the same thing at the same time. There was a parapet that overlooked that fifty foot square between the portcullis and tunnel; along its edge leaned eight men armed with muskets; they were aiming at Quorn, and a ninth man, grinning and cocksure, stood by to direct their operations. He had some knowledge of psychology, that ninth man.

"If you move we will shoot your elephant," he shouted. "You see, we found the muskets that you threw into the tank. We recovered them. Now if you don't obey us absolutely we will shoot your elephant, and we will prove that it was you who hid the muskets in the first place."

"What do you want?" Quorn asked.

But he was not interested; he only wanted time to think. He was wondering. He knew nothing about firearms, but he doubted that those ancient cartridges, supposing that they had recovered any of them from the tank, would go off after an hour or two's immersion. He remembered that the grease on them was dry and cracked.

"We want you and your elephant to march with us to the palace," the man shouted. "We are late already, but if we make haste the populace will rise in rebellion and the ranee will be deposed. Otherwise we may be caught here like rats in a trap. If that happens you shall share the blame—provided you are still alive. We might shoot you when we shoot the elephant."

But Quorn had made his mind up. Muskets and cartridges fifty years old....

"I'll give you three shots for a dime," he shouted. "And a pretty gift to take home to the wife and kiddies for him what hits the bull's-eye. Make sure you hold your muskets straight, and don't shut your eyes when you pull the trigger. Shoot, you suckers! What's keeping you?"

A bugle call answered instead of a volley—a bugle call in the street beyond the drawbridge. The man on the parapet shouted but Quorn could not catch what he said. However, the fat man at the crank understood; he began lowering the drawbridge as fast as he could sweat the crank around, and the men with the muskets disappeared like Punch and Judy puppets pulled from below.

When the drawbridge was two-thirds lowered the man on the parapet called to him in a voice from which every note of confidence and insolence had vanished.

"Mr. Quorn, we would not really have shot your elephant!"

Then the bridge thumped down into its sockets on the far side and Quorn saw at last what was happening. Siva's high priest and a little crowd of his subordinates were standing waiting. At a respectful distance behind them was the greater part of the ranee's army—about forty men in splendid uniforms, their colonel leading. Behind them was the ranee in her gold and vermilion howdah upon her second largest elephant, and in another howdah upon another elephant sat Blake, the representative of the Central Indian government.

Behind Blake, mounted upon splendid horses, were Prince Rana Raj Singh and his twelve black bearded Rajput henchmen; and behind them was none other than Redhead Bagh, ex-bandit and now minister of forests. Redhead Bagh was followed by a few score mounted peasants who looked capable of looting all Narada at a word from any one.

The street behind Redhead's men was choked, as far as Quorn could see, by throngs of children, men and women who appeared to see some humor in the situation.

OVER THE BRIDGE came the high priest, seemingly unsinged but fuming with inner flames. His frown was terrible. Quorn made Asoka raise his trunk and forefoot in salute, but the high priest took no notice. Timid conspirators, cringing, came out of the dark hole, inviting him to enter the underground temple; but the high priest muttered something and they ran to open the great gate at the far end of the tunnel.

There was scampering, shouting, thumping, while the high priest waited—then light pierced the tunnel, and Quorn heard a man say:

"She will not slay Siva's priest, who is equally guilty with all of us. It is wiser to stay with Siva's priest than to run and to be found afterwards hiding in some dark hole without witnesses."

That theory found backing. Bamjee arrived like a stage devil out of a trap, apparently from nowhere, breathless, excited and dripping with sweat, disheveled, whispering in men's ears, shoving and gesticulating, diving down the dark hole, reappearing, whispering again, persuading other men to repeat his message, and finally shouting aloud:

"To the courtyard, everybody! Everybody to the courtyard! You, Mr. Quorn, to the courtyard also!"

There was almost a stampede. Apparently nobody knew of Bamjee's secret way of escape. To flee across the drawbridge meant facing the ranee's soldiers—worse, Rana Raj Singh's Rajputs—infinitely worse, the peasants under Redhead Bagh! The thing to do was to be first into the courtyard and get a good place at the rear. And there were many more men than Quorn had seen; there must have been another hundred of them in the underground temple, who came pouring out like goblins from the entrance hole.

Quorn upon Asoka flowed into the courtyard along with the tide; and because he disliked Siva's priest almost more than the toothache, and because he was afraid that Siva's priest might find some means of vengeance for the morning's mixup, he guided Asoka back into the far corner where he had found him sulking in the shade. The high priest stood facing the well, about fifty feet away from it, surrounded by his grim subordinates; and forth from the well at intervals came Ginsberg's voice, demanding and imploring rescue.

The ranee could not ride her elephant through the tunnel because there was no room for the state howdah. She walked, accompanied by Blake and Rana Raj Singh, followed by nearly all her soldiers and the prince's mounted men. Redhead Bagh and his followers remained to guard the drawbridge.

The soldiers formed up in a smart looking square before the mouth of the tunnel. The conspirators herded themselves along the far side of the courtyard; and the ranee, supported by Blake and Rana Raj Singh, faced the high priest, with the well between them.

"Help! Help! Help me out of here!" Ginsberg's voice, hollow and booming, shot forth from the well's depths at the circle of sky.

Brazenose Blake, contriving to look only casually interested, strode toward the well and peered in. He was one of those men who could smile without moving his lips. With his hands behind him he strolled back to the ranee's side, where he surveyed the crowd with an air of exasperating calmness. Rana Raj Singh's handsome face was an enigma, but his lips moved and it appeared that the ranee listened to him, because once or twice she nodded.

The high priest grew impatient and began to speak, but Rana Raj Singh bruskly checked him. In the silence that followed Blake's voice was very distinctly heard suggesting to the ranee that Ginsberg should be dealt with first.

"You deal with him," she answered. "Mr. Ginsberg is your business."

Blake signaled to two soldiers who lowered a rope and dragged up Ginsberg, terrified, tortured by imagination, ignorant of what had happened or what was in store for him, bedraggled and without one scrap of dignity remaining. No man can be dignified when alien soldiers take him by pants and collar and deposit him on all fours in front of a seventeen year old ranee. She did not speak to him. She only smiled. It was Blake who passed sentence.

"You are Mr. Ginsberg? At least, that is the name on your passport? Do you know anything about a rebellion recently fomenting in Narada?"

"Certainly not," said Ginsberg. "How should I?"

"Quite so. Then why are you in this fort? I daresay you were studying antiquities—is that it?"

"Yes. Studying antiquities," said Ginsberg.

"Interesting, doubtless. But let me tell you, there is a treaty of long standing between the state of Narada and the central Indian government, by the terms of which all interference with antiquities in Narada is strictly forbidden. Your presence in that well is proof to me that you were interfering very impudently with antiquities. Do you admit it?"

Ginsberg had wit enough left to recognize that he was being offered an ignominious but safe line of retreat.

"I admit it" he answered. "It was foolish of me."

"Very foolish. You will leave Narada, Mr. Ginsberg. You will leave now under escort. You will take the train for Bombay. You will leave India, Mr. Ginsberg. If you should miss the next steamer for Europe, Mr. Ginsberg, your—ah—antiquarian researches might be looked into. You are perhaps the best judge at the moment of what the result of that might be. Yes, you may go now. You will find the escort waiting for you on the far side of the drawbridge."

NATIONS FIND IT hard to understand one another. Siva's high priest, one of whose subordinates had been interpreting Blake's words, thought that he recognized weakness as the cause of Blake's attitude. He knew that weakness always demands a scapegoat, and he thought he saw a chance to rid Narada of that hated Gunga sahib. He burst into speech, fiery, insolent, dictatorial.

"All of this trouble is due to that impostor—the man on the elephant. It is he who misleads the people. He plots.

He pretends to make miracles. He does damage. He drives his ferocious elephant through crowded streets at the risk of lives and property. He is a charlatan, a rogue, a devil. He is yonder. Bid him come forth. Let him answer— Who has plotted this? Who has misled these unwise people? Has he, or has he not promised to lead them to the palace to dethrone their ranee? And if this charge that I make against him is untrue, then let him show us a miracle. Aye, let him show us who truly plotted all this foolishness, and let him prove it."

It was then that Quorn remembered that roll of paper inside his shirt. He had forgotten it. He drew it forth and made Asoka take it in his trunk.

"A miracle?" he muttered. "I'm a bad bum, am I? Gee, I hope this paper ain't a testimonial for some one's cigarets. Here goes anyhow."

He urged Asoka forward. Leisurely, because he loved to take the center of the stage, Asoka swayed toward the ranee, halted before her with upraised trunk, and then, with great deliberation, put the paper into her hand. Every man in the courtyard, including the high priest, held his breath while the ranee unfolded the paper and read it, taking her own royally unhurried time. She could be as leisurely as old Asoka when she wished.

"A miracle?" she said at last, and her voice was like laughter that has not yet quite unfolded from the calyx. "How wise of you, O High Priest! I believe you knew the Gunga sahib could not fail us!"

She did not show the document to Blake and Rana Raj Singh, but she held it so that both of them could see it was a list of the names of the conspirators. And both of them could see the high priest's name, although he had not written it. It was addressed to him in the form of a sacred pledge to carry the rebellion through to its conclusion. In all the archives of the courts of all the world there could not be a more incriminating document. Rana Raj Singh raised his eyebrows to the colonel commanding the soldiers. There was a sharp word of command. They loaded rifles and fixed bayonets. But Blake whispered to the ranee:

"The worst rulers are the biggest killers. If you want my friendship, show me you can make these people eat out of your hand."

She met Blake's eyes for a moment, then glanced up at Quorn before she returned the angry glare of Siva's priest And when she spoke her voice was quiet yet it filled the courtyard and every man knew there was laughter in it.

"This list of loyal men," she said, "is something I will treasure—keep always by me to refute the slander of ill meaning people. How glad I am that I found you planning ways to seat me strongly on the throne! How willingly I welcome Siva's priest's endorsement of my stand against the tyranny of caste and superstition!"

High she held the document, the uninscribed side toward them, though all knew what was written upon the other.

"I agree that this procession through Narada that you planned is excellent. Let Siva's priest summon the temple ministrants. Let us do this splendidly. Let all Narada know how loyal and how grateful men can be whose ranee knows their hearts—and their names!"

"You win," said Blake. "I will report to the central

government that your Highness needs no troops and no commission to help you rule."

Then he stepped aside to speak with Quorn, who made Asoka kneel so that they might talk and not be overheard.

"How much of this was luck," he asked, "and how much of it your infernal doing?"

"None of it was neither, sir. It ain't luck when the sassiest she-pippin on the face o' God's earth soaks it to 'em with a sweet face full o' brains! She's the cat's pajamas, that's what she is! If you want to see life swift and sweet and snappy, put your money down on *her!*"

"Have you been drinking?"

"No, sir."

"Would you like to?"

"Thankee kindly. Me and him could do a tooth full and not hurt much."

"You and who?"

"This big bum. He's the works, Asoka is. He busted the high priest's automobile and got away with it. If that ain't worth a snifter, tell me what is!"

"I've a case of some rather good whisky, Mr. Quorn. If you'll permit me, I'll make you a present of it. I'll send it to the lines for you tonight."

AND NOW PIANO pianissimo. It must be written; and yet Quorn deserves it should be written gently without too much sense of that superiority which makes of us sober men and women heroes. Quorn was homesick. And the torchlight procession through Narada led, of course, by Asoka with the rance on his back, and followed by all the other elephants, two brass bands, and the high priest with all his elephants; by the army, and by all the conspirators carrying banners in praise of the ranee, who was cheered by a hundred thousand people until men said the sky might fall down, was a long and rather thirsty business.

There were gasoline flares in the elephant lines to make it easier to unload and picket the great animals; and the flares, the shadowy trees and the purple sky made the lines into a gorgeous place of mystery peopled with moving shadows; and in the midst there was a floor of golden light that would have tempted Greek Terpsichore. So who shall blame Quorn? There were twelve quarts and he only took two for himself. He knocked the necks off all the rest and made a glorious golden bucketful that vanished up Asoka's trunk and down his gaping throat.

Be it written then that Quorn tied strings of bells around Asoka's feet. His pipe in one hand and a bottle in the other, he backed away before the elephant and danced. A strange dance, the mahouts said, such as they had never witnessed; but a dance of which Asoka seemed to know the trick because he danced too, keeping time to Quorn's gesticulations with the pipe and bottle, and to the song that Quorn sang, whose words were doubtless magic since the mahouts could make neither head or tail of them:

"Yes—sir—she's my baby— No—sir—I don't mean maybe...."

They say that Quorn slept with his elephant that night and that none dared to interfere with either of them—not even to cover Quorn with a blanket, or to fasten old Asoka's picket ring.

www.ingramcontent.com/pod-product-compliance
Lightning Source LLC
Chambersburg PA
CBHW031158020726
47499CB00002B/414